TURMOIL AT … P
OF SECC…

HANNAH LYNN

ALSO BY HANNAH LYNN

Standalone Feel Good Novels

The Afterlife of Walter Augustus

Treading Water

Erotic Fiction?

The Complete Peas and Carrots Series

Peas, Carrots and an Aston Martin

Peas, Carrots and a Red Feather Boa

Peas, Carrots and Six More Feet

Peas, Carrots and Lessons in Life

Peas, Carrots and Panic at the Plot

Peas, Carrots and Happily Ever After

The Holly Berry Sweet Shop Series

The Sweet Shop of Second Chances

Romance at the Sweet Shop of Second Chances

Turmoil at the Sweet Shop of Second Chances

High Hopes at the Sweet Shop of Second Chances

The Grecian Women Series

Athena's Child

A Spartan's Sorrow

Queens of Themiscyra

This story is a work of fiction. All names, characters, organisations, events and incidents are products of the author's imagination or are used fictitiously. Any resemblance to any persons, alive or dead, events or locals is *almost* entirely coincidental.

First published 2022

ISBN: 978-1-915346-05-6

Imprint: Independently published
Edited by Carol Worwood
Cover design by Cherie Chapman

For the other Hannah,

CHAPTER ONE

Holly Berry stretched out her arm. She was exceedingly comfortable on the sofa and desperately didn't want to budge. Letting out a long, low groan of disappointment, she accepted that, even at full stretch, the bag of clotted cream fudge was just out of reach.

"You know you could just stand up and get them," Ben said, lifting his arm from around her waist so she could move. Holly promptly pulled it back again.

"But I'm comfy."

"So you want me to get them?"

"No! You're the reason I'm so comfy," she said, nestling her head against his chest. "If you get up, I might as well do it myself."

"Are you going to, then?"

She thought about it for a moment. Clotted cream fudge was good, but she could get plenty of that at work. However, this perfect snuggle she found herself in with Ben was just too good to give up.

"Probably not," she said.

Then, just as she had hoped he would, Ben tilted her head back and planted a kiss firmly on her lips. A long, lingering kiss that caused a warm sensation to flood through her. Yes, this was definitely better than her favourite sweet. Nothing could improve on being tucked away in Ben Thornbury's cosy living room, while the rain hammered against the window. Ben Thornbury—local bank manager, avid cyclist, all round good guy and officially Holly Berry's boyfriend.

It had been three months since they'd shared their first kiss, on a crisp, winter evening, beneath the blinking lights of the Bourton-on-the-Water Christmas tree. It was fair to say their relationship hadn't got off to the smoothest start. Their initial meeting had seen Holly knock him off his bike when she ran blindly into the road as she chased down a group of teenage shoplifters. It was then several months more before they'd considered seeing each other as more than just friends. Then Ben had nearly drowned on one of their first dates. And she could hardly forget the unexpected appearance of her ex-boyfriend, Dan.

Fortunately, Dan, along with her old life in London, was firmly in the past and as the proud owner of *Just One More*—the quaint village sweet shop that Holly had worked in as a teen—life was feeling pretty good. Even better now that she and Ben had finally found their rhythm.

At one point, she'd thought there was no chance for them, even as friends. But fate intervened, and now here they were three months on. February had thawed into March and the first bluebells were appearing in the woods around the village. And she was, spending her Tuesday night with her head resting on Ben's chest, half watching a film, and wondering how the hell she'd got so lucky.

His house was basically a mirror image of where she lived,

which wasn't surprising, given that she was his next-door neighbour, in the adjoining semi which she shared with Jamie, her landlady-slash-new-best-friend. Since they'd met, she'd been Holly's rock, helping her out of more than one tight situation and offering sound—if occasionally stern—advice.

A little spark of guilt formed in Holly as she thought about Jamie. She couldn't remember the last time the two of them had shared breakfast together or even had a conversation that wasn't just in passing on the doorstep. They still met regularly down at the pub, but always in a group with Ben and Caroline. With the nonstop rain they'd been experiencing for nearly three weeks now, they hadn't even done that in a while. The last time they spoke properly, Jamie was about to go on her third date with a guy named Fin, which for her constituted a long-term relationship. No doubt it had fallen by the wayside by now, but she really should find out. She'd do it this week without fail, she thought as she shifted the cushion behind her a fraction. She would make a concerted effort to spend some quality time with her. After all, she needed to do some washing. Spending all her time at Ben's was one thing, but doing her laundry there? Well, that still felt like a little too much of a commitment.

"Why's she doing that?" Holly asked, her attention suddenly drawn back to the television, where a woman was holding a knife against another woman's throat. The last time she'd looked, the two were laughing in a hot tub together.

"What do you mean? Did you not just hear what she said? She confessed to killing Turner."

"Who's Turner?"

"Have you been paying any attention to this film at all?"

"Not really," she admitted.

It hadn't been her choice, though to be fair, it hadn't really been Ben's either. Their tastes in television programmes, films, books and most other things in life were polar opposites. As such, finding something they could agree on to watch always proved rather difficult.

"Do you want me to recap what's happened so far for you?" he asked, running his fingers absentmindedly up and down her arm. It was a lazy movement that he probably wasn't even aware of, yet it was all Holly could focus on now.

"Not really," she said again, arching her back and twisting so that she could kiss him on the lips. "Actually, I can think of a better way to spend our time."

"Is that right?"

He returned her kiss, a little harder, and her pulse kicked up a notch.

"Why don't we turn off the television, and I'll show you."

It had been so long since she'd been in a new relationship that she'd forgotten how exciting it could be. And how the desire to be with someone so much usually resulted in another one, namely to rip their clothes off. This was another reason they stayed at Ben's. It was true, Jamie was out of the house most nights, but the last thing they wanted was for her to feel uncomfortable in her own home with their enthusiastic displays of affection.

Holly pushed herself up from the sofa and switched off the television, then reached down and pulled Ben up by the hand.

"I thought you didn't want to get up?"

"I didn't want to get up for the fudge. I own a sweet shop. I can get that anytime I want, remember? This, however," she reached up on her tiptoes and kissed him again, "has annoyingly limited availability."

"Well, when you put it that way …"

He placed his hands on her hips and pulled her closer. How was it possible she hadn't tired of kissing him yet? And how was it possible that his kisses were just so … delicious? Her productivity at work had gone down dramatically since the relationship had started. There was no sorting out the shelves now that Ben came and had his lunch with her upstairs. And her days of staying late to keep on top of the books were over, too. The minute his head appeared around the shop door in the evenings, she'd pack up her things and hurry home with him.

"We should head upstairs," he said, following the long kiss with a short one.

"After you."

Grabbing a piece of fudge and popping it into her mouth, Holly was about to follow Ben up the stairs when her phone buzzed on the arm of the sofa. She glanced down at the screen.

"Everything okay?" he called back to her.

"Just Mum," she said, rejecting the call. "I'll ring her back later. Now, where were we?"

No sooner had she taken another step than it buzzed again. Swallowing her annoyance, she took a deep breath.

"It could be important," he said.

"It's not. It'll be to do with this cardigan she's been knitting me. She's stressing about how many buttons she should put on it. I've told her twice already this week, I really don't mind. I'm not getting into that now. It'll be fine. Trust me."

"Only if you're sure?"

"I am," she replied, and this time, when she cut the call, she also switched the phone off.

"Okay, now that I've got your full attention, remind me again what we were about to do."

With Ben standing two steps above her on the stairs, the height difference between them was ridiculous, and yet as she reached up on her tiptoes to kiss him, she didn't think about it at all. His hands brushed through her hair, a twinkle in his eyes that cause her to flood with heat.

"Why do you taste of fudge?" he asked, shifting back and eyeing her suspiciously.

"You're imagining things. Now, are you going to sweep me off my feet or not?"

"You know what? That sounds like a great idea."

Before she could even fathom what was happening, Ben leapt down the steps and swept her up into his arms.

"Hey! What are you doing! I was joking! You'll drop me!"

"Don't you trust me?"

"No, I've seen you try to move furniture, remember?"

"Are you comparing yourself to a couch?"

Ninety percent certain that he was going to trip and drop her down the stairs, she clutched her arms around his neck and squeezed her eyes shut. And while he managed the first step without whacking her shins, that didn't ease her fear at all. In fact, she was so focused on what she felt was a precarious situation, that she barely recognised the sound that cut through her squeals of laughter.

"Was that the doorbell?" she asked. "Are you expecting someone?"

Ben paused, his laughter still reverberating around them.

"I never have visitors, you know that."

He tentatively turned on the spot. Holly placed one hand on the banister and one on Ben's shoulder, as she got back on her feet.

"Maybe it's Jamie," she said.

"Well, if it is, we'd better get the wine out," he replied.

Holly stayed rooted to the spot. Was it wrong of her not to want to talk to her friend at that precise moment? It wasn't that she didn't want to see her. She did. It was just that moments like this with Ben felt so special. So wonderful, in fact, that at times it seemed impossible that things could stay this good forever, and if that was the case, she wanted to make the most of each and every second.

No, she told herself. She was being ridiculous. They were a couple and a strong one at that. They had a whole future together ahead of them, and the last thing she wanted was for Jamie to feel isolated.

"You get the wine, I'll get the door," she said, straightening up her clothes, before giving him one, last kiss on the lips.

As she turned the latch and opened the front door, a cold gust of air blew in from outside, along with a spray of icy rain, stinging her face and causing a sudden burst of blinking. As she tried to wipe the rain out of her face and clear her vision, it took her a moment to see that the person standing there was definitely not Jamie. They were about the same height, but that was where any similarity ended. For starters, he was male, and secondly, he looked to be only about eighteen years old. He was wearing a oversized hoody pulled up over his head, which was soaked all the way through. Wherever this boy had come from, it was a lot further away than next door. Holly looked at him, trying to work out why he seemed somewhat familiar.

"Hi," he said, as the rain continued to beat down on him. "Is Ben home?"

CHAPTER TWO

"Er, hello," the young man tried again, as Holly continued to stare at him. "I don't mean to sound rude, but are you going to let me in, 'cos it's pretty wet out here?"

Before Holly could reply, Ben was behind her, masterfully carrying three wine glasses and a full bottle of wine.

"Toby? What are you doing standing out there in the rain? Come in. Come in. Holly, this is Toby, my nephew. Toby, this is Holly, my girlfriend."

"Hey," Toby said with a nod as he squeezed past her.

"Sorry, of course, come on in," Holly said, realising that she had been studying him with far more curiosity than was probably polite. The minute he stepped in, she saw just how soaked he was. Water was streaming from him onto the mat.

She'd never met him before, but it was hardly surprising that she'd felt she recognised him, given that Ben had several pictures of him in the house. That said, it was also understandable that she hadn't actually recognised him, either. In one photo, he couldn't have been older than five and was sitting on

Ben's shoulders as he paddled in the river in Bourton, and in another he'd been a couple of years older, maybe seven or eight, and it was a full-family photo, with Ben's parents and his sister and his niece, too. In that one, Toby had short hair and was wearing a Christmas jumper. Now, his hair was nearly shoulder length, and he was wearing baggy jeans that didn't go all the way up to his waist.

"Is one of those for me?" he asked, nodding towards the wine glasses.

"Nice try," Ben replied. "Seriously, what are you doing here and where did you come from? You haven't walked have you?"

"Just from the bus stop."

"Why didn't your mum drop you off?"

The scoff that followed told Holly two very distinct things. Firstly, that Toby and his mum's relationship was not in a good place, and secondly, that he had obviously come here for a reason: to speak to his Uncle Ben. Their fervour on the stairs of only moments ago, was long forgotten, and it didn't take a rocket scientist to realise that having Toby here meant any chance of romance that night was out the window. Besides, it was obvious the pair needed to talk.

"Do you know what?" Holly said, reaching up and grabbing her coat off the hook by the door. "I think I should probably head back to mine and give my mum a ring. She's called a few times this evening, and she'll get worried if I don't ring her back soon."

"Are you sure?" Ben asked. "Toby, why don't you grab a towel and dry yourself off? You'll find one in the bathroom at the top of the stairs. You know where it is."

"Sure," Toby said, not needing to be asked twice and kicking off his shoes. Ben waited until the bathroom door closed before he spoke again.

"You don't have to go," he said, "though this isn't like him, turning up out of the blue. I should probably let him vent."

"Honestly, it's no problem at all. I really should call my mum back. Speak later?"

She reached up and gave him one last kiss.

"I tell you what, I'll walk you home."

They kissed again, on the doorstep of Holly's house, beneath a large golf umbrella with the rain hammering down. This was a ridiculous habit they'd got into, *walking each other home.* Which actually meant stepping a full two feet out of one door to the next, but Holly loved it, not that she actually went home that often. It always made her smile, and a warmth would spread through her, knowing she had someone who would do the little things for her that meant so much. That was what really counted.

She had learned the hard way that relationships weren't about big gestures or grandiose promises, which was probably just as well, as she and Ben pretty much never discussed the future. While they talked about weekend plans and possibly going to see a new release at the cinema, that was as far ahead as they ever looked. She had vaguely broached the subject of buying a joint present for Jamie's birthday, but Ben had mumbled awkwardly something about a tradition, and Holly hadn't wanted to push it. She knew from Jamie that he'd been badly hurt in a previous relationship, and it wasn't like they needed to rush things. Maybe in a couple of months, they would start thinking further ahead, perhaps plan a holiday together, that type of thing, but for now, she was perfectly happy living in the moment. And the moments were good.

"See you tomorrow," Ben said. "And tell Jamie to stop sending me reminders about her birthday. I've known her for nearly a decade, so I'm well aware what the date is."

"I'll let her know," she said, giving him one more kiss before slipping inside the house and shutting the door behind her.

Holly had noticed Jamie's van parked on the driveway, but when she called her name, there was no reply. The light on the landing was on and so was the one in the kitchen, but that didn't mean that she was in. Leaving lights on was pretty much her only bad habit. And it wasn't like a bit of rain would bother her. She could have easily walked down to one of the pubs in the village or got a lift with someone.

Holly was about to go upstairs and check, when she remembered the phone calls from her mother and headed for the kitchen.

She had grown up in Bourton-on-the-water with her parents. This was the source of all her childhood memories, from baking with her mum and driving lessons with her dad, to her first job at *Just One More* and her first kiss with Jake Johnson. By the time she returned to Bourton, after an extended stint in London, her parents had moved to the nearby village of Northleach. The village was almost as quaint, although it lacked Bourton's distinctive river which ran alongside the High Street. Still, they were closer now than they'd been in years, both in distance and emotionally. Her parents had always been there for her, and the next stage of her relationship with Ben was going to involve introducing him to them. So far, the closest he'd got was waving at them from the car while Holly dropped off some sweets. But good things took time, and she and Ben were a good thing. Perhaps that was why her mum was ringing. After all, Holly had promised last month that she would introduce them.

In the kitchen, she picked up a bag of chocolate limes,

unwrapped one and popped it in her mouth. Her mother could talk for hours, and having a boiled sweet to suck on, while *umming* and *ahhing* at the appropriate moments, was always helpful. She'd never been a fan of them before, always finding them both simultaneously too tart and too sickly. Given the vast range of sweets that she stocked in the shop, it wasn't surprising that there were some she wasn't keen on. Yet last week, one of her customers had come in and ordered a large bag, and she'd been struck by the desire to try one again, since which, she'd been hooked.

With the sweet secure in her mouth and another one ready to go, she sat down and called her mum.

The phone only rang once before she answered.

"Hey, Mum. Everything okay?"

"Holly dear, thank you for ringing me back, love. I didn't disturb you, did I? You weren't on a date with the bank manager, were you?"

"I was at Ben's, but honestly, it's not a problem. We were just watching a film."

"Has it finished?"

"It was rubbish. And it's fine, we'd already stopped watching it and then Ben's nephew turned up."

"Right."

"Is everything all right, Mum? You sound odd."

Odd was the only word she could think of. Her mum was not a loud person, but so far, everything she'd said had been so quiet that Holly could barely hear her.

"Oh Holly," her voice quavered before the phone line went suspiciously quiet.

"Mum? What is it? Are you okay? Is Dad okay? Do you need me to come over? Mum, what's happened? Where's Dad?"

Holly could hear the panic in her voice as the worst-case

scenarios played out in her mind. She was still struggling to get past the recent loss of Verity, and she had barely even known the woman. The thought that something could have happened to her father was enough to make her blood run cold and heart race, simultaneously.

"Is he okay?"

"Oh, he's fine. It's nothing like that," Wendy said, finally finding her voice. "It's not that bad."

A sigh rattled from Holly's lungs.

"Then what is it?" she asked, alarm turning to irritation. "What's wrong?"

There was a long pause.

"He's lost his job … again," she said, finally.

CHAPTER THREE

Redundancies had plagued Holly's father throughout her childhood. Sometimes it felt like no sooner had he got a job than he was back out of work again, for no other reason than *last in, first out*, and while her mum had always worked, picking up cleaning jobs whenever and wherever she could, they were a family who'd been forced to be frugal most of the time.

That had been one of the reasons that Holly had been content to stay with Dan, working in a dull but safe job that she despised. Security. The fact that she didn't have to worry about where her next paycheque was coming from or if she was going to suddenly find herself without enough money for the rent. For years, they'd been so careful with their finances as they saved to buy a place of their own and bring about that next level of security in their relationship. That was until she discovered Dan securely in their bed with another woman.

Determined not to waste any more time planning for the future, she'd decided to take the plunge and use all her savings to try and buy *Just One More*, and she'd done it.

Her father's previous redundancy had happened before she'd started university, after he'd been working at the same place—a large, warehouse-type shop selling animal food—for years. They'd all assumed he'd stay there until he hit retirement age, and perhaps carry on a little beyond that, too, as long as his knees and back withstood carrying the heavy bags. Although retirement was still another ten years away for Arthur Berry, Holly couldn't help but wonder what chance he'd have of getting a new position at his age.

"How is he?" she asked, remembering the deep, grey clouds that settled over him the last time it had happened. He would force himself to smile and act like nothing was wrong whenever she was around, but when he didn't know she was watching she could see the heartbreak in his eyes. The thought of him suffering like that again was like a lead weight in the pit of her stomach.

"To be honest, love," Wendy continued, "he knew it was coming. I think we both did. And he's not the only one to suffer. They've let go half the staff."

It was little comfort, knowing that he was not alone.

"Why?" Holly asked. "What happened?"

"Oh, you know what it's like today. Why have a human do a job when you can use some fancy machine that can go four times faster and doesn't need any rest or holidays? And the business has been under a lot of financial stress."

The anger that Holly felt merged with guilt. She could see the sense in it from a business point of view, especially if they were struggling to keep afloat, but surely a company had to sometimes look beyond simple profit and focus on the people they employed. People, like her father, who had been loyal to them for over a decade. She drew in a lungful of air and tried to be more upbeat.

"How can I help?" she asked. "Dad's got loads of experience and local people know how hard he works. If you need any money just to see you by, I'm sure I can find some. Christmas was really strong at the shop. If you want—"

"No, no, dear," Wendy cut across her. "We'll be all right, honestly. I've still got my cleaning jobs, and your dad will get a small redundancy pay-out. He's been there a while. And it's really not that long until his pension kicks in, either. The doctor's been on about him taking early retirement with his knee playing up and everything. Besides, we've been tucking a little away for a rainy day, which I suppose we can safely say this is. No, we'll be okay for money."

"And he'll be okay?"

Given the speech Wendy had just made about their finances, Holly was expecting a quick and positive, *Yes*, but instead, silence lingered on the other end of the line again.

"It's not the money I'm worried about. It's your father. What's going on in his head. He'd hate me telling you this, darling, but he's feeling really down. It happened last Thursday, and I thought that perhaps with the weekend and everything, he might brighten up a bit. See the silver lining in it all. But he's barely left the sofa. He feels like he's got no purpose, see. Like he's too old to be useful anymore."

This was enough to make Holly's heart ache. Her father was one of the mildest, most genuine people it was possible to meet. To have him giving up hope like this was gut wrenching.

"Could he volunteer somewhere, perhaps?" she said, voicing the thought as soon as it entered her mind. "I'm sure they could do with some help at the Willows Care Home. Maybe filling his time that way might do him good? Or there's an animal shelter near you, isn't there? I know he's not much of a dog person, but if he took on some of the walking, he'd probably grow into it after a while and being outside would be better than shutting himself away indoors."

"Actually …" Wendy cleared her throat. "I was wondering if you might offer him some work."

"Me?" Holly said, not doing a good job of disguising the surprise in her voice.

"It wouldn't have to be much," Wendy added, hastily. "Just a couple of days a week or a few hours here and there."

Holly scratched her head, trying to make sense of what she was hearing. Take on her dad? The thought had never even crossed her mind, but then why would it have? He'd been happily employed, and she had all the staff she needed.

"You want me to hire Dad?"

"Well, pretend to. You wouldn't have to be out of pocket. I could give you the money from my cleaning jobs and you could pay him with that. So it wouldn't affect your profits or anything. He just needs to feel useful. I know it's a lot to ask … in fact I shouldn't have. I'm sorry. Forget it. I was just thinking out loud, that's all. I'm sorry, darling. I'll let you go."

Pretend to employ him? No. Even Holly could see that was a disaster waiting to happen, but she couldn't blame her mum for trying to think of anything that might help. The last thing either of them wanted was for her dad to slip into the type of decline she remembered from her teens.

"Just give me a minute to think about this," she said, going through the rota in her mind.

Caroline was her most regular helper now, even covering some weekends with Drey so that she could have some time off with Ben. That said, Drey was in her second term in her last year at school and would be off to university in September. She had already gone down to one day so that she could concentrate on her studies. Also, Caroline preferred to work weekdays so she could spend time with her husband and children. Plus, it wouldn't be long until the Easter stock came in, and pricing that up was a massive job. So maybe she could make use of him at weekends, although he'd need to get up to speed pretty quickly.

"Okay," she said.

"Sorry?" Wendy replied.

"I said, okay. I'll take him on, just for a few hours, though. That's all I need. It'll be mostly weekend work, but he'll have to come in on a weekday first, when it's quiet enough for me to train him up. Maybe four hours on Wednesday or Thursday. I'm not exactly sure which yet. Then, once he's got the hang of things, I can move him to Saturdays and Sundays."

"Oh, Holly darling," her mother's voice came through in a rush. "You don't know what this means to me. To him. To both of us."

"And I'll be paying him," she added, firmly. "He'll be doing proper work, so he'll earn his money. I'll put him on the same rate as Caroline. It's not much above minimum wage, I'm afraid. Would that be okay?"

"Holly love, that would be wonderful. Absolutely wonderful."

Wendy paused, and Holly could have sworn she heard sniffing.

"Right, I'd better go," Holly said, grabbing yet another chocolate lime and thinking how a soak in the tub and a glass of white wine would be the perfect complement to the moreish sweets. "I've got a couple of things to do."

"Of course, of course. Thank you, love. Oh, and just one more thing?"

"Yes?"

"You won't let your dad know I put you up to this, will you?

He won't do it if he thinks it's charity. It'll need to come from you."

Holly realised she should have seen this one coming.

"It's fine, Mum. I'll make sure he doesn't find out."

"Maybe you could come over later in the week. Make out how stretched you are, etcet'ra. And don't let him know that I told you about him losing his job, or he'll see straight through it. You'll have to wait for him to bring it up and look shocked. In fact, if you come around before five one day, when he'd normally be at work, then that would look really convincing."

A headache was blooming behind Holly's temples. This was suddenly feeling like a lot more than just giving her dad a few hours' work.

"Okay, I'll text you later in the week. I'll have to check what days the others are in."

"Thanks again, Holly. Love you to the moon and back."

"Love you too, Mum."

She ended the call and let out a long sigh.

Working with her dad? What would that be like? she wondered, dropping a handful of sweet wrappers in the bin. He was easy going and very relaxed, so it might actually be quite nice. He'd always been the one to calm her worries as a teenager, a man of rationality and logic, and someone you could sit with for hours in companionable silence, unlike Wendy. This might even be a blessing in disguise. Since she'd moved back to Bourton, she'd felt guilty about not spending enough time with her parents. Just rushed dinners here and there and occasional afternoons when she and her mum would grab a cup of tea. It had all felt very fleeting. This would definitely solve that problem.

After thinking through their conversation a little longer, she texted Ben to see how things were going next door with Toby. A minute passed and the two little ticks remained grey, signalling the message had not been opened. Ben was not one to have his phone tied to him the whole time, and with Toby over, it was probably in another room. It could easily be ages before he saw it. Luckily, she knew exactly how she was going to spend that time.

One great thing about Jamie's house was that it had two baths. Jamie's bedroom had an en suite, which meant that the family bathroom was Holly's. And for someone who had a great affinity for soaking in the tub and needed plenty of space to store all her lotions and potions, this was perfect. Armed with a glass of wine and the bag of sweets, she headed upstairs and plucked a towel off the radiator in her room. Then, with arms loaded, she opened the bathroom door with her elbow.

The first thing that hit her was a wall of steam. Stifling hot, it whooshed out through the open door, slowly clearing to reveal a man with a hand towel over his head, vigorously rubbing his hair and totally oblivious to Holly's presence. At least she assumed he was, because as the last of the steam dissipated, it became patently obvious that he was also naked.

CHAPTER FOUR

Holly needed to turn around. She wanted to turn around. And yet she seemed to be shocked into paralysis, her feet refusing to move and her eyes locked on the dripping figure in front of her. Around his neck, hung a leather cord with a wooden pendant attached and she tried to focus her attention on that. But it was more than a little difficult, given everything else that was on display. The muscles to start with. Then the perfectly toned chest that led down to chiselled abs that glistened with water droplets that trickled further south …

"Oh my God!" Holly said, realising where her eyes were heading and finally finding her voice. "Uhm … oh … I …" she stammered.

The man looked up, removing the towel from his head, and his hair fell in loose curls to just below his shoulders. He seemed surprisingly at ease with her presence there.

"Hey, you must be Holly," he said in a soft, American accent. "Fin. Friend of Jamie's. Glad to finally meet you. Let me grab a bigger towel and I'll shake your hand."

"Yes. Yes, of course. Very good," she said, her voice the very essence of British prim and properness as she turned her back on him.

"Ah," he cleared his throat awkwardly and she glanced back. "Turns out I left my other towel in Jamie's room. Sorry, you don't mind if I squeeze past, do you?"

"Erm … squeeze?"

He indicated that she was blocking the door.

"Oh, my goodness," she cried and let out a shrill, laugh. "A towel. Yes. I'll just get out your way."

And with that, she scurried back to her room, slammed the door behind her and flopped down on the bed with a gasp.

What the hell had just happened? Had she imagined it? No. There was no way she could have dreamt up that little scene. However she'd expected her evening to go, seeing an undeniably attractive man butt naked in her bathroom was a long way down the list of possibilities.

A minute later, there was a knock on her door.

"Hey," Jamie said, poking her head in and pulling a grimace. "So, you met Fin then."

"Yep, I definitely met Fin," Holly replied with a tight smile, not quite able to meet her friend's eyes.

"Yeah, he said you just got a full frontal. Sorry about that. We're in kind of a rush, and I needed to shave my legs. Didn't really want him to see that, if you get what I mean?"

While Jamie was definitely talking to her, Holly hadn't yet recovered to the point where she could comprehend speech at quite the normal pace. A few moments later and she got there.

"So, things are still on with you and Fin?"

"Actually, Finlay is my boyfriend now."

"Wow."

The shock that Holly had just received in the bathroom was partially eclipsed by the fact that her friend had just used the b-word. Stepping into the room, Jamie gave her a knowing grin.

"I know. Crazy, right?"

"That happened fast," was the only thing Holly could think of to say. Any reference to Fin's obvious physical qualities didn't seem quite appropriate.

"You're one to talk. You realise this is the first time you've been home this week?"

"It is not," she replied, indignantly. "Ben and I were over on Wednesday to play Monopoly, remember? And where was *Finlay* then? You didn't think to mention it to us?"

"It just didn't come up. Besides, that doesn't count. You were here with Ben. Which begs the question: why aren't you with him now? I thought it was a given that you'd moved in next door. I didn't think you two could be separated out of working hours."

"Of course we can. And I've not moved in," Holly said, feeling a twist of guilt. She really needed to spend more time back here. Although, by the way this Fin guy was making himself at home in her bathroom, it looked like they'd been enjoying the privacy. Still, she kept that comment to herself.

"Toby turned up, she said. "You know, Ben's nephew. He wanted to speak to him about something. Anyway, I don't want to talk about me. I want to talk about you. Tell me everything. What does he do? Where's he from? American, right?"

"Near California," she grinned, in a way Holly had never seen her do before, her cheeks rosy rounds and her entire face aglow.

Jamie had been on plenty of dates; half the guys in Bourton wanted to impress her, but no one had got to the stage where she'd referred to them as her boyfriend.

"Wow, I guess he must be pretty special," she said.

For some reason, although she'd said the words, she felt reticent. It was the way Jamie was beaming that unnerved her, she realised. Sure, it was brilliant that she'd found someone, but she'd like to know a bit more about him before she enthused. It was obvious that Jamie had fallen hook, line and sinker for a man that wasn't even from the same country as her. The last thing Holly wanted was for her to get her heart broken.

"Yes, he's great. I think you'll really like him when you get to know him. It would be good if you could see more of him."

"Oh, I've seen plenty of him," Holly muttered.

"Maybe we can arrange a double date or a triple, even, with Michael and Caroline, when we get back."

"Get back? Are you going somewhere?" Holly asked, wondering how she could ever look him in the eye again, let alone sit down to dinner with him.

Jamie looked at her watch.

"We are, and we should get moving. Our flight leaves at nine-forty. And you know what it's like checking in now. Everything takes ages."

Holly had expected her to say they were going to the pub or the cinema, or if they were being incredibly adventurous, somewhere like Bristol or Bath. But catching a plane?

"Flight?"

With another quick look at her watch, Jamie glanced over her shoulder before stepping further into the room and closing the door.

"Okay, but you can't say anything to Fin. I've booked us three nights in Amsterdam. I've got a couple of days between jobs, and he's not working at the minute. I saw a good deal and thought, why not? He doesn't know where we're going yet. I've just told him to pack a few things and some comfy shoes. We're going on a walking tour, and it's crazy long."

Holly took a moment to digest what had been said.

"You're going on holiday together?"

"I know. He's going to love it, right?"

She looked so happy, but Holly was having a hard time reciprocating. Going on holiday could be an enormous expense, as she knew from all those years with Dan when they'd stayed at home for fear of eating into their savings. And here was Jamie saying Fin wasn't even working.

"Have you paid for it all?" she asked her.

"Well, as I said, he doesn't know about it, and you can't exactly ask someone to pay if you're going to surprise them, can you? Besides, he'll cover more than his fair share when we're there. He's like that."

"Wow."

This was the only word she could conjure up as she tried to gather her thoughts together. On the one hand, she was thrilled, ecstatic even, that Jamie was this happy. And it couldn't have come at a better time, what with Holly spending all her evenings and free time with Ben. On the other hand, she'd only just met this man, and now they were going off on some European city break together, which she'd paid for entirely. Maybe the reason they'd got close so quickly, was because she'd been on her own so much more lately. Perhaps loneliness had caused her to rush into this relationship. Whatever it was, a thousand alarm bells were ringing in Holly's mind.

"Tell me how you met him, again," she said, trying to broach the subject as tactfully as she could.

Jamie's eyes sparkled, but before she could speak, there was a tap on the door followed by Fin's voice.

"Babe, don't we need to get moving? You said we had to leave here by half past. It's half past."

"Okay," she called back. "I'm coming."

She turned back to Holly and blew her a kiss.

"I promise I'll catch you up on everything when I get back. Also, if you have time to do any baking, I'm seriously missing your home-made bread. Oh, and don't you and Ben forget to keep Tuesday free for my birthday. Fin is planning something."

"Have you heard of him? I mean, she's spoken about him, but I didn't think they were serious. Certainly not enough for her to go on holiday with him, and pay for it all, too? Did I say that she'd done that, as a surprise for him?"

"You did, twice already."

Holly hadn't rung Ben to stress about Jamie, even though she'd called him the minute she and Fin had left. She'd rung to see if everything was all right with Toby and whether Ben had dropped him home yet. But she'd been barely two words in when the cascade of news started rolling off her tongue. Obviously, she mentioned the shower incident. The last thing she wanted to do was keep anything from him, even when it had absolutely not been her fault. As she'd expected, he'd found great amusement in her humiliation. But mentioning the shower incident led to the matter of the holiday, and now she couldn't stop worrying about it. She hadn't even got an address for the hotel they'd be staying at. Or Fin's surname to give to the police. If something happened to her, who would even know? She would text her the minute she got off the phone to Ben and ask for a full itinerary.

"Don't you think it's odd, though? She's been single for ages and then bam, just like that, she's head over heels."

"Like me, you mean?"

In spite of it all, Holly felt a warmth spread through her.

Head over heels was always the way Ben referred to his feelings, mainly as a running joke about her sending him flying over the handlebars of his bicycle.

"Look," he said, with a sigh. "Jamie is the best judge of character I know, full stop. If she's giving this guy her time, then he's worth it to her, and you need to accept that. I'm sure we'll get plenty of chances to get to know him soon. And here's a thought—he might be even worse at Scrabble than you are, particularly if we don't allow American spellings, and then you won't have to come last every time, when we have a games night."

"Very funny."

"I thought so."

He was right, though. Jamie was a brilliant judge of character, and she didn't suffer fools gladly. Maybe Holly would just send the occasional message, asking how the trip was going. That way, she'd be able to keep close tabs on what they were doing and where they were.

"So, how's Toby?" she asked, finally getting around to her reason for calling him. "Have you dropped him home yet?"

"It's a bit of mess, if I'm honest," he replied. "It sounds like a load of stuff between him and Jess has come to a head. I've told him he can stay here tonight."

"Oh?"

Holly's voice hitched in surprise. Jess was Ben's older sister, and though they didn't live that far apart—her home was in a small village just outside of Stow-on-the-Wold, she hadn't actually met her yet. It was something she'd more than once thought about mentioning to him, but as he hadn't been formally introduced to her family, either, it didn't seem like too much of a deal.

"Well, it makes sense," Ben continued. "He's in sixth form

in the village, so he can walk to school from here and he'll be able to have a bit of a lie in, too, not having to get up for the bus. Hopefully, it will give him time to calm down and see things more clearly. I've messaged Jess. I'm going to go over there now and pick up some of his things. I think it'll do them both good to have a time-out."

"Oh, okay," she said, unsure why she was feeling quite so irritated by this piece of news. After all, Toby was Ben's nephew and obviously in need of help.

"You're most welcome to come over and watch some TV with Toby until I get back. Or you can come with me to Stow, although I'm just going to be grabbing a couple of bags, so it won't be much fun. But it's up to you."

Her immediate instinct was to opt for the latter choice and head up the road in the car with Ben. It would be a chance to talk or just listen to the radio and simply be in each other's company. But it was still pouring outside and leaving the warmth of her house wasn't something she fancied doing, especially as a hot bath with wine and chocolates was still beckoning her.

"Do you know what? I think I might stay here," she said.

"Really?"

It was Ben's turn to sound surprised.

"I've got some things I really ought to be getting on with. The kitchen needs a good clean. Jamie never clears out the fridge properly, so I dread to think what's growing in the back of it, and there's a whole heap of washing that's been accumulating over the last two weeks."

"Are you sure?'

"Yes, of course."

"Okay, well, if that's what you want to do. See you in the morning?"

"Always."

A pause followed. They hardly ever spoke on the phone. There was no need to when they saw so much of each other. As such, Holly was unsure how to end the call. She knew how she wanted to do it and what words she'd like to hear in return. But so far, neither of them had been brave enough to say them.

"Well, sleep tight. When you get to bed, that is," she added.

"Yes, you too, Holly Berry. Sleep tight."

As she hung up, she felt a strange fluttering inside her that she couldn't quite place. After all, it was only one night apart.

CHAPTER FIVE

Deciding to stay true to her word, Holly tackled the kitchen before going for a soak. As she had suspected, the fridge was like a scene from a horror film. Plastic bags filled with what she assumed had once been salad, now contained a pungent, green mush, while a half-eaten punnet of raspberries displayed enough varieties of mould to be worthy of a post-graduate study. There were also the standard out-of-date yogurts, sprouting potatoes, and several takeaway containers which had been shoved right to the back. As peculiar as it may sound, she gained a great sense of satisfaction from washing all the surfaces and replacing everything, with the jars neatly lined up in the door and their lids screwed on properly.

Once that was done, it seemed silly not to carry on with the cleaning. She wiped down the rest of the kitchen, swept and mopped the floor and then ran the Hoover over the living room, the landing and lastly her bedroom.

Normally, she would have baked. Busy hands kept her sane when she had something on her mind. But the fact that she'd spent so much time at Ben's meant that the cupboards were nearly bare of ingredients, and her brain was too preoccupied to figure out what she could make with the last few grams of wholemeal flour and a tin of peaches. So cleaning had been the next best option.

She decided that a long bath was off the cards. It would be difficult to relax in a place where only hours before she'd seen her housemate's boyfriend utterly starkers. While she tried her hardest to settle down with a book, she couldn't get through a page without having to go back and re-read it. So in the end, she gave up and went to bed. Not that that was a success, either.

"How did you sleep last night?" Ben asked as they met outside their front doors, ready to walk in to work together, a tradition that had started long before they'd become a couple.

"Badly," Holly replied, hooking her arm around his with a sigh. "I just kept thinking about Jamie and this Fin guy. I mean, he's the type of person who walks around other people's houses naked. That doesn't say very much for him, does it?"

"And there was me thinking you were going to say you couldn't sleep because you missed me," he said, with a smirk.

"Sorry," she sighed again and leant her head against his shoulder. "Of course I missed you. Although it was relaxing being able to stretch out and have the entire bed to myself without you hogging the duvet."

"Me? I'm not the one who does that."

"You are, too."

They stopped walking and she glanced up at him with a smile. A tingle crept down her spine. Three months in, and still almost every moment like this, when they were about to kiss, felt exciting. And that's exactly what happened. Standing at the side of the road, with the morning sun reflecting in the puddles from the previous day's rain, she was kissing Ben Thornbury, her boyfriend, and it felt great.

"You know we could just pull a sickie and head back home?" he said, kissing the top of an ear and moving down to the lobe. "Toby's going to be leaving for school in a few minutes. Then we could go see who really takes up all the room in the bed."

"Ben Thornbury!" Holly's jaw dropped in mock horror. "Are you suggesting we play hooky? What have you become?"

"This is what you do to me, Holly Berry."

With the coyest grin she could offer, she slipped out of his embrace and started to walk on.

"As tempting as that offer is," she said, over her shoulder, "I'll have you know I'm a serious business owner and can't just skive off work for the day."

A massive look of relief came over his face.

"Phew. I'll be honest, I've got a load of appointments and paperwork to get through today. I didn't really think that through before I opened my mouth."

She laughed.

"I was worried about what was happening to you there for a moment. It's all right, I won't make you play truant. How about a lunch-time hot chocolate at the Littlest Cafe instead? Caroline's in for a couple of hours. She'll be fine on her own."

"Sounds perfect."

A few minutes later, they'd reached the High Street and were standing outside *Just One More,* kissing goodbye and wishing each other a lovely day at work. This really was a great life she had going at the minute, she thought. And then the niggle returned.

"Did you bring them down from the stockroom?" Caroline called from the other side of the shop.

Caroline and Holly had gone to school in Bourton together, many, many years ago, only to lose contact when Holly had moved to London. Thankfully, Caroline had been a regular customer at *Just One More,* and they'd been reunited when Holly took it over. After reconnecting over several wine-fuelled evenings, she had also become Holly's second employee.

Currently sporting the shop's trademark blue-striped apron, Caroline was standing on a small stepladder that they used to reach the sweets on the top shelves. These were the ones which weren't quite so popular as the others but they needed to keep in stock, because that's what a proper, old-fashioned shop did and was what people particularly appreciated. Things like liquorice root, Pontefract cakes and aniseed bullets. Unusually, there had been a massive run on them recently and the jars were just about empty.

"Sorry, what was that?" Holly asked, looking up from the counter.

"The sweets? The liquorice root and aniseed bullets. Did you bring them down?"

"Sorry, I got distracted. I completely forgot. I'll get them now."

Owning the tiniest shop in the village had its advantages. It was a short trip across the floor, up the stairs and back down again. After handing the bags to Caroline, Holly moved back to the counter and despite a to-do list a hundred items long, she grabbed her phone from beside the till and went back to scrolling.

"What are you looking at?" Caroline asked, leaving the jars

and coming over to see what she was up to. "Please don't tell me this is still about Jamie and this Fin guy."

Holly pouted. Caroline had said the same thing as Ben, that she was a grown woman and the fact that she usually played her cards close to her chest probably meant that he was special. But if that were the case, why hadn't he met her friends? Surely a good guy would want to do that.

"You know, I can't find him. Jamie's friends with one Fin, but it's not him. You'd think if you were dating someone, you'd be friends with them on social media, wouldn't you?"

"Unless he's not on it?" Caroline countered.

"Exactly, and what does that say about him? That he has something to hide."

"Or, that he doesn't want his personal life plastered over the internet for people to gawk at when they're trying to stalk him. Or that he doesn't feel the need to share everything from his latest meal to random train photos with people he met once fourteen years ago."

This caused a spark of annoyance in Holly. Yes, an element of what Caroline was saying was probably correct. Ben wasn't on anything, but that was because of his job and this Fin guy certainly didn't look like bank-manager material, with his long, wavy locks and leather necklace. No, he looked like the exact type who would flaunt his sculpted abs across the internet.

"You can't tell me you're not at least a little worried about this?" she said, hoping for just a bit of support.

"Yes, I can. You know, one summer, Jamie suddenly went off trekking in Nepal for a week without telling a soul. Another time, she took the train to Glasgow for a one-day whisky festival. She was back at work the next day, albeit with a killer hangover. Honestly, you don't need to worry about her. Besides, we've got more than enough to keep us busy."

With a glance out of the window, Holly saw exactly what she meant. Two coach loads of tourists were disembarking on the other side of the road and were heading straight for them.

This would become a regular occurrence now that spring had almost arrived, and Caroline was right; they had plenty to occupy their time. They had barely restocked the shelves when things started flying off them again. Jazzies and marzipan tea cakes were the most popular, along with good old sticks of rock, jelly babies and dolly mixture. Cough candy, bright orange and plastic wrapped, sold bag after bag, and Holly had to go upstairs to grab more of the crystallised ginger. By the time lunch came around, it looked like they hadn't restocked at all, which she was about to remedy when, at two minutes past one, Ben appeared.

"You ready?" he asked, looking at her, expectantly.

She returned his look with one of confusion.

"Lunch? Hot Chocolate? We were going to the Littlest Cafe," he prompted.

"Oh, of course."

With a flicker of tension, she cast her eyes around the decimated shelves. Between the influx of customers and fretting about this Fin guy, she had completely forgotten about their lunch date, let alone asking Caroline whether she minded covering. Of course, she could handle the shop perfectly well by herself; she did it every Tuesday when Holly had her day off. But that didn't mean she shouldn't have been consulted.

"Off you go. I've got this," Caroline said, before she could say anything.

"I don't mind staying. There could be another rush."

"Honestly, I'll be fine. Go."

Holly bit her bottom lip for a moment before nodding gratefully.

"Well, I'm only just over the road, so if things get crazy, give me a call. Okay?"

"Will you please just go? I'll be fine," she repeated.

"You're the best. You know that."

"I do. Now enjoy your lunch."

The Littlest Cafe had seats outside overlooking the river, with a perfect view of the bridges, the ducks and the people ambling around as they went about their day-to-day lives. However, Holly and Ben preferred the courtyard out the back with its cast iron tables and chairs, complete with dark-green parasols. Vines of ivy and honeysuckle climbed up trellises that were set against the surrounding walls. On chilly days, like this, there was a large space heater in operation which offered an orange glow and the ability to raise the temperature to a pleasant level. The place did great coffee and cakes, too, although today, they each chose a bacon sandwich.

"So, busy day then?" Ben asked before taking a bite of his.

"It really is. Hopefully, it's a sign of things to come. If it keeps up like this until Easter, it would be amazing."

Despite her positivity, he looked somewhat concerned.

"Are you going to be okay? Have you thought about maybe taking someone else on, now that Drey's cutting back on her hours?"

"Actually, it's funny you should say that."

Over lunch, she proceeded to tell him about the conversation with her mum, and how she would need to go up and see them in the week to offer her dad a job, without him realising she'd been asked to do it.

"He shouldn't have much difficulty getting the hang of things. It's not exactly rocket science. And what else can I do? He's my dad."

Ben nodded before taking a suspiciously deep breath.

"Talking about family, Jess is coming over to mine tonight. I said I'd cook dinner, act as mediator between her and Toby and hopefully help them have a civilised conversation. I hadn't realised things had got so bad between the pair of them."

"Wow," Holly grimaced. "That sounds like a fun evening."

It was his turn to pull a face.

"Actually … I was hoping you'd like to come and join us? I mean, I've wanted you to meet her for a while. I know that this probably isn't the nicest situation to be thrown into, but I'm really not good with family confrontation. By the sound of things, they've been arguing nonstop for weeks now. If you wouldn't mind, I'd like you to be there. Things always seem easier when I've got you beside me."

"You want me to meet your sister?" she asked, a warm glow taking hold of her.

"Of course I do. But only if you really don't mind, though. If you'd rather wait for a better moment, I'd completely understand."

"No. I mean, yes. I want to. Today would be good. Today sounds great, in fact."

The flush of heat transformed into a swarm of butterflies. Dropping her sandwich, she leant forwards and kissed him firmly on the lips.

She was meeting her boyfriend's family.

This was getting serious.

CHAPTER SIX

Whilst Holly still felt extremely concerned about having Jamie away on a trip with a man she knew nothing about, she was at least relieved that she had a genuine reason to message her, without it looking like she was checking up on her. After all, she really was desperate for advice. After Ben had dropped her back at the shop and Caroline headed off to pick up her children from school, she grabbed her phone and started typing away.

Help! Meeting Ben's sister! What do I need to know?! You've met her, haven't you?

She watched as her message was delivered and then, to her surprise, was immediately read and replied to.

Yay! Jess is great. You'll love her.

Only a few seconds later, another message came through. This time, it was a photograph of Jamie and Fin who were, by the looks of things, on a boat trip. Their heads were squashed close together in a selfie, although it was difficult to make out much of him with his stubble, sunglasses and baseball cap. A hint of annoyance flashed through her. Sunglasses and a hat in

March? Was it really that bright in Amsterdam at this time of year? Maybe he needed to wear them because of an eye condition. Either that or he was just a poser. Still, Jamie's face was glowing.

Fin says hi, she'd written underneath.

Can't wait to meet him properly, Holly messaged back, grateful that Jamie couldn't see her gritted teeth as she typed. *And wish me luck for tonight.*

No luck needed. She'll love you, like we all do.

Holly finished with a string of smiley-face emojis. Jamie was still alive. That was something. As for the evening with Ben's sister, she felt quietly confident. Although she'd found herself suffering a constant stream of butterflies since the lunch time invitation, it was mainly due to the excitement of reaching the next level in their relationship.

She was only mildly concerned about meeting Jess. She'd never had any problems with other people's parents, who'd always seemed to love her, if that was anything to go by. Dan's mother had been the most possessive parent possible, who thought no one on the planet could be good enough for her wonderful—and only—son. And yet she had soon come around to his relationship with Holly. Before they broke up, she would often message her with pictures of outfits she'd bought, asking her opinion on shoes and accessories, or for suggestions of nice places to go when she and her husband were up in London. Not that Holly had ever been an expert on such matters. She doubted getting on with a sibling would be very different to that.

Determined to make a good impression, she chose a nice selection of sweets to take along with her that evening. Ben loved anything that involved lemons: sherbet lemon, lemon pips, lemon bonbons—the more citrusy the better. But she didn't know what Jess's taste in confectionery would be, so she selected some quality items, including dark chocolate-covered Brazils, chocolate gingers and a new pecan fudge that was new in. It was so melt-in-the-mouth that she'd probably eaten a pound or more already. She'd even put together a little golden box filled with Belgian chocolates, too. Then, having cashed up and shut the shop for the day, she headed back home to have a shower and put on a fresh outfit, ready for the big meal.

Jess was due to arrive at seven thirty, and after much debate, Holly decided that she'd feel more comfortable already being there when she arrived, rather than making a grand entrance. Ben's house was where she spent most of her time, and it seemed silly pretending otherwise. She checked her reflection in the hall mirror at least half a dozen times, then grabbed the sweets and a bottle of wine from the rack and headed next door at ten past the hour.

It was strange having to ring the doorbell. Normally, she went straight in with Ben after work and left again with him the next morning. There was no need to have her own key or knock on the door. In fact, she couldn't remember the last time she'd had to wait outside in the cold like this. Thankfully, it didn't take long for the door to swing open.

"Toby!" Holly said in surprise. "How are you doing? Is Ben here?"

"Just through in the kitchen, cooking," he replied. "Come in."

She took a step inside. Coming from just next door, she hadn't bothered with a coat, but the chill outside had quickly settled on her and was at extreme odds with the central heating.

As Toby slipped back into the living room, she went in search of Ben. While most of the house was an exact mirror image of her place next door, the kitchen was the one room that was set out entirely differently. There was no large island in the centre and no wooden cabinets, either. Everything here was sleek and white. Not a door handle was visible, and the place was so pristine that the first couple of times she had gone to cook something, she'd been terrified. Once, she would have even worried that leaving a bag on the worktop might upset the feng shui. But those days were well past her now. She had baked fresh bread to go with her homemade soups and even fried several full-English breakfasts. And her sweets now had their own little cupboard space.

The oven light was on, and the scent of roasting meat and herbs filled the room. Ben was busy fussing with something on the hob, an apron tied around his waist and a sheen of sweat gleaming on his brow.

"Something smells good," she said, wrapping her arms around his waist. "What's cooking?"

"Lamb shank. The same recipe I used when I first cooked dinner for you."

"You mean the one that ended up burning because we got too distracted?"

Holly grinned as he turned around to her.

"I don't think it was burnt," he mumbled.

"I think we both know it was," she insisted, pressing her lips firmly onto his.

Kissing in a kitchen while her man cooked her dinner. Did life get any better than this? she wondered.

"You know what, that's not the main thing I recall about that night," he said, breaking away briefly from the kiss, only to return to it almost immediately.

"No?" she asked, pulling back just a fraction. "What is it then?"

"When this evening's over, I'll remind you."

The heat was undeniable and wasn't just coming from the oven. Three months in and they were still firmly stuck in the honeymoon period. It was a shame that he'd already got changed from work, though. There was something she liked about loosening his tie and slipping it over his head the moment they got indoors. The memories of that first dinner were still clear in her mind.

She was just recollecting exactly how that evening had gone and how nervous she'd been, when a throat cleared behind them and they hastily backed away from each other.

"Sorry, I just came to get a drink," Toby said, looking sheepishly from the doorway. "I can wait if you need some alone time?"

"Um, uh, no ... no, of course not. You should get a drink. Yes. Of course," Ben stuttered.

As Holly retreated to the other side of the kitchen, brushing down her skirt and then trying to tidy her hair, she wondered if she looked as embarrassed as Ben, who was currently turning crimson.

"We were just talking about the food your uncle's cooking," she said, coming up with nothing better.

"Yeah, it looked like it," Toby smirked.

"No, honestly, he made it for me before. It's very good. Great, actually."

Holly could feel the hole she was digging herself into getting deeper. This was what she did when she was nervous. She babbled.

"I mean it wasn't the best. That could have been because it got a bit burned, but I'm sure—"

The shrill ring of the doorbell cut her off mid-sentence and she wondered if she had ever been more grateful for an interruption.

"Thank God," she muttered, as Ben shot her a sideways smile.

"Saved by the bell," he said.

"Or not," said Toby.

Any trace of amusement that had been lingering on his face vanished, and he suddenly looked a lot younger than he had before, far more like the small boy in the photos she'd seen. Whatever argument there'd been between him and his mother, Holly was now a little unsure that she wanted to be there to see how things turned out.

"Time for you two to meet," Ben said to her, and the way he spoke, sent a whole new level of terror through her.

It was fair to say that in the excitement of being introduced to Ben's family Holly had forgotten the reason that he wanted her there: as moral support to help buffer the tension between Jess and Toby. She had started to envision a jovial affair, where they drank wine, chatted and laughed over anecdotes from Ben's childhood. However, judging by the grey tinge that both Toby and Ben's complexions had taken on, that wasn't going to be the case. A silence descended upon the room, that was abruptly interrupted by another shrill blast of the bell.

"Is anyone going to get that?" she asked.

"Not me."

Toby's answer was immediate. He directed his next words at Ben.

"You're the one who invited her here. You should go."

"I can't answer the door. I'm busy cooking," he replied, making a random grab at a nearby saucepan that had nothing in it.

"Should I, then?" Holly offered, sensing that neither of them was going to back down anytime soon.

"That would be great. Thank you," Ben said, putting the saucepan down again.

The relaxed confidence of earlier had evaporated entirely and been replaced by a nervousness that they all seemed to be sharing. She strode towards the front door, taking uncharacteristically deep breaths. There was nothing to worry about, she reminded herself. Hadn't Jamie said that Jess was lovely? Besides, she had brought her chocolates, and that was always a sure-fire icebreaker.

Holly fixed a smile firmly in place and opened the front door.

CHAPTER SEVEN

Holly had not been alone in experiencing *that look* from another woman every now and then. Sometimes, it would come from someone you hadn't seen in a long time, assessing how you'd changed—for better or worse—between meetings. Other times it would come from a woman you didn't know, doing a quick assessment of how you compared to her in age, attractiveness or style. Or it could be a colleague, inspecting how you'd dressed for a meeting or event. Like every other woman she knew, she'd been the victim of the full body scan, the analysing glance in which the other person made a dozen judgements about you in less than two seconds. She had worked in London, after all. But back then, it hadn't bothered her. She couldn't have cared a jot what people thought about her wearing the same top two days in the same week or a jumper from three seasons ago that she'd picked up in a charity shop. But never had she felt a scrutiny so intense as this.

As she opened the door, Jess's eyes barely met hers before they scanned down her and back up again. Every muscle in

Holly's body tightened. Finally, when the woman's eyes had returned to her face, she offered a wide smile.

"You must be the new neighbour, Holly," she said.

The comment was said with a warmth that didn't quite reach her eyes.

Neighbour. Holly's mind tripped on the word. It was true she lived next door, but she wasn't exactly new anymore. Besides, *Ben's girlfriend* seemed like a more suitable epithet. But before she could clear matters up, Jess had slipped passed her into the hallway and was unbuttoning her coat.

"Ben?" she called out, not offering Holly a second glance as she strode into the house.

"We're in the kitchen!" he called back.

A stunned moment followed, in which Holly felt like she had just missed something important, yet she couldn't for the life of her figure out what it was. Assuming she must have read too much into a mere seven-word sentence, she closed the door and raced to get back to the kitchen, following behind Jess.

The scene had barely changed from a few moments earlier, except that Toby was now even greyer, and Ben's saucepan actually contained something. Crossing over to the dining table, Jess slipped off her grey, woollen coat and slung it on the nearest countertop, before turning to offer Ben a swift kiss on the cheek.

"Wow, you weren't joking when you said you were going to cook dinner. That smells delicious," she said.

Just as with Toby, Holly had seen plenty of photos of her around the house, but again, like her son, she'd been substantially younger in them. They also tended to be taken on holiday, or during big family get-togethers and had an air of frivolity about them. Something that was currently completely absent.

If she had to pick one word to describe Ben's sister, it would be severe. Tall and slim, she wore her dark hair in a sleek bob, cut at a sharp angle to her chin. Like her coat, her jeans and top were grey. She would bet that her underwear and socks would be grey, too. Whilst taking this in, she tried to recall what Ben had said she did for a living. Was it something in finance or accounting, perhaps? She was sure there were numbers and money involved, just like with his job.

Having addressed Ben, Jess turned to Toby.

"Tobias," she said, in a less than affable voice.

"Mum."

Tension rippled in the air. Unsure of what she was supposed to do, Holly looked towards Ben and thankfully caught his eye.

"Jess," he said, stepping away from the hob and towards her. "I've been wanting you to meet Holly, my girlfriend."

That same forced smile as when Holly had opened the door to her, was now firmly back in place on Jess's face.

"Yes, we met. She let me in."

Feeling she had to be the one to make the first move, Holly stepped towards her and held out her hand.

"Pleased to meet you. Ben's spoken so much about you. And Toby. And Patrick," she added, praying she'd got her husband's name right. "The whole family, really."

The smile remained fixed.

"Well, I'm sure we'll have an opportunity to catch up in the future."

Everything she said was clipped. It was setting Holly's teeth on edge.

"Actually," Ben said, coming behind Holly and slipping his arm around her. "Holly's joining us for dinner."

She couldn't be sure whether she'd sighed out loud with relief or just felt it. She hadn't realised how tense she'd become until Ben's arm and words had loosened her up. Whatever

Jamie's opinion, she had the distinct feeling that this would not be an easy evening.

"She's staying for dinner tonight?"

Jess responded to Ben's comment with a further stiffening of her shoulders.

"I don't think that's a good idea at all, Ben. We've got things to discuss, family things."

"Don't be silly. Come on, let me get you a wine. White?"

"I have to drive us home."

"You can have one small glass."

She made a sound that was halfway between a tut and sigh, although her shoulders did relax a fraction.

"A very small one, then. Somehow, I think I'm going to need a drink to get through this."

As he moved to the fridge, Ben caught Holly's eye and offered her a small smile that said he was there for her. That she was okay. A sudden thought struck her. Something that would hopefully put his sister in a slightly better mood.

"Jess, I brought you some things from the shop. Let me just fetch them."

Holly was grateful for a moment away from the kitchen. Reaching the hallway, she took a couple of deep breaths. She could do this. She'd be fine. Half an hour and a couple of drinks later, they'd all be laughing like old friends. Maybe she could offer her a bed next door, so she didn't have to drive back, if that was what she was worried about.

Confident that there were many ways to turn things around, she collected the bag she'd brought from the shop and returned to the others.

"I picked out a few things you might like," she said, handing it to Jess with her widest and warmest smile. "The pecan fudge is amazing. So are the dark-chocolate Brazils.

They're really moreish; trust me. I've eaten far too many of them."

Given how these were some of the nicest items she stocked and were obviously not cheap, she expected a nice thank you. Perhaps even a hug—no, maybe not. She felt that Jess was definitely not a hugger. Instead, her reaction was somewhere between a pout and a grimace.

"I know pecan fudge sounds a bit weird, but it's incredible," she tried again, feeling the awkwardness level rising. "You can ask Ben. I've brought him loads home. He loves it, too."

"Mum's allergic to nuts," Toby said, from the other side of the room. "Can't eat anything at all with them in."

"Oh," Holly said, feeling as deflated as if she'd been hit by a rock. "Oh, sorry. I didn't know. There are some other things in there, some Belgium Chocolates, for example."

Jess's smile tightened.

"That's sweet of you. Have they been hand boxed?"

"Yes. I picked them out myself this afternoon."

"Then I probably shouldn't risk it. Cross contamination can be a killer. Besides, if there were a praline in there, it would be a disaster."

"No, no. Of course not, silly me. Well, maybe Patrick would like them?"

"He's prediabetic," she replied. "Under strict dietary instructions from the doctor. Extremely limited carbs. Ben knows all of this. I guess he hasn't told you much about us at all," she added with arched eyebrows.

Desperately wanting to maintain an air of positivity, Holly had to force herself to not look upset by these comments. Particularly the last one. You'd have thought that Ben's sister having a severe nut allergy would have come up in conversation, even if his brother-in-law's prediabetic condition hadn't. It was also more than a little irritating that he'd not come to her aid at any point during this conversation, but then he was currently busy opening every kitchen cupboard in search of something.

"Do you know what? I'm just going to lay the table," she said, making a dash for the cutlery drawer. "I don't think food is going to be too long now, is it, Ben?"

Not waiting for a reply, she grabbed handfuls of knives and forks, not even bothering to count if she had the right number, before racing out of the kitchen and into the dining room.

Closing the door behind her, she shut her eyes and drew in several, deep breaths, Jess's voice still echoing around her head. *I suppose he hasn't told you much about us at all.* Had she been deliberately trying to get a rise out of her? Aiming to upset her? But what on earth would be the point of that? Perhaps she was just one of those people who couldn't help being blunt, no matter how rude it came across.

Wondering if she could make a sudden excuse and leave, Holly was just about to place the first knife on the table, when the door opened.

"Hey," Ben said, looking flustered. "I don't know where my gravy boat is. I know I have one somewhere."

A lump came to her throat. He clearly had a lot on his mind with this dinner, but she genuinely wasn't sure that she could make it through an entire ·meal if this woman continued to speak to her the way she'd done in the last few minutes. At the very least, she needed to be reassured that she hadn't done anything wrong.

"It's next door, at mine, remember?" she said, somewhat startled. "We had a roast there about a month ago. I don't think I brought it back.

"Ben, about Jess—"

"She's great, isn't she?" he enthused. "I knew you two would get on like a house on fire. Would you mind going and grabbing it? The food is ready, and I don't want it to spoil."

Holly swallowed. *Like a house on fire*? That is one way to describe his sister, she thought. Unapproachable and a danger to your wellbeing. Yet Ben was smiling enthusiastically at her. What could she say? That she didn't think his sister liked her and the feeling was mutual? That he should have told her about the nut allergy?

Maybe Jess wasn't being unreasonable. She obviously had a lot of things going on with Toby, and they had rather sprung Holly being there on her. No. Jamie had said she was great, and she had to believe her. She was probably just being overly sensitive about making a good impression, that was all. Everything would be much better during the meal, she told herself. Yes, everything would be great.

"I'll go and fetch the gravy boat for you now," she said with a smile, giving him a quick peck on the cheek as she left.

CHAPTER EIGHT

Despite Holly's desperation to believe that Jess's lack of civility had all been in her head, things did not improve over dinner. The food was great. The lamb shank was decidedly more delicious than when Ben had burned it the first time around. But the company left a lot to be desired.

It quickly became apparent that Toby and Jess had no intention of talking to one another and the air of hostility in the kitchen only deepened when they were seated close together. Apart from a couple of curt *thank yous* to Ben for the food, the first few minutes around the table passed in complete silence. Chewing a mouthful of meat, Holly considered whether she should risk being the one to strike up a conversation. On the plus side, dinner would be over far quicker if no one said anything. But that was why Ben had invited her there, she remembered. To help relax the situation. Just as she was about to open her mouth, Jess spoke

"So, you work in a shop," she said, somewhat dismissively, while stabbing a potato with her fork.

"I don't just work there, actually. I own it. It's the sweet shop in the centre of the village: *Just One More.*"

"Ah yes, I remember Ben mentioning it when you first moved here. *Ridiculously irresponsible* was what you said, wasn't it?"

Ben's cheeks flushed a deep red.

"Well, that was before I got to know Holly," he replied, although this sounded a pretty weak line of defence, even to her. Unfortunately, there wasn't any time for her to defend herself, as Jess was back in with her next question before she even had time to draw breath.

"And why did you leave London? It was London, wasn't it?"

"It was," Holly replied, wondering exactly how much Ben had told her, and how much she could skim over. She certainly didn't want to discuss Dan.

"I just needed a change. You know how it is. This is a beautiful part of the country and I think that, somewhere deep down, I'd always planned on moving back here."

It wasn't exactly the truth, but Holly didn't care. Nothing Jess was saying was improving her opinion of her, and the sooner this meal was over, the better.

"I knew it. I think I remember you from school. You did go to school here, didn't you? Were you in the Debating Team? Or the Orchestra, perhaps?"

"Yes. I mean yes to going to the school, but not to the other things. I wasn't in any of the clubs."

Jess sniffed. Obviously, not being a member of the School Debating Team or a musician was a valid enough reason to judge someone fifteen years later.

"Not everyone can be head of two sports teams and the Chair of the Debating Society," Ben said, teasingly.

"And First Violin. You forgot First Violin."

"Jesus, Mum."

While the words had come from Toby, Holly shared his sentiment. The boy had barely spoken two words during the meal, other than to ask her to pass him the gravy, and given how Jess had been pointedly ignoring him, she assumed that would continue. But Jess placed her cutlery down on the table with a loud smack.

"Well, why don't we talk about your school accomplishments, Tobias?"

A long sigh rattled from his lips.

"Great, I was wondering when you were going to get to that."

"That is the reason we're here, isn't it? Because you decided you need a mediator to speak to your own mother."

"That's because my mother won't listen to me. My mother won't listen to anyone."

Holly threw a glance at Ben. Considering how tightly she was gripping her cutlery, she was surprised that he wasn't intervening at all. He didn't look happy with this sudden, passive-aggressive outburst from his nephew, but he wasn't doing anything, even though a full-blown argument looked only moments away.

"Fine, I'm here now and I'm all ears," Jess responded. "So why don't you explain to me how you think it's a good idea to throw away everything you've worked for and not go to university?"

"I don't know why you think that. It's an amazing chance for me."

"One that doesn't offer you any security, like a degree would. For goodness' sake, you haven't even completed your A levels yet!"

"But I don't need to! I don't understand why you can't see how brilliant it would be."

Holly was well and truly lost. She'd figured out that all this angst was something to do with his education, but that was pretty much it. Thankfully, Ben at last noticed her bewilderment and explained.

"Toby's been offered an internship at a web designers in Bristol," he said.

"It's a paid internship," Toby came in quickly. "A proper, paid job. I've already got loads of the skills I need, like scripting in HTML5 and CSS, but they'll train me up to do other things, too. This could set me up for life."

While the words—or rather the acronyms—that he had used went entirely over her head, and she would be the first to admit that she knew absolutely nothing about web design, he had done a brilliant job on the website he'd put together for the shop, when she first took it over. She'd even had customers commenting on how good it looked and how easy it was to navigate and place an order on it. There was also no denying that he was seriously enthusiastic about whatever this job entailed.

"That does sound like a great opportunity," Holly said.

"Exactly." Toby raised his hands. "Anyone can see that. Anyone, except my mother."

"Oh, I'm sorry. Perhaps we should just consult a few more random strangers for their opinion on your future, if that's what we're doing here."

Whether she'd meant the words solely as an insult to Toby, Holly wasn't sure, but it certainly sounded like a personal attack on her now. *Another* attack on her.

"Look Mum," he said, lowering his voice a little. "I know you're just worried about me, but I don't need a degree. Loads of people working in my line don't have one. Even the old guys at the top."

"But you won't be going in as an old guy at the top. You'll be the lowest of the low. And when the company reshuffles—as all businesses do, Toby—when that happens, who do you think is going to be the first out the door? And with nothing to fall back on. You need to think of your long-term future."

Holly shrank back in her seat. This was obviously a rerun of an argument that had happened several times before and was undoubtedly the reason that Toby had appeared at Ben's door in the first place.

Silence engulfed the table. Holly returned to her food and speared a piece of lamb as quietly as possible, but her chewing felt conspicuously loud. Ben opened his mouth several times as if he were about to speak, only to close it again, obviously failing to come up with a suitable line of mediation between his nephew and his sister without upsetting either of them. Jess and Toby simply glowered. How long would this go on for? Holly wondered. She wasn't good at silences. They made her intolerably nervous, which always led to her trying to fill them with inanities. And even as she tried not to, telling herself that it really wasn't a good idea, she could feel the words spilling from the end of her tongue.

"I hear internships can be really competitive these days," she burst out. "I read something about it online. Lots of the really big companies are going down that path now. Trying to recruit the best people before they're even out of school."

"See!" Toby said, slamming a hand down on the table.

While he may have been grateful for Holly's input, Jess obviously wasn't.

"Well, thank you very much for that utterly insightful overview. But if you don't mind, this is a family matter. I'm not even sure why you're here at all."

These words were more than blunt and Holly felt cut to the quick. She sucked a lungful of air in through her nose, clenching her fists under the table. How dare she? How dare she march in here, to the place that was almost her home and speak to her like that? Maybe it was a family matter, but she'd been invited to join them for dinner by the person who owned the bloody house. And maybe she wasn't some hot-shot accountant, or whatever the hell it was that Jess did, but she was a mildly successful business owner, not to mention the fact that she was Ben's girlfriend.

It was this thought that made her look straight at him. He was surely going to make his sister apologise for what she just said, wasn't he? He couldn't possibly let her speak that way. Jess was also staring at him, as if daring him to contradict her, but there was no way he was going to let her get away with such rudeness, Holly thought with a surge of confidence.

Yet no sooner had the thought entered her mind than Ben shrank down in his seat, his eyes avoiding them both.

"Perhaps everyone just needs a little time to sleep on it," he said.

CHAPTER NINE

Holly was fuming. Beyond fuming. She was livid. Every ounce of willpower she possessed was currently being put to the test, to stop her from walking out there and then. It was a miracle she hadn't done that immediately or thrown a piece of cutlery across the table at the bloody woman. Or at Ben. Yes, on second thoughts, he would be the target of the blunt knife she was trying to cut her meat with.

Mouthful after mouthful, she stabbed her fork into her food while grinding her teeth together as she chewed. She wasn't the only one who was hacked off, either. While Ben now tried to drum up conversation—were they doing anything for Easter? Had they seen his parents' new conservatory—every question he asked was met with a single-word reply from Toby, Jess and Holly.

When the meal was over, Holly didn't wait for anyone to say anything. She just stood up and started gathering the plates together.

"I'll take these," she announced, desperate to get out of the room.

"I'll help," Ben said, about to stand, but her look was enough to keep him in his place.

"I said, *I'll* take these," she repeated, with a tone that implied Toby, too, should definitely stay put.

In the kitchen, she dumped the plates in the sink and turned the tap on full blast.

She screamed internally as she added an obscenely long squirt of washing up liquid to the water, which was spraying up and over the edge of the sink. She watched as the foam grew to mammoth proportions. When Ben came into the kitchen a few minutes later, her arms were lost all the way up to the elbows in bubbles.

"Toby's going to go home with Jess," he said, hovering in the doorway. "They're leaving now, if you want to say goodbye."

Holly dropped a knife into the cutlery drainer.

"Goodbye!" she yelled, not moving from the spot.

He looked at her quizzically, obviously expecting her to offer a more formal farewell. After taking a second to realise that wasn't going to happen, he headed back out into the hall. A minute or two later, the front door closed, and he returned.

"Well, that didn't go quite as planned. Still, I'm sure he'll come around soon. It's easy to jump at the first opportunity when you're young."

"Mmm-hm."

Holly couldn't even look at him yet. She was still too mad. Instead, she grabbed a tea towel and began to dry the bubble-coated plates.

"But Jess should have learned that he doesn't listen to her when she gets cross like that. He never has."

"Mmm-hm."

Despite her offering the same two-syllable response, it was

only when he came up behind her to kiss her neck and she turned rigid beneath his touch that he finally twigged something was up.

"Are you okay?" he asked. "Is something wrong? Is it Jess? She's a tough nut to crack, sometimes, I'll admit. I promise, once she warms to you, she'll love you."

This was enough to make her blood boil.

"I don't give a rat's arse about Jess. I mean, she's impossibly rude and frankly a bit of a bitch and how she raised someone as nice as Toby, I have no idea. But I really don't care what her opinion of me is."

"So you're not cross with Jess?"

"With Jess? No, not particularly."

It still took another minute for the penny to drop.

"You're cross with me?"

"Well done."

She tossed the tea towel to the side.

"Would it have hurt you to stick up for me, just once?"

"I didn't think you needed sticking up for?"

"No? What about when she said that I wasn't part of the family?"

"Well, you're not."

She could see he didn't mean to hurt her. And looking at the bare facts, it was true. She and Ben weren't married. They'd only been together a little over three months, and yet when they'd got together, she'd thought there had been an unspoken understanding between them that this was it. That after all the heartache each of them had gone through in previous relationships, they would never put each other through anything like that again. That they were committed. The L-word hadn't been said yet by either of them, but it didn't mean she didn't feel it, and she thought the same applied to him. Only now, she wasn't so sure.

"What am I, Ben?"

"What do you mean? You're a sweet shop owner?"

"I don't mean what job do I do. I mean, what am I to you? You said I was your girlfriend, and I thought I was, but you don't even tell me the most basic things about your family. Like the fact your sister has a massive nut allergy."

"Did you want to know Jess had a nut allergy?"

"Aaaargh!"

This time Holly let the scream escape into the outside world. How could he be that obtuse? It was either that, or he was being cruel, and she knew he wasn't that. No, he was just thick. She picked the tea towel up again and twisted it in her hands, only to drop it back down on the counter a moment later.

"Do you know what?" she said. "I've got some more washing to do. I think I'll stay at mine tonight."

"But you did that last night?" he said, sounding utterly confused by her reaction. "Look, I'm sorry you're upset. Why don't you come upstairs, and I'll make you feel better? I promise," he offered, giving her *the look* that he'd used countless times since that first kiss in the snow.

Sometimes they'd be sitting on the sofa together or having dinner alone. Other times, they'd be at the pub, and it would be followed by a hasty exit to get back home and upstairs. There had never been a time when Holly had not responded to it or at least wanted to. But right now, she didn't want him to throw her onto the bed. In fact, she'd rather throw something at him, instead.

"I'll see you tomorrow," she said and picked up the bag that Jess had left on the countertop.

After all, there was no point in letting good sweets go to waste.

It was fair to say that Holly had become a bit of a comfort eater since owning *Just One More,* and when morning came, the boxes of fudge and chocolate Brazils lay empty, although her bad mood remained.

I'm sorry you're upset. The words whirled around and around in her head. That's what he'd said to her: *I'm sorry you're upset.* Not, *I'm sorry I upset you.* He hadn't even been willing to admit what an arse he'd been. Three months in, and they'd barely bickered about anything. If they did, it would be about something trivial, like which type of takeaway they should get. Well, this was certainly making up for it now. He couldn't fix this with a quick apology. No, this would require extreme grovelling.

Even after a morning cup of coffee, her mood failed to lighten, and she'd done so much pacing that she feared she'd wear a groove in the wood flooring if she wasn't careful. However, there was one silver lining. Not having a boyfriend to kiss and cuddle and get distracted by made it far easier to get herself ready, and despite it being twenty minutes before they normally left for work, she was ready to go.

Pausing at her front door, she took out her phone. Ben had sent her a goodnight text—to which she'd churlishly not responded—and then another saying he missed her, which she had replied to, but only with a single x. Normally, their messages ended with at least three, so he should have been able to tell that she was still cross with him.

She thought for a moment, before swiping the screen and typing, *Gone to work early. See you later.* Then, because it felt wrong not to, sent a further one with a kiss on it. He wouldn't see if for a while. She knew that. He always left his phone downstairs when they went to bed and used a proper alarm clock, so that he wouldn't get distracted by messages and emails during the night. So Holly knew she could get to work before Ben saw it and wouldn't risk coming across him. It didn't seem that long ago that she tried to engineer bumping into him. Now she was doing the opposite. Hopefully, after a day of not seeing her, he would realise the error of his ways and give her the apology she deserved.

At the shop, she found that things were pretty much sorted for the day, so after a quick trip to the bakery to grab a cinnamon roll, she flicked the sign on the door to *Open* half an hour earlier than usual to accommodate a particularly eager customer.

As she was serving, a familiar figure appeared in the doorway. Not that she acknowledged him. She continued serving the customer with her normal, bright, cheery smile.

"Hi," Ben said as the customer left.

"Hi," she replied, in the most off-hand tone she could muster.

"I missed you last night. I don't like this. I like you being in bed beside me."

"Is that right?"

"Of course it is."

Even though he wasn't apologising, Holly could feel her resolve weakening. Her determination to stay mad at him until he apologised properly was starting to waver. He stepped into the shop and walked slowly up to the counter.

"You know, two days is the longest—"

"I know," she replied, immediately cutting him off.

"Look, I'm sorry last night was so tough. I guess I hadn't

really thought through how Jess might feel about having you there. And I'm sorry for how she reacted. She can be rather defensive of me, you know, after everything that happened before. I guess I've just got used to it and don't tend to hear it anymore."

He slipped behind the counter and reached out to take her hands. Holly, however, didn't shift.

"You know you still haven't actually apologised, don't you?"

"What do you mean? I just did."

"No, you apologised for last night and how your sister treated me. You didn't apologise for your behaviour. For how you made me feel."

"Look, I understand you're upset," he said, dropping her hands. "But I don't get what you want from me. I know you were upset when Jess made that comment about you not being family, but what could I say? We don't know what the future holds right now. Maybe in a year or so, if we're still going strong, then it could be something we'll discuss."

"Wow, this is romance at its finest," she said. "So you don't actually want me to be part of your family, Ben? Is that where this is going? And if not, why the hell am I wasting so much time on you?"

"Holly, don't be like that."

"Be like what? Wanting answers. Wanting a grown-up, committed relationship?"

Her anger was bubbling back to the surface. She was also going against Agnes's number one rule of not bringing bad feeling into the shop, but Ben was well and truly making that impossible.

"I am committed to this relationship," he said. "I'm here now, aren't I?"

"And what about the future? Can you say you see me as part of that?"

It took less than a second for him to open his mouth, but when he did, no sound came out. She now just wanted to get away from him and the worst apology in history, but she was penned in behind the counter and her only way out into the shop would be to barge past him. Thankfully, she was in barging mood, and he jumped back just in time.

"Great," she said, marching over to the door and opening it, showing in no uncertain terms that she wanted him gone. "Well, at least I know what your kind of commitment means. You need to get to work, and I have a shop to run. If you don't mind, I think it's time you left."

"Holly, please, can we not just talk about this?"

"What's there to talk about? Your face said it all. And there's no point coming down to walk me home today. I've got to visit my parents. You know, *family stuff.*"

For a moment, Ben didn't move. His brow furrowed, and he stared at her with an intensity that she could have sworn bore into her very soul. And then a moment later, he shook it away.

"I guess I'll see you when I see you, then," he said, and left.

CHAPTER TEN

"I don't know what to do, Mum? Am I blowing things up out of all proportion? He had a point. I'm not family yet."

"You don't need to be married to someone to be family, love. It's about how they make you feel. And how they feel about you."

It had been a long day, trying to honour Agnes's rule, while dealing with customers who complained how jelly babies were so much smaller than they used to be in their youth, and how American hard gums were much harder than they thought they should be. Maybe if someone else had been working alongside her, it would have been bearable. She could have been distracted by news of Drey's university applications or what chaos Caroline's children had caused at home. But it was Thursday, and she was all on her own, and her anger continued to simmer.

At 4:45, fifteen minutes earlier than normal, she shut up the shop, walked home and got in her car and set off for Northleach. With all the drama going on in her life, she'd forgotten about the arrangement with her mum to offer her dad part-time work in the shop, and it was only when she saw him at the far end of the back garden with a large basket on his knees that she remembered.

Apparently, he had at last decided to try and find ways to occupy his time. Today's activity had involved going into the forest to forage for mushrooms. It wasn't something his wife was too keen on.

"Honestly," she said. "I give him a week before he tries to feed us something poisonous. What I could actually do with is him cleaning out the shed, but I don't think that's going to happen anytime soon."

Holly offered a sad little chuckle in response, although she was grateful her dad was now getting out and about. She hadn't given any more thought to how she was going to raise the idea of the job without it seeming like charity, so it gave her and her mum time to talk it over alone. Although it didn't take long before she was spilling out all her own frustrations over a cup of tea and chocolate-dipped shortbread.

"I know it's ridiculous to be this upset. We've not been together that long."

"Time means nothing, you know that, dear. How long were you with Dan before you knew he wasn't right for you? Besides, think of your Aunty June."

"Aunty June?"

Holly wasn't sure how her mother's sister fitted into this discussion.

"Well, she met your Uncle John on the Wednesday night when he came into the pub for a game of darts. Two months later, they were married, and she'd got your cousin Henry in her belly. The pair of them just shared their ruby wedding anniversary last year. No, I don't think time matters. If you know, then you know."

"That's the problem. I thought I did, but Ben obviously doesn't feel the same way."

Wendy let out a sigh as she laid her hand on top of Holly's.

"You need to take some time off and think about yourself and not all these men that have been causing havoc in your life. When was the last time you had a holiday?"

"I have a day off every week, Mum," she replied, taking a bite of shortbread, crumbs tumbling onto the table.

"That's not a holiday, is it?" Wendy said as she brushed the crumbs into her hand.

"I don't have the time or the money for a proper break."

"Well, maybe with your dad on board, we might be able to change that."

A noise came from outside as Arthur attempted to pull his boots off before coming indoors, and Wendy lowered her voice to a hushed whisper.

"Remember, it's not come from me," she said.

A second later and the door swung open.

"Is that Holly? I didn't know you were coming over today, love."

Her dad certainly looked like he'd been foraging. His hands were caked in mud, and he was wearing his old black coat with wide pockets and a thick, metal zipper that she remembered from her childhood. There were several green and brown patches on it now where her mum had fixed it up over the years. The sight of it made her smile almost as much as seeing her dad again.

"Let me get washed up and I'll give you a hug," he said, slipping the coat off and hanging it on the back of the kitchen door. A minute later, the sound of running water came from the utility room.

"Not from me," her mum whispered again, her eyes wide with nerves.

Holly nodded. As if she needed anything else to stress her out.

"I guess you'll be wanting a cup of tea and some short-bread, now," Wendy said, when Arthur returned.

"Only if you're offering."

"Go on you. Sit down. I was going to put the kettle on again for us, anyway. Oh, I've just remembered, we've used up all the milk. I tell you what. I'll pop up the shop now. You'll want another cup before you leave, won't you, Holly love?"

"That would be nice," she replied, realising that was the only answer she could give.

"I'll just be two ticks," Wendy said, grabbing her coat from the hook. "I should probably get some more tea bags, too, while I'm out."

A second later, and she was gone. It had obviously been her plan to leave Holly and Arthur on their own like this, so it didn't look like the idea had come from her. But while Holly knew what she needed to do, going straight in with a job offer seemed too obvious. She had to talk to her dad first and address the elephant in the room.

"I guess your mum told you why I'm home and not at work," he said.

There was no point playing ignorant and at least he'd got the ball rolling.

"Yeah, she told me what happened. I'm so sorry."

"I'd be lying if I said I hadn't seen it coming." He sighed. "To be honest, I'm amazed they didn't let us go before now. Mitch, my boss, well my old boss that is, is a nice enough young lad. I know he tried hard for us. But when Head Office gives the orders, there ain't much you can do." He sighed again. "I'll be honest, I thought the days of job hunting were past me now. But something'll turn up soon."

Was now the moment? she wondered. She didn't want it to seem contrived. Her mother was right. If he had any inkling that the offer was coming because of her, he'd see it as charity and refuse, immediately. But it seemed silly not to say something when he'd just given her the perfect opening.

"Did you use tills at the warehouse?" she asked, trying to sound casual.

"Tills? For money?"

"Yes."

"No. Stuff's not done like that in wholesale. It's all invoices. Money moving through the phone lines, you know, that type of thing. No, I've not used a till in a long time, not since I was a lad when I worked in a paper shop."

Holly groaned inwardly. That could have gone better. If he had worked with them recently, it would have made offering him a job more natural. She'd have to work harder to get to the point.

"I can't imagine they've changed that much. I remember Maud and Agnes had an old one when I first went to work at the shop. The electric ones are actually much easier."

"Is that right? I wouldn't know."

How on earth was she going to shoehorn this in? she wondered. They could end up going around in circles like this for hours if she didn't ask him soon. Then again, what was stopping her?

"Why don't you come and do some work for me at the shop?" she blurted out, trying to make it sound as spontaneous and unrehearsed as possible. "I've got some hours I need filling."

Arthur paused and rubbed his forehead with a knuckle.

"Did you mother put you up to this?" he asked. "Do you think I need some sort of charity?"

"No!" she protested, shaking her head perhaps a little too rapidly.

Her father's frown deepened.

"You've turned up here, off your own bat, to offer me a job?" he said, sceptically. "When we haven't seen you for near on a month, what with you cooped up with that fella of yours? You just happen to come up this week? Funny coincidence that, isn't it?"

It was Holly's turn to rub her temples. Her dad wasn't one to easily have the wool pulled over his eyes, but she could still do a better job at making this sound convincing.

"Ben's the reason I'm here," she said gloomily. "I know I've been a rubbish daughter. I didn't realise quite how useless I'd been. I'm sorry. We had our first fight—Ben and I—so I came to talk to Mum about it. She told me about your job and everything and I just thought … well, I need some extra help … and you … well, it just makes sense, that's all. But forget I said anything. If you don't fancy it, I can always put an ad in the window."

Her dad's eyes narrowed, but it seemed his interest had been piqued.

"You're serious?"

"Drey's had to cut back on her hours so that she can concentrate on her studies. She only does one day at the weekends, now. And Caroline's fabulous, but she can only do a full day once a week and she has to fit her other hours around the kids. It would be nice to have some help, especially getting ready to open up some mornings, just getting the stock straight and stuff. I was going to ask Drey if any of her friends wanted the work—it's only minimum wage—but I haven't mentioned it to her yet. I get that it might not be the type of thing you're after, and it's not exactly great pay …"

Arthur puffed out his cheeks.

"You know me, Holly. I'm not proud. And I don't need much."

"So you are interested? I'll be your boss, remember and there'll be no family favours. I can be a hard taskmaster and I'm not afraid to sack people. Well, I haven't had to yet, but I'm still not afraid to do it."

After a moment's pause, Arthur let out a short, gruff laugh that stopped abruptly as his eyes narrowed on her again.

"And you swear your mother didn't put you up to this?"

"How would she?" she replied, feeling slightly bad for lying through her teeth. "She didn't know I needed anyone."

The probing gaze lingered for a moment longer before a half smile twisted at the corner of his mouth.

"When do you want me to start?" he asked.

With the perfect timing that could only come from a sixth sense, the front door opened and closed, and a moment later Wendy strode into the kitchen, swinging a plastic bottle of milk in her hand.

"Right, I'll get the kettle on now. So tell me, what have you two been chatting about?"

Arthur's eyes went to Holly, who nodded with a smile.

"Well, Holly here was just telling me how she needed someone extra to do a few hours at the shop. And with me being available, we thought I might give it a go."

"Really?"

Wendy's eyes went wide in mock surprise. The whole thing

was starting to feel like a bad amateur-dramatics performance. Surely her father could tell that she was faking it, although from the look of bashful pride on his face, he was buying it all.

"Well, that's wonderful. What a spot of luck that is. When are you going to start?"

"As soon as possible would be good," Arthur said, looking to Holly for confirmation. "When do you think?"

Today was Thursday. Whilst she didn't want him to have to wait for ages, if his first shift came at the weekend that would be a very busy time for him to manage. Firstly, Drey would be there, which would mean she wouldn't actually need him, but also it would be far too busy for her to show him the ropes.

"I guess tomorrow morning," she said, suddenly wondering what she was getting herself into. "But if that's too soon, we can wait until next week. I still need to sort out the exact hours, and I guess you might want the weekend to get your head around the idea of working for your daughter."

"No. Not at all," he said, sitting up. "Trust me. I won't let you down on this, love."

A wave of apprehension rippled through Holly as she considered what the practicalitics of working with her dad would be. But the sheer joy in his face helped to dispel her worries just a fraction.

"Then tomorrow it is," she said.

CHAPTER ELEVEN

Holly left the house once she could extricate herself from all the hugging that then ensued, particularly from her mother.

"Thank you," Wendy whispered in her ear as they walked to her car. "You don't know what this means to us both."

She had never been one for such demonstrative gratitude and felt really awkward, especially with it coming from her parents. As she hurriedly strapped herself in, switched on the engine and started to drive away, she found herself in a complete quandary as to what to do next.

As ridiculous as it was, considering how angry she'd been, there was no doubt that she was missing Ben, and the last thing she actually wanted was a third night on her own in the house. But she was still mad. And even more so as he had made no attempt to contact her again. Okay, Dan had been a Class A idiot, but at least he'd had the common sense to grovel and apologise when they'd had a fight. He wouldn't go so far as to buy flowers or any other peace offering—he was far too cheap for that—but he'd normally leave messages or turn up outside work to walk her home. Since he'd dropped into the shop that morning, Holly had not heard a word from Ben. No calls. No texts to check if everything was okay, even after she'd told him she was closing up the shop early.

She spent the entire drive back wondering if she should knock on his door and demand he apologise. But why on earth would he feel the need to do it now, when he hadn't that morning? She could go round anyway and not even mention the argument, with the hope that they could just enjoy an evening together, sweeping the whole thing under the rug. After all, did she expect them to never have a difference of opinion? Still, not confronting problems didn't seem a particularly healthy way to go.

By the time she'd turned off the Fosse Way into Bourton, she'd decided she would text him and invite him over to hers for a takeaway. Maybe spending so much time at his house was the problem. Perhaps he felt she was invading his space too much. Maybe the fact that it already felt like they were living together had led to her getting way ahead of herself. Takeaway at hers felt like a happy compromise.

That all changed when she turned into her driveway.

At first, she assumed that the brown box sitting directly in front of her door was an online delivery that Jamie had ordered. It certainly looked like that. Great, she thought with a smile. It would give her a *genuine* reason to check up on how the city break with the mysterious Fin was going. She also needed to fill her in on the disastrous meal with Jess, although she didn't feel quite up to that yet.

However, when she got out of the car to inspect it, she discovered that there was no address label attached to it or even a name. Just a message scribbled in black pen, in Ben's handwriting.

I thought you'd like this type best.

She stared at the parcel, which stood above knee height, and wondered what on earth could be in it.

A brief glance next door revealed a light on downstairs. He would never leave one on unnecessarily, meaning he was probably in the kitchen, fixing himself something to eat. Maybe she should knock on his door and let him tell her what it was. Or she could just take it into her house and not open it straight away, out of sheer stubbornness. These thoughts lasted less than a couple of seconds, as curiosity got the better of her and she used her front door key to slice through the tape. She eagerly opened the box to peer inside, half expecting—simply because of its size—a lavish display of blooms. Instead, she discovered it was full of paper packets. Reaching in, she pulled the first one out.

"You bought me flours?" Holly said when Ben opened his front door. "Actually flours? You do realise it's normally fresh flowers—you know, the type that have petals on and look pretty in a vase—that people give each other?"

"Of course, but I thought this sort would suit you much better. Didn't you read the note?"

She did again and laughed as she pulled out one bag after another.

Spelt, wholewheat, almond, self-raising. The list went on and on, and with each package, her laughter grew and the anger she'd been feeling slowly evaporated.

Fearing rain, she opened her door, and they manoeuvred the box in, having realised lifting it might risk a back injury.

"To be honest," he said, once it was safely in the hallway, "I thought I might benefit from this type of flour as well. Assuming you still like me enough to offer me some of your baking?"

It took all her willpower not to answer immediately.

"Well, I suppose I still like you a little bit," she said, with deliberate reticence.

"Just a little bit?" He smiled coyly. "Well, what do you think I can do to improve on that?"

The positive side of having their first argument, Holly discovered, was the fact that their first make-up sex followed it. To be fair, she'd rather that they hadn't fallen out in the first place, but as she lay there, nestled in his arms, she had almost forgotten what it was all about. Almost, but not quite. Still, it didn't really matter. In the grand scheme of things, she told herself, what counted was that they were solid.

"I've got my dad starting at the shop tomorrow," she said.

"Really? Will that work?" Ben asked.

"I think so. It'll be nice to spend more time with him. I know I see them much more than when I was living in London, but they miss not seeing me regularly."

"It must be difficult with there just being the one of you. I can't imagine not having siblings. Jess has been there for me through everything, you know."

She bristled at the mere mention of his sister. She shifted herself a little and forced a smile as she turned around to face him.

"I was thinking, perhaps we could go away for a weekend

soon. We could get a last-minute deal like Jamie did. I'm sure there are plenty available."

"You want to go away with me? Isn't that a bit serious?"

He grinned at this deliberate wind up. With an exceptional display of maturity, she refused to rise to the bait.

"I've always wanted to go to Vienna," she suggested, "or Paris?"

He scrunched up his nose.

"No? What's wrong with Paris?"

There was a shift in his expression and his shoulders tensed. It was not the response she was expecting during a discussion about their first holiday today.

"Paris just has some …" he paused, apparently needing to find the right words, "… some memories for me."

She raised her eyebrows.

"Memories?"

The atmosphere in the room had suddenly changed.

"I proposed to Ella in Paris."

"Oh."

She sat up.

"Yeah, like I said, memories."

The hurt was still evident in his eyes. They'd both come to this relationship with baggage, and she'd be lying if she said that, now and then, Dan didn't slip into her thoughts, usually in a bad way. But the pain she saw in Ben's eyes looked so raw, as if the betrayal he'd suffered had only been yesterday.

"Well," she said, moving on top of him and placing her hands on his bare chest. "We could make some new memories there. Or we could go somewhere completely different."

But his expression didn't change, and his gaze seemed distant.

"Ben?"

"Do you mind if I have some time to think it through?" he said, finally.

"Going away for a weekend?"

"Yeah. Is that all right?"

She looked at him. He seemed strangely detached. What was this? One minute he was buying her a thoughtful present and the next he was saying he needed to think about going away for a damned mini-break. It wasn't like she was asking him to marry her, for crying out loud.

"What are we doing, Ben?" she asked.

"What do you mean?" he said, blinking, like he'd just realised she was there in the room with him.

"Am I just a person you're using to fill in time with until you feel ready for a proper relationship? Or will you never be ready to risk it again? Maybe it's just to save on the cooking."

"Holly, that's not fair."

"No. What's not fair is not knowing where I stand."

"You know where you stand. You mean the world to me."

"You mean the world to me. What does that actually mean? Do you love me?"

"I … I guess," he stammered.

"You guess?"

"I would say so. Yes. You're a lovable person. I mean, I've always loved parts of you, your generosity, your free spirit."

Considering he was supposed to be complimenting her, his words sounded incredibly disjointed. Like he was having problems recalling facts for a school test.

"Okay, so I have lovable features," she said, trying to keep her voice steady, "but are you actually in love with me? Can you answer me that?"

He frowned and his discomfort was obvious. She didn't move a muscle, just stared at him, waiting.

"Why do you need to do this?" he asked. "Why can't we just be fine as we are? Taking things as they go?"

She dug her fingers into the duvet beneath her, trying to calm the rage that was growing inside her.

"I need to know this is going somewhere, Ben. I'm nearly thirty. I want a family. I want a house. And I don't want to wake up in six months, or a year or two, to find you were just using me to distract yourself from Ella, the girl you still wish you were with."

"That's not fair," he said again.

"Is it not? You can't even stand the thought of going to the city you went to with her."

"Things happened there."

"I get it. You proposed. You've already said that."

"No. It's not just that …" he started, only to shake his head and dry up. "You can't expect me to just forget about my past."

"I don't expect that, but I want to think about the future."

Whatever reaction she had expected, it wasn't for him to start laughing. And it wasn't a pleasant laugh. It was nasal and mocking.

"This, from Miss *Living-in-the-Moment.* I'm only doing what you've encouraged me to do. You were the one who told me to be spontaneous. Not get hung up on the future."

"Sorry for thinking I would be worth getting *hung up* on."

Tears were stinging her eyes as she jumped off the bed and grabbed her jeans from the floor.

"You're going?" he asked, scrabbling to keep the sheet from falling.

"As surprising as it may seem to you, sleeping next to someone who can't even bear the thought of going on a mini-break with me isn't how I want to spend my night."

He was now standing up, too, struggling to put his boxer shorts on.

"So that's it, then? You're going to leave again. This is becoming a habit of yours."

"Yeah, well, it's a habit I'm about to break, because this is the last time," she spat. "We're done."

CHAPTER TWELVE

Holly was too angry to cry. She was too angry to do anything, really, other than bake. That was her normal go to in times of crisis, but the only flour she had were the packets in the big box that Ben had given her and she sure as hell wasn't using that. She'd thought about putting it back outside to get ruined in the rain, but on reflection, she'd realised that was just childish. Even if she couldn't bring herself to cook with it, she could take it to the food bank collection point in the supermarket. Yes. That would be the best thing to do with it.

Picking up her coat and bag, she pushed the box back out onto the drive, where she somehow managed to heave it into the boot of her car.

Although it was dark, she was surprised to discover that it was already nine o'clock when she arrived at the superstore in Stow-on-the-Wold. It was the biggest one in the area, and there would definitely be somewhere there to drop off Ben's unwanted gift and replace it with some cheap, value flour, ready for an all-night, therapeutic baking session. Cinnamon rolls.

Chocolate blondies. She was going to make herself the most sugary, buttery treats and love every bite of them.

However, when she parked up the car and went to lift the box out of the boot, she hit her first snag. Yes, it had taken more than a bit of effort to get it out from her hallway in her house and into the back of her car, but the distance involved was only a few metres, and through sheer strength and bloody mindedness, she'd managed it. Now, however, she was at least twenty metres from the shop entrance, and she couldn't even get a decent grip on it to pull it out of the boot.

"For crying out loud!" she yelled, kicking her wheel, which had no effect whatsoever other than causing pain to shoot all the way up to her knee. "Oh, for God's sake!"

This discomfort, overlaid with frustration and her continuing anger brought tears to her eyes. This was all down to Ben, but she was not going to cry because of him. She wouldn't. After all, it was her own stupid fault. She'd dived headfirst into the relationship, despite the fact that he'd given up so easily when Dan had come back on the scene. That should have been an early warning signal. She was probably lucky to have got out now, before her heart was completely broken. Still, none of that helped with the problem of getting this damned box of flour out of her car.

"Come on!" she said, trying and failing again to lift it over the lip of the boot. Maybe if she just tipped it over? That could work.

"Excuse me, can I help you with that—" the speaker paused. "Well I never, if it isn't Holly Berry."

She froze, certain that she must be mistaken. That voice. That perfectly refined British accent. Just hearing him say her name sent a fresh surge of anger through her veins. Of all the people she didn't want to see today, or ever, he had to be number one on the list.

"Giles Caverty," she said with all the venom she could muster.

"You look like you could do with a hand there."

His grey eyes twinkled under the carpark light, and his mouth was lifted in a smile that she would have found utterly irresistible and charming at one time, but at that exact moment made her want to slap him.

"I don't need anything from you," she spat. "You tried to get my business shut down the last time I trusted you."

He'd got ridiculously close to achieving his goal, too. If it hadn't been for the security cameras in the shop, she would never have realised that he'd planted a mouse amongst the sweets, and she would have lost *Just One More* for good. His scheme had started by him befriending her, wooing her to the point she actually thought he was genuinely interested in her.

Shuffling his feet, Giles shifted his gaze to the ground.

"Holly, I know you won't believe me, and I understand you must despise me—which I thoroughly deserve—but I am genuinely sorry. I really did enjoy spending time with you. I was ... well, let's just say it was a difficult time for me back then. I'm not proud of who I was."

"You'll excuse me for not believing a word you say."

"I would be worried about you if you did," he said, with a smile playing on his lips. "Can I at least help you with that?" he said, gesturing to the box.

For a moment, she considered refusing, out of pure stubbornness, but she really was going to end up getting injured if she tried to move it herself.

"It needs to go inside, to the food bank drop-off point," she said, stepping back.

In one easy motion, he reached in and pulled it out.

"Are you coming with me?" he asked, nodding towards the supermarket doors.

She considered what this might lead to. She and Giles always got on so easily. Yes, part of that had been his desire to learn as much about her business as possible, but they'd had some good times, and if ever she could do with a laugh, it was now. But she shook the thought away.

"No, I'm heading back home," she said, decisively.

Then, before he could say anything more, she shut the boot, got back in the car and drove home.

Still lacking the key ingredient she needed for baking and with the added trauma of bumping into Giles, she decided it was best all round if she poured herself a glass of wine. Unfortunately, all that she could find was a half-empty bottle of red in the back of a cupboard, that could have been there for months for all she knew. Still, needs must, and at that moment, she needed a drink. The first mouthful was like vinegar and confirmed her suspicion that she'd opened it months ago to cook with, but she didn't care. By the third mouthful, it was becoming almost tolerable, and by the time she was ready for a top-up, the burning at the back of her throat had almost stopped.

So that was it then, she thought as she sat alone at the kitchen table. They were over. She should have realised that Ben was still hung up on Ella. After all, she would often find herself absentmindedly commenting about the things that Dan used to do. Not because she missed him, but because he had been the biggest part of her life for so long that it was impossible for him not to crop up in conversation now and again. But Ben never spoke about Ella. Ever. Not even in passing. Knowing how painful their breakup had been, she had never quizzed him. But even on the occasions when she had asked something innocuous—like if they'd played board games together—he would immediately shut her down, changing the subject or simply saying that it was a long time ago and he couldn't remember. At the time, she had thought that not wanting to bring an old relationship into a new one was understandable; but now she felt it wasn't that at all. Maybe the reason he'd been so standoffish when they'd first met wasn't because he was afraid of getting his heart broken again. It was because his heart was still somewhere else. It had never been hers to have in the first place.

It was tough to know whether the headache that throbbed behind Holly's eyes when she woke up the next morning was caused by the dodgy wine or dehydration from the quantity of tears she'd cried. She suspected it was the latter, although there was a definite hint of nausea, too. Her throat was dry, and her tongue was coated with what felt like fur, leaving a horrible, bitter taste in her mouth.

A silver-grey light was stealing through a gap in the curtains, casting a pattern on the floor. Looking at it for too long made her eyes go all fuzzy.

Groaning, she momentarily wished for the old days of being an employee with sick pay, when she could call someone higher up the ladder and explain that she wouldn't be coming in that day, roll over and go back to sleep, free to spend all morning tucked up under the duvet feeling sorry for herself. Maybe she could open up half an hour later than normal. It would hardly be the worst thing to have happened.

Having reset her alarm for an extra thirty minutes, she'd just dropped her head back onto the pillow, when the high-pitched chime of the doorbell cut through the quiet of the house.

"You have to be joking," she muttered, massaging her temples and checking the time again on her phone. When seven-fifteen glared back at her, she grabbed her pillow and put it over her head. Unfortunately, that didn't stop the ringing.

"Go away!" she shouted, believing it must either be an early rising delivery man or Ben coming to apologise. Well, if that was the case, he could take his apology and shove it somewhere very uncomfortable indeed. A minute later, the ringing had changed to knocking. Hard, loud knocking.

With a huff that would have put any teenager to shame, she jumped out of bed and stormed out of her room

"Go away, Ben!" she yelled down the stairs, assuming that the delivery-man option was a lot less likely. But the knock came again … and again … and again.

She marched down the stairs. She was wearing her Harry Potter pyjamas, which had been unwashed for an indeterminate length of time, and her hair resembled that of a wind-swept scarecrow, but none of this mattered to her as she swung open the door.

"What do you want?" she spat, before doing a double take. "Dad? What are you doing here?"

Arthur was dressed more formally than she could remember seeing him for years. His blue shirt was neatly ironed and combined with a navy-and-white tie, which he'd secured in a large, double-Windsor knot. And the clothes were only a part of it. His hair had been slicked back and gleamed with wax, not to mention the fact that he smelt of aftershave. Had she not known better, she would have thought he was on his way to a wedding.

"I hope you don't mind me coming here first," he said. "I was just worried the later bus wouldn't get me in on time. I thought I'd come a bit earlier and we could walk down together. But if it's a problem, I can always head down to the village and feed the ducks for a while. It's quite a pleasant morning."

Still struggling to comprehend what was going on, Holly finally took in what her father had just said. He must have walked from the bus stop in the centre of the village. That would have taken ten minutes at least, for someone his age, and the bus from Northleach was slow. How early must he have left to get here at this time? she wondered.

"Sorry Dad, of course it's all right. Come on in."

She stepped back, allowing him room to enter.

"You can fix us both a cup of tea while I get dressed."

"A cuppa sounds good," he said, rubbing his hands together, before stopping and looking a little more closely at his daughter.

"Are you okay, love? You look a little … unkempt."

She was about to reply that everything was fine. That she had just woken up and hadn't slept very well, but as she opened her mouth, she found that those words wouldn't come out.

"No, I don't think I am," she said.

CHAPTER THIRTEEN

As nice as the cup of tea was, what Holly really needed to offset her current queasiness was something really stodgy and starchy. Unfortunately, there was no food in the house that fit the bill. So, Arthur's first job when they arrived at the shop, was to immediately leave again on a trip to the bakery, while she sat upstairs in the stockroom and cradled her head.

"Say you're working over at *Just One More,*" she'd told him. "You'll get a discount that way."

"Working at a sweet shop and getting discounts at the bakery. I'm liking the sound of this. What do you want, love? Chocolate croissant? You always liked those when you were little."

She thought about this. The cinnamon rolls they did there were utterly divine, and the almond croissants were great for a sugar fix, not that she often needed one of those in her line of work, but the prospect of eating either of those caused a fresh wave of nausea to surge through her. In fact, the idea of eating anything at all had the same effect. Even the thought of her normal hangover go-to of a ham and cheese croissant, left her feeling light-headed.

"Actually, don't worry about me, Dad. I'll pick something up later. Maybe if you could just grab me a black coffee? And make sure the sign still says Closed on your way out."

She regretted that wine even more now as she headed for the stairs to get a large glass of water.

"No problem."

"Oh, could you pick me up a wholemeal roll, too. Not filled, just plain. And obviously get yourself whatever you want."

"You might regret saying that," he replied, with a wink, before disappearing out the door.

As it happened, the wholemeal roll was too dry for her to stomach and even the black coffee tasted excessively bitter. It was a shame, she thought, tipping it down the sink. It was unlike the bakery to have an off day. So instead, she filled her glass with water again and sipped at it tentatively.

At twenty to nine, Holly knew she couldn't hide upstairs much longer. Besides, she thought, if her dad got the hang of things quickly, she could go back up to the stockroom and catch forty-winks during a quiet spell. So, she put on her apron and headed down to the shop floor.

"Okay," she said to Arthur, who had been waiting patiently, looking at all the different sweets displayed on the shelves. "The main thing is hygiene. The best thing to do is to tip the sweets directly into the bag, or if you need to, use the scoop. If the sweets don't have individual wrappers make sure you wear gloves. No bare hands."

"No bare hands. Got it."

"Now the lids are screwed on pretty tight. That's deliberate. We can't have children unscrewing them and sticking their hands in."

"Are those barley sugars?" he asked, having wandered across the room away from her.

"Pardon?"

"These, are they barley sugars? I can't remember when I last had one of those."

"Oh, yes," she said, having now lost the thread of what she was saying. "If you want one, you can help yourself. They're in wrappers, so you can take one out by hand."

Smacking his lips together, he unscrewed the jar and pulled out a bright-orange sweet, then pulled the ends of the wrapper, causing it to spin open, before popping the contents into his mouth.

"Oh, these are good. Do you want one, love?"

"No. No, I'm fine. Okay, if you put those back, I'll talk you through the till."

She turned towards the counter as he replaced the jar, only for him to call out again.

"And are those cough candy? It's been years since I had one."

"How about we go through what all the different sweets are once I've shown you how the till works?"

She tried to make her voice sound as jovial as possible, but tension was starting to build up along her shoulders. She had invoices she wanted to send out, and bills she needed to pay. If she had to go through every item on the shelves with her dad testing them all as they went, then she would never get around to doing anything.

"Of course, of course," he said, hurrying over to her. "It's just all very exciting, you know. I guess you could say I'm like a kid in a candy shop."

She tried to smile as if it was the first time she'd heard that one.

To give Arthur his due, he listened to her explanation of how the machine worked without any interruptions. It was all very simple: type in the number on the price ticket, press the category that the item belonged to, then finally hit enter. There were no barcodes to worry about. No complicated computer systems. He did a few practice runs, including removing things and correcting the prices as well, just to be sure.

"Okay, time to put what you've learned into practice," she said. "Here comes Mr Moore. Now, it's a Friday, which means he'll ask for a hundred grams of chocolate ginger and a hundred of black jacks, plus something else, perhaps pink shrimps, for the grandchildren. But wait for him to ask first. He doesn't like it if you assume anything."

He nodded and stepped up to the till.

"Good morning, sir," he said, in a charming lilt he normally kept hidden. "What can I get you today?"

Mr Moore stopped in his tracks. He was one of Holly's most regular customers, arriving like clockwork three times a week, minimum, more if there was a special event on the horizon. Although he was somewhat abrupt and barely said any more than the bare minimum, he knew all the women who worked there by name and had even dropped off a Christmas card addressed to them, signed *Mr Moore*.

"A new face?" he said. "You are not one of the regular ladies."

"I'm a new employee," Arthur replied. "Arthur Berry, pleased to meet you."

He stretched out his hand, which the elderly gent took and shook.

"Berry, a relation of Miss Holly here, I assume," he said.

"Yes, indeed. This lovely young lady is my daughter."

Arthur glanced back at her, a glow of pride lighting up his face.

"Well, isn't that something? How wonderful, helping your daughter out like that."

Arthur's smile increased.

"Oh, it's a mutually beneficial situation, believe me. But it's nice to spend some extra time with her."

Mr Moore nodded thoughtfully in reply. Holly had never seen him in such a chatty mood, and it was certainly the longest he'd gone before making an order. He hadn't even got his wallet out.

"I envy you. My three have all flown the coop. The last one left, oh, must have been twenty years back. We've got two grandchildren, already, if you can believe that."

"That must be grand," Arthur said, leaning forwards a little onto the counter. "All the fun, then you get to give them back before they start whinging."

Mr Moore sighed.

"I wish that were the case. We see them twice a year, if we're lucky. It's not Henry's fault—that's my son—no, it's his wife. Upset Mrs Moore something terrible the last time we saw them. Said she didn't trust us to be responsible around them. Like we hadn't already raised three by ourselves."

"That sounds terrible. Your poor wife."

Holly wasn't entirely sure what was going on. Not only was Mr Moore gossiping, but he appeared to be unloading on her father. It wasn't unusual for a customer to do this—a sweet shop was a long way from a bar or a hairdressers, but there was something about the nostalgia of the place that made people feel at ease—but this was quite out of character. Normally, she wouldn't have minded, but there were now two customers waiting behind her father's new friend.

"Excuse me, Dad, would you mind taking Mr Moore's order, and I'll serve the next person?"

He frowned at her momentarily before turning back and shaking his head.

"I'm sorry. It's the way of today, isn't it? All rush."

"Tell me about it."

With the men still mid-discussion, she peered around Mr Moore's shoulder to the woman behind him.

"Can I help you?" she asked.

By the time she'd served four customers, Mr Moore was finally on his way out.

"What an interesting man," Arthur said. "Did you know he spent three years in Malaysia, working as a dive master."

"No, Dad, I didn't."

She wasn't sure how to phrase what she needed to say next.

"Dad, it's great to chat with a customer and everything, but you have to make sure that you aren't ignoring the others."

His face fell.

"I don't think I was doing that at all. There's nothing wrong with people having to wait a little."

"Maybe not, but you hadn't even taken his order and there were three people behind him."

His face fell further, and guilt swelled in her chest. Is this what people felt like when they had to tell off their children? she wondered, before trying to rephrase her comment.

"It's fine, Dad. I'm sure Mr Moore really enjoyed talking to you. Just try to go a little quicker, okay? Some customers are in a rush. They might be on their way somewhere or have a bus to catch, and they'll leave if they have to queue for too long."

He nodded.

"Course, go a little quicker. I've got that."

It soon became apparent that doing things quickly was not

her dad's style. By lunch time, she knew that Mr Brown was suffering from gout and that his youngest had put him on a diet that was simply impossible to survive on, hence his visits to the sweet shop. She'd learned that Kate, who owned the gift shop down the road, had booked a holiday to the Seychelles for June and was hoping it would be sunny enough to get a tan, as she was going to be a bridesmaid three days after she got back. And those were only the details she overheard and could remember. Never in her life had she known her father to talk so much. Unfortunately, it meant she was having to do all the running around.

"Okay, Dad," she said, "I'm probably good for the rest of the day. You were only going to stay for a couple of hours, weren't you? Do you want to get off now?"

She smiled broadly. The sooner she could get the shop to herself, the quicker she could sort out all the jars that he'd put back in the wrong places.

He looked at his watch.

"What do you know? I've just missed the bus. It's another forty minutes until the next one. Is there something else I can do, instead?"

She pulled down a jar of chocolate limes from the shelf. They seemed to be the only thing she could stomach right now, and she'd already had half a dozen that morning. Popping one in her mouth, she considered what she could give him to do that wouldn't end up with him chatting away on the shop floor.

"Okay, Dad, there are some boxes of fudge upstairs that need pricing. Would that be okay?"

"I think I'll be able to handle that. Do you not want to get some lunch before I go, though? You didn't eat any breakfast."

Holly wrinkled her nose. Her stomach had settled, but she still wasn't ready to risk anything substantial.

"No, I'll be fine with a couple more of these," she said, lifting the jar a little for her dad to see.

"Chocolate limes?"

It was his turn to wrinkle his nose.

"Oh, I can't stomach those anymore. Didn't use to mind them, though. It's your mum's fault."

"Mum's fault? Why?"

Holly wondered how on earth her mother could have put him off a sweet.

"Well, they were all she'd eat when she was first pregnant with you. Morning, noon and night. Even now, the smell takes me back. I guess having them around the house all the time put me off them. But she'd chuckle to know that you like them. Honestly, she never touched the things before you were due."

Holly looked at the cellophane wrapper in her hand, and suddenly her stomach upset took on a whole new meaning.

CHAPTER FOURTEEN

Holly slowly placed the jar of chocolate limes back on the shelf behind her, taking a moment to steady herself. A sudden weakness in her legs was causing her knees to tremble, and she was desperate not to let her dad see this.

"Really?" Her voice came out as a high-pitched squeak. "Mum liked chocolate limes when she was pregnant? I never knew that."

"Cost us an arm and a leg," her dad continued. "After three months, though, she moved on. Then it was all about the spaghetti hoops or was it the cheese and onion crisps next? I can't remember the order of all those cravings—they never lasted more than a couple of weeks—but those chocolate limes, well you didn't forget that in a hurry when you had to go to Stow-on-the-Wold at three-thirty on a Sunday because you've already bought all the ones in the local shop."

Unable to form an immediate reply, she hoped the fact that she was still looking up at the shelves meant her father wouldn't notice how pale she'd turned. Pregnant. No. She couldn't possibly be. Could she? No, of course not. Lots of women liked particular sweets, and it didn't mean they were all expecting, did it? It was a coincidence; that was all.

"Excuse me. Have you got any chocolate mini eggs? I know it's not Easter yet, but I was hoping you'd get them a bit early."

The voice from the doorway brought Holly back to the moment. Standing just inside the shop, a customer was looking at her, hopefully.

"Chocolate mini eggs?" The woman prompted her.

"Oh, yes, yes," she said, finding her voice again. "They came in last week. Let me just go and get a jar from upstairs."

"Thank you."

She wasn't sure how her legs made it to the top of the stairs and into the stockroom. Her knees were still trembling so much that she couldn't go any further. She dropped down onto the small stool.

Could she actually be pregnant? It was true she and Ben had been at it like rabbits all the way to the breakup, particularly at the start. But they'd been careful, hadn't they? And she'd gone on the pill only a few weeks after getting together with him.

Knowing that the customer was waiting downstairs for her, she pushed this thought to the back of her mind, sucked in a deep breath and picked up the jar of mini eggs, managing to push her cheeks up into a wide smile as she reached the shop floor.

"Here you go," she said. "Now how many grams can I get you?"

When the woman had left the shop, she realised her dad was still hovering. Closing her eyes, she rubbed the bridge of her nose.

"Dad, weren't you going to price up those boxes of fudge for me in the stock room?"

"I was," he said. "I've got the hang of that pricing gun. Very clever little gadget, isn't it? But I just wanted to check you meant that big box. I don't want to do anything wrong."

Were sudden headaches a sign of pregnancy, too? she wondered, as her dad's voice bore through her skull. She pushed that idea away quickly. No, she wasn't going to start on a downward spiral now, when she didn't even know if there was anything to worry about.

"Holly dear?"

"What Dad? Oh yes, sorry. It's all up there. I was doing it yesterday. If you could just finish the box I started."

Despite receiving quite clear instructions, he remained where he was.

"Are you all right? You look a little peaky all of a sudden."

While there'd been times in her life when her father was the person Holly had opened up to, this was definitely not one of them. So, despite how she was actually feeling, she replied. "I'm fine, Dad. Absolutely fine."

While Arthur worked away upstairs, Holly thought about dates, trying to calculate her way out of the situation, for which she had no evidence other than a possible over-fondness for chocolate limes. But, sod's law, the shop became the busiest it had been all day, and she barely had time to breathe.

"Well love, if it's all right with you, I'd better get off. Bus leaves in ten minutes."

"Sorry?"

"I'm going now. Is that okay?"

She looked at her watch. It felt like only a couple of minutes had passed since he'd popped upstairs, but he was right. Nearly half an hour had gone by.

"Yes. Yes, of course," she said. "You get off."

Yet he lingered, his faced creased in a frown.

"What day next?"

"Sorry?"

"For me to come in. When do you want me again?"

"Oh, yes. Uhmm …"

She thought about this. Today hadn't been a total success, but it hadn't been a disaster, either, and she'd promised her mum that she'd take him on for at least a month, then reassess.

"How would Monday work for you?" she said, although quickly remembering the early morning wake-up call he'd inflicted on her, adding, "But the afternoon, not the morning? Would one o'clock be okay?"

"That sounds grand. All right love," he came around and squeezed her shoulders. "And you make sure you're looking after yourself properly. If you need to get me in for longer, just say. That's what your old dad's here for."

"Thank you, Dad," Holly said, looking over again with longing at the chocolate limes. No. It was all in her head. All of it. Except the nausea that was very much in her throat and stomach.

For the rest of the afternoon, she remained in a daze, moving between the shelves and robotically filling bags with sweets. She smiled at customers and bid them a good day, but more than once, she made a mistake weighing out too much or too little and having to restart the order. She got one customer marzipan teacakes instead of coconut teacakes and another one floral gums instead of wine gums. By the time she locked the door, her feet were aching, and her stomach was growling from the lack of proper food. Perhaps she could manage some bread and soup, she thought, turning the sign on the door. Unfortunately, if she wanted to eat anything at all, it meant a trip to the supermarket was needed.

Not wanting to drive all the way to Stow, she settled for the Co-op in Bourton which was only a short walk away and usually had everything she needed, although when she stepped into the carpark, she couldn't believe the sight in front of her.

"You have to be joking," she said, as she strode up to the shop entrance. "Are you following me?"

Giles Caverty was standing beside a dark-green sports car, dressed almost entirely in tweed. When he saw her, his eyes lit up in a sheepish grin.

"Considering I'm just leaving, and you're just arriving, I'd say it's you that's doing the stalking."

It was true. He had several wine boxes and bags which appeared to be filled with bottles of spirit at his feet, but the fact that he was right, didn't make things any better. Seeing him the first time was bad enough, but twice in as many days, and coinciding with her breakup with Ben? It was safe to say that it felt as though the fates were taunting her.

"So, you're back then," she snapped. "Back in the Cotswolds?"

"I am. I can't say how long it'll be, but I have more than a few things to make amends for, so I guess we will see how much time that takes."

She let out the most derisive grunt she could muster, expecting a quick retort from him, but instead, he pressed his lips together and did that shuffling thing with his feet again.

"Holly, I meant what I said. I really am sorry. If you're free, I would love to take you out for meal, or a drink."

"Well, I'm not free. I'm—,"

I'm what? She asked herself. *With Ben* was what her instant reaction had been to say, but she wasn't. She was alone, utterly alone.

"I'm not interested in hearing any more of your lies," she said and swept past him into the supermarket, where she selected a small tub of soup and a very, very large one of ice cream.

By the time she finally got home, it was gone six o'clock and her anger had reached a whole new level. She was angry with Ben and Giles. Angry with her dad for waking her up when she needed to sleep and angry with herself. Most of all, she was angry with herself.

As she pushed open the front door, the shoes were the first thing that caught her attention. Placed smack in front of the door, she nearly went flying as she stepped in. Two pairs of large, hiking boots, one pair female, one very definitely male, and a brightly coloured skateboard lay there.

"A skateboard? Really?" she muttered.

So, not only was Fin taking advantage of Jamie, but he also appeared to be a man-child. Brilliant. Although she had to admit that the artwork on it was fantastic. A series of mandalas overlapped in different colours, and she felt herself drawn to them before she shook the feeling away and returned to her previous state of annoyance. Would it really have taken that much of an effort for them to have put their boots on the shoe rack? It wasn't like it was far away. And they had a perfectly good shed for the skateboard.

"Jamie?" she called out. "Are you back?"

It took a moment before her friend appeared at the top of the stairs. It may have only been six o'clock, but she was currently dressed in a thin dressing gown and looking decidedly dishevelled.

"Hey, I didn't expect to see you," she said, straightening

herself up. "How come you aren't next door? Are you planning on staying here tonight?"

Holly took a deep breath. This was it, she realised. This would be the first time she was actually going to say it out loud, but the sooner she faced it, the better.

"Ben and I broke up," she said.

"What?" Jamie's eyes bulged.

"Yup. It's over."

A moment of silence followed, before Jamie walked down the stairs towards her. She was expecting a hug and a barrage of questions. But instead, when she reached the bottom step, Jamie pulled a face that could only be described as a grimace.

"Well, that makes the timing of my news just the worst," she said.

CHAPTER FIFTEEN

Holly was nursing her glass of wine. So far, she'd taken exactly six sips. Six tiny sips. Although she'd inhaled the aroma so much that her nose was starting to sting. Was even inhaling wine bad if you were pregnant? she wondered, trying but failing to cut off the thought before it was fully formed. She wasn't going to keep doing this. She didn't even know she was pregnant. If having a craving for a certain type of sweet or chocolate was genuinely a sign, then most of her customers were expecting. It was all the trauma of the breakup. She was just fixating.

Content with this rationalisation, she took a more sizeable gulp and immediately felt considerably better.

Jamie had ushered her into the living room before getting them both drinks.

"What's your news then?" Holly asked, tucking her feet under her on the sofa. "I take it Amsterdam was a success?"

"We'll talk about me later. What happened? I thought you two were completely loved up. You looked like you were."

"I thought we were, too. Turns out, Ben's not there yet."

Holly fought back the tears. "I think he's still in love with his ex."

"Ella?"

"Yup. I thought he'd moved on. But then I mentioned about us going away for a weekend, and he started saying how he wasn't really thinking about the future for us. It was more just a here-and-now thing."

"Surely he didn't mean it that way?"

"Oh, he meant it. You should have seen him at that meal. He didn't even bother defending me when his sister said I shouldn't be there taking part in a conversation with them, as I wasn't part of the family. I bet she'll be delighted to hear she was right all along."

"Oh Hols, I'm so sorry," Jamie reached out and rubbed her knee. "I can't believe him. Really, I can't. I'm going to go over there and give him an utter mouthful."

"No, don't do that. It's not worth it. I just need to forget about him," she said, glancing down at her glass.

She noted that it was less than a quarter full and swigged it back without pausing for breath.

"Anyway, that's enough about me," she said, forcing herself to sound jovial. "Tell me more about you? Amsterdam. How was Fin?"

Did he pay for things? Was the actual question at the front of her mind, but asking that bluntly could easily put her friend's back up. She would try to slip it into the conversation later, more subtly. Maybe asking about expenses, cost of food, that type of thing.

"It was incredible. Honestly, so beautiful," Jamie replied, with a wistful sigh. "All we did was walk and eat. Actually, that's not true. We went on one of those boat tours through the canals, and one afternoon, we hired bikes. Everyone cycles there, honestly. The infrastructure is amazing. We got completely lost, though, and then it started to pour down. It should have been a disaster. We had no idea where we were, and we were soaked to the skin, but then we stumbled into this little pub in, of all things, a windmill. I mean, of course it had to be a windmill, right? So, we had some food and a couple of drinks next to the fire and then a couple more drinks, too. We must have been there for a good three hours, and it was still raining, and we still didn't know where we were, but we'd drunk way too much to ride our bikes back. Well, Fin being Fin, he'd already made friends with half the pub—knew them all by name and everything—and the next thing I knew, we were in the back of a pickup with our bikes next to us and some farmer was giving us a lift to our hotel while we finished our drinks! It was crazy. Honestly, I don't think I've ever laughed so much on a holiday."

"Sounds great."

"It was."

"And you two seem to have really hit it off."

It was the first time since they'd started talking that Jamie looked uncomfortable. She shifted on the opposite sofa, mirroring Holly's position with her feet tucked under her, before changing her mind and putting them back on the floor again.

Holly's grip on her wine glass tightened.

"But is everything okay between you?" she asked, feeling that her suspicions of this mystery man were right. Jamie certainly looked apprehensive. "If he's done anything, you know you can tell me."

"What? Fin?" Shock immediately registered on her face. "No. He's great. We're great. Seriously great. I've never felt like this before."

"That's brilliant," Holly said, trying to stifle her jealousy and concern and just feel pleased for her friend. "I'm so pleased. I guess I'll be getting to see a bit more of him then?"

Rather than the quick response that she had expected, Jamie's discomfort increased, and she picked at her fingernails. A new sense of unease churned in her stomach. Whatever she was about to say next, she knew she wouldn't like it.

"Is something wrong?" she asked. "What is it? What is it you said you needed to tell me?"

"It's tough, you see," Jamie said, dropping her hands in her lap. "I didn't know about you and Ben. If I had, I wouldn't have said anything. I just assumed that, you know, you two were moving in the same direction as Fin and I."

"The same direction?" Holly said, wondering where this was going.

What did that mean? What direction were they moving in? It didn't take long for Jamie to clarify

"I asked Fin if he would move in with me. Move in here."

CHAPTER SIXTEEN

Breaking up with her boyfriend and then being told she was about to be kicked out of the house she considered home was rather a lot to take in one twenty-four-hour period. Holly blinked rapidly and cleared her throat.

"Wow, that's fast."

She probably should have said something a bit more congratulatory. After all, Jamie hadn't had any more luck than her for a long time with dating. She thought they were moving fast with their holiday together, but this was a whole new level of commitment. There was also the added kicker of needing to find somewhere else to live.

As if reading her mind, Jamie reached out and took her hands.

"Please don't think this means I want you to move out. I don't. That was never on the cards, I promise. I thought you'd been spending most of your time next door, but this is still your home. For as long as you want it to be. I mean, I would be perfectly happy for you to stay here until Fin and I are married with three kids, although we might have to make one of them live in the cupboard under the stairs when we run out of room."

She smiled at Holly, looking for some kind of positive response. And Holly tried to reciprocate, but Jamie's words had just struck another chord in her. Another, painful one.

"So you and Fin have talked about it? About getting married and having kids?"

Jamie shrugged.

"Only in the way that you do, you know?"

She tried to make it a throw-away remark, but Holly could see it in her face. She had this glow about her. Something she'd never seen before. Her friend was well and truly smitten.

"Wow, that's great."

"I guess at our age there's no point beating about the bush with things like that, is there? I mean, it's all a bit of a joke at the minute. Silly drunken conversations. I'm not even sure if I want kids, but he's happy either way. He's open, you know. We're on the same page. That's what matters in the long run, isn't it?"

Isn't it just? Holly thought. But somehow every relationship she'd had, she seemed to be in an entirely different chapter, if not book, to the guy.

"Of course it is," Holly said, forcing herself to smile. "So, when's the big day? When's he moving in? I guess he's got a fair bit to sort out, first."

Jamie took a deep breath.

"This weekend."

"This weekend? As in … tomorrow?"

"As in tomorrow. It's going to take him a while to get everything across from the States. He's got to arrange shipping for a few things, but yup, he's going to call this home as of tomorrow. Crazy isn't it?"

The words echoed around in Holly's head. Tomorrow. Tomorrow Fin was moving in. She picked up the bottle of wine next to her, topped up her glass, and swallowed half of it in one long gulp.

"Yup," she said. "It's definitely crazy."

"Are you okay? That's the third time you've put a jar back in the wrong place in the last half hour. And don't take this badly or anything, but you look kind of well … crap."

If nothing else, Drey was honest. And most of the time, Holly appreciated it. But today she was finding her comments less than helpful. She was struggling. There were too many things in her head to keep track of.

Thankfully, this latest development of Fin moving in had forced her to push thoughts of her own calamitous life to the back of her mind and focus on Jamie's instead. A visa—she'd decided last night—that was the reason why things were moving so fast between them. Fin wanted a way to stay in the country. How often did you see something like this on television? The young, attractive man would woo some lovely, trusting woman, marry her to get his permanent residency and then scarper the moment it came through.

Well, Fin had obviously fallen on his feet with Jamie. Young, successful, not to mention hot as hell. It would also be the reason for his lack of social media presence. He wouldn't want anyone snooping about and finding info about his life back at home and his abandoned wife and family who he wasn't paying any support for. No, the guy was dodgy. She might have only met him the once, albeit briefly, but she was certain she was right on this, and she would not let Jamie get played the same way Giles had played her. Giles, who she had assumed was out of her life for good.

Given that Drey was right about the mixed-up jars, if nothing else, Holly switched them around on the shelves and straightened a few others. The chocolate limes were calling to her again, and she'd been alternating between feeling ravenous and not wanting any food all day, but she was determined not to give in to the craving. Not that it really mattered. She wasn't pregnant. She couldn't be.

Despite these determined thoughts, a wave of sadness momentarily washed over her. She'd wanted children, but even if she had, by some deplorable miracle, fallen pregnant, she could hardly bring up a baby at Jamie's. It might have made sense before—with her baby's daddy right next door—but not now, with Fin moving in. She'd have to move out, but to where? Her parents? That could be a possibility. Could she manage to juggle keeping the shop running and childcare?

This was all speculation, of course. She couldn't actually be pregnant.

"Earth to Holly? You've been holding that jar of mint imperials for the last two minutes. Are you sure you're okay?"

"Sorry?" she said, turning to Drey. "Did you say something?"

With her head tilted to the side, Drey offered her the most scrutinising look.

"Yeah, I said, *earth to Holly*. Look, you're clearly not feeling right. Why don't you go upstairs and sit down for a bit? I'll be fine on my own."

She hesitated for a moment before making up her mind.

"Actually, I think I will," she said.

She placed the jar of mint imperials on the floor and

trudged slowly up the stairs, her mind feeling distinctly disengaged from her body.

When she reached the top and saw her handbag sitting there, she picked it straight up, took out her phone and sat down at the table. She opened up a webpage and typed in, *Effectiveness of the pill.* An answer popped up immediately. The contraceptive pill was 99% effective. That sounded good. 99%, meant ninety-nine times out of a hundred, no one got pregnant. But what about that other 1 percent? One person out of every hundred on the pill did get pregnant. How many did that mean each year?

Holly clicked on another page.

Her heart missed a beat.

This website claimed the effectiveness was more like 91%. That was definitely not as good. Had she been forgetful about taking it? She didn't think so. There'd possibly been one or two days when she'd got up late and rushed to work ignoring her usual morning routine, but she'd normally remembered, hadn't she?

With every word she read, she could feel herself getting hotter. She scanned through more and more pages. *The first signs of pregnancy. Tell-tale giveaways a baby is on the way.* And to make matters worse, these articles were interspersed with tales about people who had given birth not even knowing they were pregnant!

She dropped her phone on the table. The nausea that had been plaguing her for the last twenty-four hours returned with a vengeance and she rested her head on her arms. This was ridiculous, she chastised herself. She was working herself up for no reason at all. She was not pregnant. Still, she needed to be sure. She'd go to the chemist and get a test.

Picking up her bag again and dropping her phone back in it, she took the steps two at a time down to the shop floor.

"I'll be back in a minute," she called to Drey, already halfway out the door.

Bourton's pharmacy was set a little way back from the High Street, with a small patch of green in front of it. The narrow shop had been there since Holly had been at school and was the place she bought her first lipstick and mascara after earning money at *Just One More*. For a while in her youth, she'd visited regularly to browse the different shades of eyeshadow and boxes of hair dye, even if she was reluctant to spend her money on them. Since moving back, though, she had barely been inside it. Ben liked a particular brand of medicated mouthwash that he could only get there, and she had picked that up for him once, along with a pack of Lemsip for a cold she felt burgeoning, but apart from that, she'd been fortunate enough to remain in good health this last year. Doubly fortunate, as the last thing she wanted was one of the women who served there to remember her.

Typically, the shop was full, and she had to let three people out before she could even get inside. She threw a quick glance at the counter, checking that she didn't recognise either of the faces there from the sweet shop, before heading back to the first aisle in hunt for test kits.

"Pregnancy tests," she muttered to herself. "Where would they be?"

She moved past the nappies on her right. Seeing the pictures on the front of them made her heart lurch unexpectedly. Suppose she was pregnant—not that she would be—but suppose she was. Could she do it? Could she raise a baby on her own? It wasn't worth thinking about. She was getting herself all worked up for no reason. In twenty minutes, she'd be laughing at her paranoia and be enjoying a chocolate lime in peace.

From nappies, she moved past soaps and shower gels to dental hygiene, feminine hygiene and then, just beneath the condoms, the pregnancy tests. She laughed cynically to herself. Perhaps it would be a good idea if they displayed these items the other way around or at least gave more prominence to the cracked nipple cream.

Like everything nowadays, there was a vast selection of brands to choose from. Deciding that one would be as good as another, she was steeling herself to pick up the closest packet, when a throat cleared behind her.

"Holly?"

She didn't need to turn to know who was there. Her heart hammered in her chest as she swivelled slowly around on the balls of her feet, straightening her back and keeping her hands by her side.

"Ben," she said.

CHAPTER SEVENTEEN

He was holding a shopping basket, which contained two bottles of his favourite mouthwash, along with a set of replacement heads for his electric toothbrush. Silence bloomed. An awful, uncomfortable one during which she wished the ground would just swallow her up. She should say something, she thought. Explain why she was hanging around this part of the store. But what could she say? That she was looking for condoms? That would hardly be any better.

Thankfully, her trademark babbling hadn't started, but if someone didn't say something soon, then it probably would.

Please Ben, just get out of the way, she wished as hard as she could. *Just move to the side and let me pass.* But no sooner had she thought the words than he spoke.

"I've been meaning to text," he said. "Have you been okay?"

The temperature of the air around her soared. The aisles were narrow, and it felt as if they were closing in around her. She could feel the sweat building up on the back of her neck. She swallowed, trying to find something to say.

"Jamie's back," she said, aware that she was ignoring his question entirely. "And Fin. He's moving in. Today actually."

"Oh."

"I'm sure you'll get an invitation to come around, at some point. For drinks or something. From Jamie, I mean."

"Right."

She paused. Why was this so difficult? There were so many things she wanted to say. She'd held at least a hundred conversations with him in her head over the past two days, in which she'd confronted him with all the things she needed answers to. Like why had he carried on with her for so long if he was never even considering a future with her? And had he known he was still in love with his ex when they'd started dating, all those months ago? What about when they'd stood in the snow together, next to the lights of the village Christmas tree and he'd told her how special she was to him? Had he known he was still in love with this Ella then? That he hadn't got over all the hurt she'd caused? But she couldn't ask any of those now. Instead, what she said was.

"I assume you can do bingo on your own next Monday?"

She was, of course, referring to the regular night when they volunteered at the Weeping Willows Care Home.

"Oh?" His eyes widened a little. "If that's what you want. Or you could do it. Or …"

His voice trailed off.

What was the last or? she wanted to snap. There was no third *or.* There was no chance they could get it together again. There wasn't even a friendship between them anymore.

"The old ladies prefer it when you do it," she said. "You should go."

"Okay."

His eyes locked on hers. Those eyes that she'd looked into so many times in the last three months. Normally, when their gaze met with this amount of intensity it was just before their lips met, or they'd be sitting across from one another at a pub or restaurant table.

Her hands were still at her sides, and only now did she realise that they were trembling.

"I should get back to the shop," she said. "I left Drey by herself."

"Okay."

She looked around herself and hesitated. There was no route out that didn't involve going past him. The other end of the aisle was blocked with people already queuing up for the till. Trying to get by them and their baskets would end up causing havoc for everyone. She pressed herself as close to the shelves as she could, aware that she was fortunately blocking his view of the pregnancy tests behind her.

"Do you want to get past?" she asked him.

"Aren't you queuing?"

She shook her head.

"No. I've changed my mind. Don't need it after all."

She stood her ground, waiting for him to get the hint and move on, but for a moment, he stayed there, just looking at her. Then he finally left.

It was a tight squeeze, and as he passed her, she could feel the warmth of his body and caught the smell of his deodorant. She held her breath, closing her eyes. When she opened them again, he had already joined the queue. A moment later, she was out of the door, gasping for air.

Back at the shop, she mainly stayed upstairs, occasionally coming down to restock the shelves with boxes of fudge and other things that sold particularly quickly at the weekend, but by two o'clock she was done in. Maybe it was the—hopefully imaginary—pregnancy, but it was far more likely the fact that she hadn't slept properly for the last three nights. She was having trouble focusing on anything, even when Drey asked her a direct question. More than once she'd sat down at the stockroom table and found her eyelids drooping. At three o'clock, she pulled on her coat and headed back down.

"Are you okay to close up tonight?" she asked Drey, when the shop was empty. "I'm not feeling so great. I can ask Caroline to come over and cash up if that would help?"

Drey studied her with obvious concern. Though still in her teens, she had been a lifesaver on many occasions and Holly was truly worried about what would happen when she left for university and was no longer able to help at the shop. But that was something to deal with another day. She had more than enough to cope with for now.

Drey shook her head.

"Don't worry about calling Caroline. I'll be fine. It's fairly quiet for a Saturday. I can manage."

"You're sure?"

"Positive. I'll lock the takings in the safe, like normal."

"That'd be great. And if it gets too busy, or there's a problem, just call me."

"Sure, of course," she replied, although Holly had a sneaking suspicion that should anything go wrong, she would ring Caroline and not her. But right now, she was happy with that.

"Do you want me to do a couple of hours tomorrow, too, if you're not feeling good? I've got plenty of time tonight to get my essays done. I can open up if you'd like a bit of a lie-in."

She was about to refuse, then changed her mind. After all, she was exhausted, and that sound very appealing.

"That would be great. Thank you."

As she left, she considered going back to the chemist to pick up that test, but she couldn't face it. The first attempt had been traumatic enough, and there was no way she was in the right mindset to deal with whatever the result would be today. She'd see how she was feeling tomorrow and give it a go then. So instead, she headed straight home.

The sight of Jamie's van parked outside the house made Holly's heart sink. The last thing she wanted was to have to deal with questions about why she was back early. If she said she felt ill, even though she did, Jamie would think it was because of Ben. Maybe she'd be able to sneak straight upstairs to her bedroom, she thought. That could be doable.

Her key turned in the lock, and she pushed the door, only for it to get stuck. She pushed again, but something heavy was behind it, stopping it from opening fully. With an almighty shove, she tried again, but whatever was there wasn't budging.

"Great," she muttered to herself.

After nearly a year living there, she still hadn't got a back-door key cut. There just hadn't been any need. She never went in that way, even in summer. Either she got this door open herself or she'd have to ring the bell and get Jamie to come and sort things out. As she didn't want her to know she was back, that left only one option.

With a new determination, she put all her weight into moving the door, and after several, strong pushes, it finally started to shift, not by much but a bit, at least. Two minutes later, she'd created a gap large enough for her to squeeze through in an ungainly manner, although getting inside was only the start of the problem.

The entire hallway was jam-packed. A mixture of brown packing boxes, duffle bags and even crammed bin bags filled the hall right up to the staircase and spilled over into the living room, too. Given what a stickler Jamie was about fire hazards, she was amazed to see the chaos. Something must have happened for her to leave it like this. Thinking that was more important than being able to creep in unnoticed, she was about to call out when a sound stopped her in her tracks. A heavy, thumping noise coming from directly above her. From Jamie's bedroom.

She knew that sound well, she thought with a sinking feeling. Her own, Ikea bed had been beating the same rhythm when she'd walked in on Dan and his bit-on-the-side.

"Brilliant. Bloody Brilliant."

Not only was she now single and possibly, but not likely, pregnant, but she was going to be living with a man she didn't know who was almost certainly out to scam her best friend. And on top of that, she'd have to put up with what all newly-moved-in-together couples got up to when they first moved in together. Well, maybe she'd be able to cope with that at some point but that was not today.

Pulling some of the boxes away from the door to make a little more room, she opened the door as wide open as it would go and then slammed it back closed with as much force as she dared.

"Jamie, I'm home," she called.

CHAPTER EIGHTEEN

The noise from upstairs stopped almost immediately, but it was a couple more minutes before her friend appeared at the top of the stairs, tying her hair into a ponytail as she walked. Her skin was decidedly flushed.

"Hey, Hol. You okay? We weren't expecting you home for a couple of hours."

"Yeah, I'm fine. Just wasn't feeling myself. That's all. And the shop was quiet. Drey quite likes it when I leave her to her own devices, so I thought I'd come back and maybe watch some television."

She tried to make her way through to the kitchen but having moved things around to make room for slamming the door, there was now even less room in the corridor.

"Sorry about that," Jamie said, bounding down the stairs and lifting one of the boxes out of the way. "We've just brought everything in from my van. We were going to get started carrying it all upstairs."

"It's no problem," Holly lied, trying to navigate a path between various suitcases.

"Here, pass me that, Babe. That's heavy."

Fin was standing above Jamie, thankfully dressed today, wearing a pair of ripped jeans and a T-shirt, his arms outstretched waiting for her to pass him the box. Holly held her breath. If there was one thing Jamie didn't like, it was men doing things for her, or even offering, because they assumed she wasn't strong enough. Particularly as she could probably dead lift substantially heavier weights than them at the gym.

As expected, she raised her eyebrows.

"You know I'm perfectly capable of carrying this."

"I do. But I also want to make a good impression on Holly here. I can't have her thinking her new housemate isn't a gentleman. So, are you going to let me take that or not? In fact, why don't I sort all this stuff out, while you both have some of the cake we bought?"

Jamie turned back to Holly and offered her a sideways smile.

"I told him you bake far better than anything the shops have on offer, but he insisted on buying something."

"You can't meet a new housemate for the first time empty handed," he said. "Besides, it isn't from any old bakery. It's made with organic flour, raw palm sugar and Himalayan sea salt."

"Oh," Holly said, wondering what the significance of that was. "I feel like I should have brought something from the shop now. There are probably a couple of bags of chocolate raisins in the fridge. Feel free to help yourself."

"Sweet, thanks."

"He brought bubbles, too," Jamie added.

"Champagne?" Holly said, feeling that maybe an afternoon drink would be the exact thing she needed to perk up her mood.

"This is better than Champagne," Fin said. "It's loaded with probiotics and pre-biotics. I guess it's a little like a kombucha."

"So not alcoholic?" Holly said, bluntly.

While Fin didn't pick up on the slightly snarky tone in her voice, Jamie looked at her through narrowed eyes.

"Come on. We'll go into the kitchen and let Fin clear up his mess."

Holly hesitated. While she did want to know exactly why Himalayan sea salted cake was that much better, she would also be forced into further conversation, probably leading to how she was feeling, and she just wasn't in the mood to do that with Fin around.

"Actually, I need to have a lie down. You know, home from work early and everything."

"Sure," Jamie said. "Shall I come and check on you later?"

"That would be great," she replied, forcing herself to smile before heading up the stairs.

Halfway up, she met Fin bounding down again.

"Bad luck to cross on the stairs," he said, cocking his eyebrow before breaking into a grin. "Only joking," he added, bounding back up to make room for her to pass. "After you."

He was still smiling as she moved past him, but she didn't reciprocate. There was no way he deserved that.

Despite desperately wanting to sleep, Holly found her mind far too active to drop off, so instead she spent the rest of the afternoon trying to read a book before giving up on that and watching short clips on YouTube.

Since she'd started living there, she'd never spent any time alone in her room like this. The conservatory was a lovely place to read, and the television was in the living room, where she and Jamie had previously watched films together. The kitchen, as in most houses, was the heart of the home, where she spent most of her time, particularly as the long benches around the table were almost as comfortable as settees. Her bedroom was used primarily for two things: sleeping and changing. Not that it wasn't nice. The large window looked out onto the garden below and although it wasn't a bay, like the rooms at the front of the house, there was a pretty, cast-iron fireplace with a mantlepiece and large mirror above, where she put on her makeup. Maybe if she was going to end up spending more time in here, she would improve the space. Get some nice throws and cushions. Some of those scented candles with the crackling wicks that made a room smell like a spa.

She was considering what colour she could paint the walls, when there was a knock on the door.

"Holly, are you okay? Can I come in?"

She shifted herself on the bed, sitting up a little.

"I'm up," she called, and a second later, the door creaked open.

"Hey," Jamie said, stepping inside the room. "How are you doing? You still look a little peaky, you know."

Holly sat upright, stretching out the cricks in her neck.

"I'm okay. Maybe a bit hungry, if I'm honest."

"That's great," Jamie replied, apparently extremely pleased by this news. "I was just coming to ask if you wanted to get some food with us. Fin and I were going to get a takeaway. Celebrate his first night here and everything. We thought we'd crack open that bubbly, too. And he's paying."

Holly was about to refuse. The last thing she wanted was to

accept Fin's generosity. It was bound to come back to bite her eventually, even if Jamie couldn't see that now. But before she could speak, her stomach growled, loudly enough for her friend to hear.

"Perfect. Chinese, Indian, or Thai? Your call. We're fine with any of them."

Holly and Ben's go-to had been Indian. A good butter chicken and tarka dahl were, in her opinion, unbeatable. She always went for the creamy options rather than the chilli varieties that Ben preferred, but right now, she fancied something spicy. Really spicy.

"I think I'm up for Thai," she said.

"Brill, well decide what you want, and I'll pick it up."

Then, unexpectedly, Jamie stepped further into the bedroom and pushed the door closed quietly behind her. In all the time they'd been housemates, she had never once done this, and it didn't make Holly feel good.

"Look, he wouldn't want me to say anything, but Fin would like to spend some time with you while I go for the food. I know he's worried that he's not made the best impression on you, what with flashing you in the bathroom and everything. But it's so important to me that you two get on."

She sat down on the end of the bed, seeming oblivious to the fact that Holly's feet were already there.

"I know you're probably not in a good place at the moment and that him moving in here with me must be the worst possible timing, given the situation with you and Ben, but do you think you could try? Honestly, I know you'll love him. He's … he's …"

Holly watched as the glint in Jamie's eyes reached a whole new level of bliss.

"He's a little different, I'll admit. But I just know you'll really like him, that's all. You'll give him a chance, right? For me?"

As she waited for an answer, Holly could hear him whistling as he moved around the house. And because she knew that there was nothing else she could say, she lifted her cheeks in a smile and said, "Of course I will."

CHAPTER NINETEEN

They were sitting in the living room. Fin was on the sofa that Holly usually occupied, and it didn't feel right to take Jamie's, so instead she was in the armchair that she never used and with good reason. The thing was like a rock. No wonder Caroline and Ben always made beelines for the sofas. She felt sorry for Michael now, who always ended up with it when they came around. Maybe she would mix it up now and again, give him a chance on the sofa. Then again, maybe there wouldn't be room for all of them now that Fin was here. Although she couldn't imagine Ben was going to come over for a board game any time soon.

Jamie had been gone for over ten minutes, which seemed more like twenty, but waiting times at the Thai restaurant were notoriously long and there was still at least double that to go before she'd return. It didn't help that Holly's hunger was making her even grouchier. She'd ordered a Thai green curry, hoping that the spicy flavour would ease this new craving for chilli she seemed to be developing. As for it being Fin's treat, that concept had evaporated when he'd realised that his wallet was back at his old place, leaving Jamie to foot the bill. How she hadn't seen through his ploy to part her from her money yet, Holly couldn't imagine.

"So, tell me, do you have any secrets, Holly Berry?" Fin asked, leaning forwards.

"Sorry?"

"Secrets. Are you the type of person who keeps secrets?"

"Um. Uh."

If she'd ever been in any doubt, she was absolutely certain that she did not like this man, and the feeling was increasing by the second. Did she have any secrets? What kind of question was that? Everyone had secrets, and she certainly wasn't going to start spilling any of hers to him.

But what she actually said was, "No, I don't think so. I'm a pretty open book."

Obviously satisfied by this answer, he nodded approvingly.

"Great, that's great. I know I sometimes come across as a little intense, but I think it's important we show our purest self when we meet someone new. Don't you?"

"I suppose."

He nodded some more, apparently unaware of her look of utter confusion.

"Jamie said I'd like you," he continued. "You know, she's so pure, so straightforward. And I think that's healthy. Being who you are. Not hiding parts of yourself you think people won't like. The older I get, the more I've learned that bad thoughts, deceit and lies, all block the energy channels within you. It can cause real damage to your mental health and your physical health, too."

"Blocked energy channels?"

"Exactly. When I look at life now, I know that anger and bitterness have no place in a happy person. They hold you back.

You can never be free, not in business or in love or just in yourself if you hold onto these things. Do you agree?"

This had to be subterfuge, Holly said to herself. No one actually talks like this, do they? Not unless they were on a reality-television show, claiming to have spent twenty months in some hidden ashram followed by two years in a Buddhist monastery and then found the meaning of life in a temple on the mountain slopes of Bhutan, all by the time they were nineteen. There was no way Jamie could have possibly fallen for this, surely?

"I think keeping some secrets is quite healthy, actually," she said, asserting herself a little more.

Fin shuffled forwards slightly on the sofa.

"Really, like what?"

Holly thought about it momentarily.

"Like the tooth fairy. And Father Christmas. I mean, how disappointing would Christmas be if you told all the kids that Father Christmas wasn't real, just because you didn't want to keep a secret from them?"

"But how much more grateful would they be," he came back, "knowing that their parents did something so special for them each year? How much more appreciative would they be of the gifts if they knew they'd been bought with their parents' hard-earned money, rather than thinking they'd been built in some imaginary workshop at the North Pole or Lapland or wherever you Brits think it is that Santa lives? Don't you think that would be better? That knowing the presents and the love they were given with came from real people would have a greater effect?"

She considered her own childhood Christmases. With her parents' financial struggles, Santa had always been a little more frugal with her than her friends. Rather than cassette tape players and the latest fashion accessories, her stocking used to contain satsumas and home-made knitted gloves. By the time she realised why, she'd already grown out of believing in Father Christmas, anyway. Would it really have made a difference if she'd known the truth? It was hard to tell.

"Well, I believe some secrets are worth keeping and stop people from getting hurt," she said, with an air of finality.

"In the short term."

"Not necessarily."

She could feel herself bristling. For someone who was so into peace and tranquillity, he didn't seem very open to different opinions. Apparently, it was his way or not at all. Great.

"Now, my turn to ask you a question," she said. "Why did you leave the States? California, wasn't it?"

"Ahh, California."

His lips curled in a smile, exposing his perfectly straight, bright-white teeth. He really was an attractive man. There was no denying that. She could easily imagine him on some pin-up calendar, maybe wearing a checked, lumber-jack shirt, open to display his muscular chest or else holding a handful of puppies, going for that cute, caring look.

"Well, I actually have dual citizenship. My mum's a Brit. She was born in Colchester. Do you know it?"

"Vaguely," she replied, truthfully.

She knew it was on the east coast, but her geographical knowledge was limited to the Cotswolds and London and the area between, with not much north or south of that.

"Essex, right?"

"Right. I've only been there once or twice. She mainly stays around this area when she comes back. We used to visit every couple of years when I was young, to catch up with the grand-parents and cousins and people. Anyway, I figured it had been a long time since I'd been over, so I decided to come by myself in the New Year. And that's when I met Jamie."

"So, you were visiting? Where've you been living these past months?"

"Well, here a lot of the time. I left some stuff at my grans, but I was at my cousins to start with. He's got this house up in Chipping Norton."

He continued talking about his cousin, who worked in finance or something, but Holly was only half listening. She found herself feeling totally vindicated in her decision not to like him. It was obvious from this conversation alone that he was only moving in with Jamie because he had nowhere else to go. No doubt the story about his mother and his gran and dual citizenship was a lie. She gave it a month before he went for the whole proposal thing. Assuming she hadn't managed to send him packing before then.

"So, Jamie said you used all your savings and bought a sweet shop. That's radical. Really brave."

She sniffed.

"Maybe. But I didn't just *buy it.* I had worked there before. And lived here, too."

"Oh yeah, she said that. But still, it's rad."

Rad. She had heard her decision to buy *Just One More* called many things, but *rad* had never been one of them.

"So, what do you do?" she asked.

This was the first occasion when he'd looked as if he needed time to consider his answer. Stretching his arms out over his head, he let out a short yawn before lying back on the sofa.

"I'm actually between things right now," he said. "I sold my company just before leaving the States. It was one of my reasons for visiting, actually. Travel always helps free my mind, you know? Gives me a bit of perspective to decide what I want to do next."

"So, you don't have a job?"

"I have ideas. I figure I'm going to use this time to work out what direction I want to go in next."

It was exactly the type of vague nonsense that Holly would expect from a conman. All this stuff about secrets being toxic. What a great way to disguise the fact that he was pulling the wool over Jamie's eyes. A burst of anger surged through her. She was done with this.

"What do you want out of this? Out of this relationship with Jamie?" she asked.

"What do I want?" He sat forward. "What do you think I want?"

"I don't know. That's why I'm asking."

He pressed his lips together and ran his hands through his blond mop of hair, which fell perfectly back into place, like he was on a photoshoot for some aftershave magazine.

"Well, I guess I want it all."

"What does that mean?"

"It means exactly what it says. I want to make her happy. I want to grow old with her. Have kids, maybe, or not. I know she's undecided about that, but that's cool. I figure we could just pack up and travel the world if she'd like to do that. Dive in deep-blue waters and climb white-capped mountains. Bathe under waterfalls and camp under the stars. Whatever she wants."

What absolute drivel, was all Holly could think. What complete and utter codswallop. The ease with which these words spilled off his tongue was like he'd rehearsed them or, more likely, used the same spiel a thousand times before.

"Wow, you sound like the perfect man, willing to give up everything for her."

"Isn't that what you do when you love someone?"

"So you love her?"

It was the first time that his easy-going, Californian attitude shifted. He sat up again.

"You know what, I've answered a lot of questions," he said. "I think it's time you answer another for me."

Reverberations from her teeth grinding rattled through her skull. Whatever was coming, she knew it wasn't going to be good.

"Go on, then," she said.

"What have I done to upset you?" he asked.

She snorted. It came out far more abruptly than she'd expected. Almost aggressively. She tried to disguise the noise with a half laugh.

"What makes you think you've done anything to upset me?"

"Your energy, it's very … tight."

"Tight? And next you're going to tell me that my energy paths are blocked, too?"

A look of annoyance flashed across his face. It was the first time since they'd started talking that she'd seen him anything other than calm and collected. The expression was fleeting, though, and a moment later he was smiling again.

"Look, I'm sorry you feel it necessary to belittle someone else's beliefs. I'm only here to make her happy. That's it. And I don't want any toxic attitudes in this house. Bad energy is contagious, and Jamie and I don't want that."

"Wow. Way to lay claim to the house."

"That's not what I'm doing. I didn't mean it that way, Holly. I only want peace."

She shook her head. Really, this guy was even more unbelievable than she'd imagined.

"I tell you what: I'll tell you exactly what I don't like about you. It's—"

She wasn't a hundred percent sure what she was about to say first. There was certainly a whole menu to choose from. Top of the list might be the way he treated Jamie, like she was incapable. Then there was how he let her pay for everything without a second thought. And also the manner in which he'd infiltrated their lives so completely in such a short time. There were a dozen other things she could think of, too, right off the top of her head, but none of them left her mouth as no sooner had she gone to speak, than the front door clicked open.

"I hope you guys have been getting on," Jamie said, on her way past to the kitchen. "Now let's get this dished up. I'm bloody starving."

CHAPTER TWENTY

Holly could only eat half her curry and eventually consigned the rest of it to the fridge for the next day, assuming she'd be able to stomach it then. Fin was acting quite normally, offering her smiles and chatting away. Not a hint of animosity, which she found quite unnerving. Having fetched the plates, he'd dished up his food, filled their glasses and kept the conversation flowing. It was clear that Jamie was smitten, as she lounged against him, brushing crumbs of spring roll out of his stubble and feeding him forkfuls of her pad Thai. They were now watching TV, and he continued to be the epitome of the perfect gentleman. But something about him still set her on edge.

"I think I'm going to call it a day," she said, standing up.

"Are you sure?" Jamie asked. "We can put something else on if you prefer. Or we can play a game. I was going to teach Fin that new board game. He's never played it before."

"Honestly, I need to get a good night's sleep. I'm on my own in the shop tomorrow," she accidentally lied, only remembering afterwards that Drey had agreed to open up.

"Okay, if you're sure."

In the kitchen, she poured herself a tall glass of water and took a mouthful. Her favourite toothbrush was still at Ben's house, she realised. Along with a fair few other things, like pieces of jewellery and some of her makeup. She should really go and get them but wasn't sure she was ready for that yet. Maybe he'd drop them over.

"Holly?"

Fin's voice behind her made her jump. For a moment, she'd forgotten all about him. Yet there he was again, holding a small box in his hand.

"Sorry if we didn't get off on the right foot earlier. I know I can be a little intense when you first meet me. It's a fault I'm working on. Great for business meetings, not so good for socialising. Jamie has warned me about it. So here."

He held out the box to her.

"What's this?" she asked, not moving to take it from him.

"Just a little housewarming gift."

"I think you're meant to give gifts when someone moves in. I already live here. Besides, you brought the cake and the drink."

"Which you barely touched. Besides, this is something a little more special. Go on, take it."

She hesitated a moment longer, then reached out and took the box. It was heavier than she'd expected, particularly given its size.

"Go on. Open it," he instructed.

Sensing there was no way around this, she lifted the lid.

"A candle?" she said, making sense of the shape inside.

"Yup. It's homemade. Not by me, though. One of my friends creates them. They smell amazing. This one's sage and rose quartz. It has actual pieces of quartz embedded in it. If you burn it while you meditate, it helps to unblock your energy channels."

Bloody energy channels, again. Holly felt her jaw tighten. She somehow managed to disguise her grimace as a smile, if a somewhat brittle one.

"Thank you," she said. "That's very kind of you."

A second later, his arms were around her, squeezing her into a bear hug, the likes of which she'd not experienced before. Was this how they all behaved in California, embracing your girlfriend's *girlfriend* so intensely? she wondered. If it was, she wasn't planning on taking a trip there anytime soon.

"Look at you two getting on so well. I knew you would," Jamie said, watching them from the doorway.

Then, before Holly could extricate herself from his grip, she leapt across to them.

"Housemate group hug!"

Between Fin and Jamie's arms and the box digging into her ribs, Holly could now barely breathe. Her face flushed with heat.

"Okay, well, that's me done," she said, wriggling her way out of their grasp. "Early night and everything. Sleep well," she added, then grabbing her glass of water, bolted out the door.

When she woke up the next morning, Holly felt marginally better. She had, against her previous better judgement, decided that maybe some ambient, low light wouldn't go amiss to relax her and had lit the candle Fin had given her and let it burn on the windowsill for half an hour before she settled down to sleep. She really didn't buy into all that stuff about unblocking energy channels, but it certainly smelt divine, and she found herself reading with a better level of concentration than she'd managed in days. Her mum would definitely love it. Maybe she could get her one for her birthday, assuming he was still around by then. He might have already got everything he wanted from Jamie and fled.

Although she was planning on having a lie in, only half an hour after her alarm went off, she remembered she had two party platters due to be picked up that day. She'd already bought all the required confectionery and the jars and pots to display it in, but she hadn't got around to assembling it and there was no way she could expect Drey to manage something like that by herself and get the shop ready to open.

So, by nine-thirty, she was upstairs in the stockroom, filling little glass jars and stacking them in boxes ready to be collected. Considering how busy the shop was, she considered asking Drey to stay and work a full day, but she quickly thought better of it. Drey's father had spoken to Holly, shortly after Christmas. He wasn't rude or unkind, but he did mention, in no uncertain terms, how he was worried that spending too many hours at the shop was affecting the standard of work she was producing and that this year was so important, with her applying for university.

So, by one o'clock, she was on her own, serving the steady stream of people who came through the door.

"These are fantastic value, aren't they?" a customer said, as Holly rang up her purchases on the till.

She was so preoccupied with everything on her mind that she'd barely been looking at what she was selling. As such, this was the first time she paid any real attention to the item in her hand. It was a fudge box with a postcard of Bourton on the front. This particular one showed a winter scene, with snow falling around the mammoth Christmas tree. She felt a surge of anger at the image. Would there ever come a time, she wondered, when she'd be able to look at it without thinking of Ben? She had loved that tree, and she'd be damned if he was going to ruin it for her. She was about to place the box in a bag, when she noticed something, and rather than her blood boiling, it damn near froze.

These consistent best sellers sold at two pounds and ninety-nine pence. The mark up on them wasn't particularly good—they certainly weren't as profitable as the sweets they sold by weight—but she bought them in sufficient quantity that made it worthwhile. But the label on it didn't read two ninety-nine at all but ninety-nine pence.

"I'm sorry," she said, checking the box below and the next one.

The woman had picked up seven in total, all incorrectly priced.

"These are wrong, I'm afraid," she said. "These should be priced at two ninety-nine."

The woman stiffened.

"It says ninety-nine pence."

"I can see that," she replied, "but there's obviously been a mistake. I promise you; these boxes are two ninety-nine."

She moved out from behind the counter to the shelf where they were displayed. Her heart plummeted as she saw more and more labelled ninety-nine pence. In fact, it wasn't until she was nearly halfway to the back of the shelf that she actually found one at the right price.

"Here," she said, pulling it out so that the customer could see. "They're meant to be like this."

"Well, I don't want them at that price. These say ninety-nine pence and that's what I want to pay. You can't just change your mind. That's not how to run a business. I'm surprised you get anyone in here at all, if this is the way you treat people."

Several more shoppers had filed in by this time, and she could see that they were all watching with interest. There was no way this woman was going to pay the right price, and why should she want to? Holly thought. She wouldn't. But it was plain that there was going to be an even bigger scene and she would also have to go through all the rigmarole of cancelling off the items from the till. She would just have to suck it up.

"Fine," she said.

She then rang them up and bagged them in record time so that she could dive back to the shelf and remove all the wrongly priced boxes. How on earth had that happened? She tried to think back to when they'd come in. The delivery had arrived early last week, but she hadn't started pricing them until later on. That's when it hit her; her dad had finished the job and she'd been so preoccupied, she'd just told him to carry on. Did he not at least think about checking the price of the ones in the box she'd already labelled or notice the difference when he'd put them on the shelf?

Anger rippled through her, directed solely at herself. It was a good job the bank wasn't breathing down her neck so much anymore, she thought. Thankfully, it didn't take too long to sort out the error and soon the popular boxes of postcard fudge were on offer at the correct price.

Unfortunately, the chocolate-lime craving remained just as strong as the previous day. She had to do a pregnancy test and put her mind at ease, but at this time on a Sunday, there was nowhere to get one, and while she might be able to pick one up at the local garage, she knew several of the people who worked there, through Caroline and Michael, and to say they weren't discreet would be putting it mildly. No, she'd be better off waiting until tomorrow. Her dad would be back in for a couple of hours then, and she could slip out and get one.

She walked home, wondering if Jamie had done any food shopping or whether she'd need to search the cupboards for a tin of soup to eat. Tomorrow, she would definitely do a food shop of her own. Maybe she'd get up early for a change. Perhaps being single again would allow her to be one of those people who liked to start the day at 5:30. Then again, that had never happened before, so it seemed unlikely.

As she neared home, the level of noise suddenly struck her as unusual. Banging, interspersed with what sounded like the whir of an electric saw, was coming from somewhere close by. Lots of people around her house were into DIY but rarely on a Sunday night. Given how she was feeling, constant hammering was the last thing she wanted.

She arrived at the house and was pleased to see that Jamie's van was missing. At least that meant she wouldn't be interrupting any adult alone time again. With a bit of luck, Fin would be out, too. Remembering that she had some left-over takeaway in the fridge, she opened the front door and stopped dead in her tracks. The banging was louder now. Feeling decidedly apprehensive, she walked into the kitchen and stared out the double doors that led onto the garden.

"What the hell!"

CHAPTER TWENTY-ONE

"What the hell are you doing?" Holly demanded, as she raced out the back door. "What the hell?"

Fin was standing at the far end of the garden. The shed end. The shed where Jamie kept all her work tools securely padlocked away and even had a small camera on it—the same type that had caught Giles planting a mouse in the shop—to make sure nothing was stolen. But at that moment, she wasn't looking at the shed, she was looking at her raspberry bushes, or rather at where they had been, between the shed and Ben's garden hedge.

It was like a scene from a disaster movie. Upturned earth. Plants torn up by their roots and trampled on the ground. Not a single thing left standing. For a moment, she couldn't even speak.

"My raspberry bushes," she said when she finally found her voice again. "What the hell have you done?" she said, looking around. "My gooseberries too!"

Angry tears pricked her eyes, seeing how far spread the destruction was.

"What on earth were you thinking?"

Fin stood motionless.

"These were plants?" he asked, looking bemused.

Never before had his Californian drawl grated so much.

"Of course they were plants. They were *my* plants. My *fruit*."

He stood there, gawping like a fish out of water.

"I thought … I thought … I think I might have made a mistake."

"You think?" she said, heat burning her cheeks.

He had obviously been busy. Not only had he cleared her raspberry and gooseberry bushes, but almost all her blackberries and red currents, and the bed she'd covered in straw to keep her strawberries protected from the winter frost, had been entirely dug up. Basically, everything she'd planted last year when she'd first moved in, had gone.

"I'm seriously sorry. I didn't realise."

"Why are you even out here?" she spat.

She knew she had to share her home with this man, but did that include the garden? There had been an unspoken understanding between her and Jamie that this was her domain. Not only did she tend her herbs and fruit, but she mowed the lawn and kept the weeds under control, too. Jamie used the shed and would sit on the patio when the weather was good enough, but that was pretty much it.

Now, however, all that seemed to have changed.

"I screwed up," he admitted, as he sat at the kitchen table clutching a mug of herbal tea that smelt like a mixture of compost and eucalyptus oil. "Jamie and I were talking earlier. I said how I needed a workshop—you know, to do my stuff, not to mention somewhere for my yoga gear. And she said that she thought her shed was a bit small and maybe we could kill two birds with one stone and put up a bigger one and have a shared space. Well, I just thought it would be a nice birthday surprise for her if I got on with it. I was hoping to have all the clearing done by tonight and get the shed up in time for her birthday on Tuesday. They just looked like bushes."

"That's because they *were* bushes," she said, angrily. "Fruit bushes. Expensive ones."

"I can give you the money. Whatever they cost."

He pulled his phone out of his pocket.

"This is not about the money," she snapped.

He nodded.

"I understand. I do."

She expected more grovelling, but in an action that was utterly unexpected, he reached across the table and took her hands.

"Tell me how you're feeling?"

"What?"

She was too stunned to move. Surely it was bloody obvious how she was feeling? She was feeling bloody furious. Even more so now that he was touching her.

"It will help. I promise," he said, closing his eyes. "You know, if you hold it in, you'll find it'll only make things worse. Your energy—"

"Don't you dare. My energy channels were completely fine before you ripped up my garden," she said, pulling her hands away from him. "I think this is something that Jamie and I will need to talk about. In private."

And with that, she exhaled loudly, stood up and retreated to her room. To spend the night by herself.

It was gone nine when there was a knock on her bedroom door. She'd been expecting it. Jamie had already messaged her, saying Fin had spoken to her, but she hadn't replied. She was worried she would end up saying something she would regret.

"Can I come in?" Jamie called, although she didn't wait for an answer. "Fin told me about the fruit bushes," she said, taking a seat at the end of Holly's bed. He feels terrible."

Holly huffed. She didn't want to vent her anger on Jamie, but maybe if she'd taken the time to get to know the guy better before moving him in, things like this wouldn't have happened.

"Honestly, he feels awful. This has hit him really hard. It's so important to him that you guys get on. It's important to me, too."

She paused, like she was expecting Holly to say something at this point, but she didn't have it in her to reply, and Jamie was the one who wanted to talk, after all.

"He was going to order you some new ones online," she said, "but wasn't sure they'd be the right thing. Could you come down and check?"

It was the first direct question she'd asked, and Holly answered her immediately.

"You can see I'm already in my pyjamas," she said.

"And? You used to spend most of your days off like that."

"Yeah, well, that was before."

Holly wasn't sure what kind of response to expect to this, but she assumed that Jamie would at least take the hint and leave her alone. Instead, her housemate stood up, placed her hands on her hips and glowered. It was probably the first time she could remember her looking at anyone like that, let alone her.

"Look, I know things aren't going great for you at the moment. I do. But Fin's important to me. He made an honest mistake. That's it. And if you can't see past your own ego to realise that, then there's a bigger problem with the living arrangements than I thought there would be."

Wow. Holly let out a sigh. Jamie was the most chilled-out

person she'd met. She took everything in her stride, except Giles, but then she had been right to warn Holly about that one. Only now did she realise just how much of a prick she must have seemed.

"I'm sorry," she said. "You're right. I'll come down and look at the bushes."

"Thank you."

Jamie's frown loosened a fraction. As Holly pulled down her pyjama top and shifted off the bed, something else ran through her mind. Probably not the best time to bring it up now, but she knew if she didn't ask then and there, it would just be eating her up when she was supposed to be looking at plants and showing gratitude to Fin for doing something that any normal human being would if they'd just trashed someone else's belongings.

"Have you spoken to Ben?" she asked.

Even from behind, she could see the shift in Jamie's posture. Like she'd known the question had been coming.

"Only briefly. He rang me earlier. He wanted to know how you were doing."

"He did?"

She tried to sound disinterested, but knew she was failing miserably.

"What did you say?"

"I said I thought you were doing okay. Of course, that was before you were a bit of a bitch this evening."

She threw a smile over her shoulder, indicating that she was only joking. Holly was relieved. She could do without another relationship failure right now.

"He also said he'd understand if I didn't want him at my surprise birthday party on Tuesday."

Having been so preoccupied with the destruction of her property, Holly hadn't taken in what Fin had been saying about putting a new shed up for Jamie's birthday. Jamie's birthday, when they were all meant to be going to dinner together.

"You know it's technically not a surprise party if you're the one who invites everybody. It's just a party," Holly told her.

"I know, but Fin wanted it to be a surprise. He just didn't know who to invite. And I'll look suitably taken aback. That's what counts, right?"

She wanted to smile at this, but she didn't have it in her. Not with the way she was feeling. Not until she knew what she might be facing.

"Ben won't be coming, will he," she asked, hearing the tremble in her voice.

"Of course he will," Jamie replied. "He never misses my birthday."

"I thought you might ask him to give it a miss, this time."

"That's ridiculous. He's one of my closest friends and I want him there. I want you both there."

This felt like a knife to the chest, temporarily stopping her breathing. She clenched her jaw, fighting back all the things she wanted to say. It wasn't Jamie's fault. Of course, she'd want Ben there, just like she'd wanted her boyfriend to move in, even if he was clearly trying to scam her out of all her money and destroy her property. But all of a sudden, it felt like she'd been abandoned. Like a ship that has come away from its mooring, just drifting with no destination.

"They'll be plenty of others there," Jamie said. "Caroline and Michael are both coming. And a couple of guys I sometimes work with. I figured you could sit at opposite ends of the table. You could sit next to Fin. I'd love it if you could get to know him a little better. Maybe it would actually be good for you and Ben. You know, to see each other out, just as friends again."

"Maybe."

She didn't want to get upset. There was nothing to cry about. She was an adult for goodness' sake. She could handle one dinner in the company of her ex-boyfriend. And yet, for some reason, the urge to cry was overwhelming. Maybe it was her hormones, she thought, only to wish she hadn't. That reminded her of what her dad had said about the chocolate limes and, even though she was sure it was all in her head, it was still too much. Three seconds later, there was no escaping the tears, as they cascaded down her cheeks.

"Oh Holly," Jamie sat back down on the bed and pulled her into a hug. "Don't worry. You're going to be fine. You're going to be absolutely fine. I promise."

CHAPTER TWENTY-TWO

Looking for replacement fruit bushes that evening went as well as could be expected, given that Holly didn't really know what she needed. Last time, she'd gone to the garden centre, where the people there had advised her what to plant. It was much harder to tell from small pictures on a screen. Still, she knew that Jamie really wanted her to do this. Although any chance Fin had of getting back into her good graces disappeared the moment it came to pay.

"Damn, my card won't go through. Can I use yours? I'll transfer it later with my share of the rent."

"Sure."

"Thanks my little Jam Jar."

Jam Jar? Holly felt sickened by this new nickname and the fact that she'd handed over her card without a second's thought. Then there was the comment about his share of the rent. Did that mean her own rent was going to be reduced? Because that would be great if she was going to start saving for a deposit on another place.

When the payment finally went through and she'd accepted

a tight and lingering hug from Fin, she headed back up to bed, wondering what the next week was going to throw at her.

The next morning Holly awoke to an unfamiliar aroma. It wasn't particularly unpleasant, just … out of place. Stepping out of bed and stretching, she made her way downstairs, where it quickly become apparent that the smell was coming from the kitchen. Jamie usually ate a slice of toast or a bowl of cereal in the morning, unless Holly cooked something more substantial for them both, and this didn't smell like bacon and eggs or even pancakes or waffles. Her stomach dropped with the realisation of what it meant.

Bracing herself, she stepped into the kitchen.

"Morning sleepyhead," Fin said, in the irritating way people who are abnormally chirpy first thing do. "Ready to start the day? I thought I owed you an apology breakfast."

Still rubbing her eyes and wondering how someone could have so much energy so early, her jaw dropped when she finally took in the sight in front of her. The kitchen, *her kitchen,* was an absolute mess. She would never have considered herself the tidiest of bakers—in fact there was barely a session where she didn't get flour or sugar down her at some point—but she had learned through the years that it was far easier to clean up as you went than deal with chaos at the end. And chaos was the only word she could come up with to describe the state of the place at that moment. Chopping boards, knives and bowls were all over the countertop, while pans were stacked haphazardly in the sink. Just looking at it was causing her throat to tighten.

"I need to go to work," she said, wondering if perhaps he'd

invited half a dozen other people over to join them, judging by the quantity of food.

"Not before eating, you don't," he said, pulling out a chair for her to sit on. "Your body needs proper nourishment. Besides, Jamie said you like your food. I thought this might go some way towards making amends."

This had to be a dream or, more accurately, a nightmare, Holly thought walking over to him as if her body were on autopilot and numbly sat down. Jamie was already sitting opposite her, with a wide grin on her face.

"I told you he was great, didn't I? He's been up for two hours making all this."

"Well, I get up at four-thirty most days, so it's good to spend the time being useful. Besides, there's something crazily invigorating about skating in a morning frost."

"Or just crazy," Jamie replied.

Holly had to agree. Skateboarding on an icy surface sounded like a quick route to A&E.

Fin brought a heavy, cast iron-pan from the hob, which he put down in the centre of the table on heat proof mats. However, rather than sitting down and joining them, he closed his eyes and took in a deep breath. Several seconds went by and he hadn't moved. Only when he opened his eyes did Jamie offer an explanation.

"Fin likes to meditate for a moment before he eats. I know. It's weird. I've told him that, repeatedly, but he still does it."

"It's not weird to want to feel your best self before you nourish your body," he said, taking a seat next to Holly. "Nor is it weird to be at one with the earth that provided you with your sustenance. I can't help it if you Brits are lax on your spirituality."

"Just ignore it," Jamie said to Holly, with a smile. "That's what I do. Now, can we tuck in?"

"Absolutely," he replied. "So, this is Galayet Bandora."

He pointed to a dish of chopped tomatoes.

"It looks really plain, but trust me, I could eat this forever. I used organic tomatoes, obviously, and wild garlic that I foraged with my cousin on the land around my grandmother's house. You know lots of people don't realise you can do that in the UK. Honestly, the taste is so much better. Not to mention the antioxidant level. You know that the farmed, white garlic you buy is so full of chemicals it's doing your body more harm than good. And I really don't see why we need to ship things thousands of miles when we're perfectly capable of growing them in our climate. I mean, the UK's not California, but you can do anything with a polytunnel and a bit of motivation."

Holly had to almost bite her tongue. If every meal was going to start with a lecture on farming methods and the inappropriateness of her purchases, she'd be eating out much more.

"Is that so?" she said, forcing a smile.

"There's also a dahl. I know you have it as an evening meal from the Indian takeaway sometimes, but in many parts of the world, it's a breakfast dish. I wish I could make the roti to go with it, but I'm afraid my skill set doesn't stretch to breads. I fetched some fresh, English bread from the bakery, though. You know they have a selection made with organic flour, if you ask for it?"

Holly wasn't sure whether it was the constant stream of rhetorical questions or simply the abrupt start to her morning, but she couldn't focus. Under normal circumstances, a meal like this would have been amazing and she could probably have polished off most of the food on her own. But all the smells were heady and strong, and she wasn't used to them so early. It was making her feel more than a little queasy.

"I think I'll just start with some bread," she said and picked up a piece from the plate in front of her.

By the time she left the house, she was running twenty minutes late. After the initial slice of bread, her appetite had picked up and she discovered that dahl really was great for breakfast, although the tomato dish was probably her favourite. She only hoped that the extra food would give her the energy she needed to get through the day. When she reached the shop, there was already a queue waiting for her.

"I'm so sorry," she said as she wiggled past the customers to unlock the front door. "It's a long story. A bit of an emergency at home."

"Oh no! Is everything all right?" one asked. "Nothing wrong with your father, I hope. Will he be here again today?"

"No, no, it's all sorted now. Just an issue in the garden," she replied, switching on the lights and turning the sign around to Open. She considered this to be only a half lie. After all, it was the apology breakfast that had been the cause of her lateness. She pulled off her coat and tucked it under the counter, not wanting to go upstairs to the storeroom when there were so many customers in the shop.

"Okay," she said, switching on the till, ready to go. "Who's first?"

The late start put her on the back foot all day. With no time to check the calendar, she forgot to email the order for more sticks of rock, and they were already running very low. She also forgot to put together an order of individual Belgium chocolates that a local couple wanted as wedding favours. Running a business was all about organisation, and right now she was utterly lacking it. When her dad walked in, she didn't know if she felt more stressed or relieved. That was until he started serving.

"Here, let me help you with those. How much would you like?" he asked a woman who was after Everton mints.

He took the jar from her, weighed out the requisite amount, rang it up and took her money, with nothing more than general day-to-day pleasantries. Holly let out a small sigh of relief. Maybe this was a good idea, after all.

She was feeling almost normal, when a young family came in.

"We need to get Granny and Chad some chocolate," the younger of the two girls told her, having raced into the shop ahead of the others. "Dad? Dad? Can we get them some chocolate? You know they'll like it."

The rest of the family arrived at the counter.

"Abbie, keep an eye on Mabel, please. Make sure she doesn't end up trying to buy everything in the shop," the father said.

"Stop fussing, Eric, they're fine," the woman chided him, good humouredly.

Just as she'd been asked, the older girl guided her sibling around, making sure she didn't touch any of the glass jars. But it was the couple that Holly found herself most drawn to. They were holding hands, fingers entwined, and they were so at ease with one another, she thought as she watched the woman drop her head onto her partner's shoulder. And when her gaze moved further down, to the swell of her belly, tears pricked at her eyes.

Why was it so difficult for her to find something so simple as a peaceful, happy relationship? she wondered. Or rather, why was it so difficult?

As she watched the family looking around the shop, she felt a strange pang in her abdomen. Her initial thought was that it was gone lunchtime, and she hadn't eaten anything except for a couple of gummy bears since her enormous breakfast. But as her eyes were drawn back to the woman's stomach, a flutter of nerves grew within her.

"Dad," she called up the stairs. "Would you be okay to cover the shop floor for a bit? I need to pop out and get something?"

Her dad's head appeared out of the stockroom door.

"You want to leave me? On my own?"

"You'll be okay, won't you?"

Pushing his shoulders back, Arthur straightened his tie and came down.

"Of course I will. In fact, I'll be better than okay. I'll be grand."

Comfortable that the worst-case scenario would involve finding a massive queue when she returned, she grabbed her bag and slipped past the family out into the High Street.

It was only when she entered the chemist that she realised her mistake. Not only was it the tail-end of many people's lunch breaks, but it was also a Monday, meaning that everyone who'd needed to pick something up yesterday but couldn't because the shop was closed, was there today. The queue was almost twice as long as it had been when she came in before. She considered coming back later, but something else was bound to distract her and it would end up being another day before she got the pregnancy test. No, she needed to get it now. There was so little she felt she had control of in her life at the moment, and getting over her paranoia would give her one less thing to worry about.

Joining the back of the queue, she waited patiently, moving slowly forwards and casually picking up a test packet on route, along with a lipstick, for old time's sake.

Her hands were shaking as she reached the counter and went to pay. Did the sales people here take particular note of what customers were buying and who they were, like she did in her shop? she wondered. Probably not.

"That's nine pounds ninety-eight, altogether," the assistant said, without looking up. Holly tapped her card on the reader, took the bag and quickly left.

The bag was white and made of incredibly cheap paper, meaning that it was practically transparent, and the words *Pregnancy Test* shone through as clear as day. So she slipped it under her jumper before stepping through the door of her shop. The bell jingled above her and the familiar scent of sweets and chocolate wafted around her. She breathed it in, relieved that no one was there to see her as she slipped around the counter and tucked the bag securely out of sight. That was when it struck her. There was no one there to see her. The shop was *completely* empty.

CHAPTER TWENTY-THREE

"Dad?" Holly called up the stairs, trying to suck back her annoyance that was, once again, aimed at both herself and her father. She hadn't told him not to leave the shop floor even if something needed restocking. She would have preferred him simply being unable to offer it to the customers than leaving the place unattended. After waiting a moment and getting no reply, she called a second time.

"Dad, you really shouldn't leave the shop for this long."

His lack of response led her to assume that he must be in the toilet and her irritation grew. If he'd been that desperate that he couldn't wait a few minutes, he should have said something before she left. But as another minute passed and there was still no sign of him, a feeling of panic started to bubble up.

"Dad! Dad! Are you okay?"

She took the stairs two at a time, yet it still felt too slow. Had he collapsed? Her mother was always going on about what perfect health he was in for his age, but he was in his sixties, after all. Her mind started racing away with images of what she was going to see when she reached the top of the stairs. After losing her friend, Verity, at the end of last year, she wasn't sure how much more she could cope with. Yet, when she reached the stockroom, he wasn't there.

"Dad?" she said, pushing open the toilet door and finding it empty, too. Her concern kicked up another notch and her pulse was starting to pound in her ears.

"Dad!" she yelled. "Dad! Where are you?"

But there was no point. The shop was so tiny that you could even hear the ringing of the doorbell from up here. So where the hell was he?

She bounded back down the stairs, immediately checking behind the free-standing displays, worrying that maybe he'd collapsed behind one of them, but there was still no sign of him. Her heart was pumping fast now, and her chest was becoming tight. Where could he be? It was as if he'd vanished.

The bell above the door jingled, and a voice said, "Excuse me. Are you open?"

She turned, to see an elderly couple peering in.

"I know you've got your lights on and everything," the woman said, "but the sign on the door says, Closed."

"Um … we're … we're …"

Holly's brain was performing acrobatics as she tried to answer and at the same time work out what the hell she was supposed to do. Her dad was missing, and there were customers at the door, asking if they were open.

"Sorry," she said, giving the woman a little more attention. "What did you just say?"

The woman looked at her, confused. "I just wanted to check if you were open, because the sign on the door says, Closed."

Holly approached them. She was right; it did say that. But she always turned it around in the morning. It was automatic, part of her routine. She had been in a rush today, but that was why she recalled doing it so clearly, as there had already been customers behind her at the time. And it was a sturdy sign on a substantial chain and couldn't easily be accidentally flipped. No, someone had deliberately turned it to face the other way.

"I'm sorry," she said. "Yes, yes … come in. Come in. I'm just …"

She stepped quickly outside, scanning up and down the road. Could her father really have left the shop like that? Surely not? The till had over half a day's takings in it, and the door hadn't been locked. He would never have done that, she thought, until she caught sight of the figure walking alongside the river, swinging his arms as if he had all the time in the world. As he reached the opposite side of the road to her, he offered a short wave.

"Excuse me, can I pay for these?" the woman called from inside the shop.

"Of course, I'll just be one minute," she called back with a smile.

She stepped across to stand in front of the window, allowing herself a perfect view of the till.

"Where the hell have you been?" she hissed at her dad.

"Ah, well, you see Mrs Jenkins had her arm in a sling. Slipped down the stairs, apparently. Not the first time she's done it either, she said. Well, she'd got all these bags, and she was only going a little way across the road. You know, where the Kingfisher pub used to be?"

"Dad, you left the shop unattended."

"Only for a couple of minutes."

"You can't do that. Anyone could have come in and emptied the till or stolen things or trashed the place."

"I switched the sign on the door to, Closed. I'm sure nobody would go into a shop when the sign says that."

Holly was absolutely flabbergasted. Had it been another employee, she would have sacked them then and there, but at that moment, she couldn't even speak.

"Excuse me? We've been waiting rather a long time."

The customer had come to the door.

"If we could please just pay—"

"Yes, of course."

"I can do that," Arthur said, moving towards the till, but Holly put her arm out to stop him.

"Actually, Dad, I think you've been here long enough today. Why don't you get your things? I'm sure there'll be a bus soon."

His chin wobbled as he looked at his daughter.

"Oh, okay, if you think so. When would you like me next? Friday again?"

She flexed her fingers then stretched them out again, to the point where the tendons became visible.

"How about I give you a call?"

"And what's really crappy is, I'm left feeling as if it's me that's done something wrong. I've given him a job, when I didn't even need him, and I had to lie about it, and honestly, I am so bloody exhausted, I feel like closing the shop for a week."

"Or you could just take a full weekend off, go to a spa and let me and Drey take the reins. And why are you drinking lemonade? This definitely feels like the type of day when you need a gin, or twenty."

Caroline was right. Holly had rung her from work and asked if she was free. With her two eldest at taekwondo and gymnastics and the youngest parked with her parents, she had thankfully been able to spare her half an hour. Holly had spent the entire twenty minutes they'd been together in the pub venting about her frustration with her dad. In fact, she'd been so preoccupied with this that she'd barely even thought about Ben or Fin or any of the other disasters in her life.

"I'm doing dry January," she replied to Caroline's question.

"You know we're already halfway through March?"

"Well, I didn't start it on time."

Obviously sensing that this was something she didn't want her to pursue, Caroline shifted the conversation.

"So, how's the new housemate? Jamie told me about the fruit bushes. She feels terrible. She thinks you don't like him."

"I don't. I can't stand him."

Caroline arched an eyebrow.

"He can't be that bad. Not if Jamie likes him. What is it?"

Holly ran her tongue over her top teeth as she tried to put into words exactly what it was about Fin that wound her up so much.

"To start with, he's always smiling. He's constantly upbeat but also ridiculously chilled."

"And that's a bad thing?"

"No one can be that positive all the time. It's just not possible. Either he's faking it, or one day he's just going to snap and hack up more than my raspberry canes."

She sank back into her chair and took a long sip of lemonade.

"I don't know. I just don't trust him, that's all. He's always talking about sharing feelings and not having secrets. It's weird. And he has crystals in his candles and meditates before he eats."

"Well, I for one am very much looking forward to meeting him tomorrow evening. Michael's parents are having the kids overnight, so we can stay out as late as we want."

"That's good," Holly said, trying to muster some enthusiasm.

She'd actually been wondering how she could get out of this birthday meal. She'd concluded that she couldn't. It shouldn't matter that Ben was going to be. Nor should the fact that she thought Jamie's boyfriend was as slippery as an eel influence her. It was Jamie's birthday. Jamie, who she loved dearly.

"You guys will protect me, won't you?" she said to Caroline, feeling unbelievably pathetic.

"You can sit between me and Michael. That way you don't have to speak to anyone else all night if you don't want to. Although, just to warn you, this will be his first night out in over a month, so he might end up drinking rather too much. You know he can't handle it the way he thinks he can."

"Trust me, sitting next to a drunk Michael is infinitely more appealing than sitting with Ben or Fin," Holly said, relieved that now she had some sort of survival plan in place.

"You know you don't need to look so worried," Caroline said. "It might not turn out anywhere near as bad as you think it's going to be. Have you decided what to wear?"

"What to wear? I didn't even want to be there."

"Which is why you have to look as hot as possible. Make Ben see what an idiot he is for letting you go. You should wear those knee-high boots you picked up at the charity shop the other month. I still haven't seen you in them yet."

"That's because I haven't been."

The boots had been a bit of an impulse buy having seen them in the shop window opposite the motor museum. She'd never owned anything like them before and always felt envious of women who could carry off the look so confidently, strutting around in such high heels. On the spur of the moment, she'd decided to check their size, and on discovering they were a six and also only seven pounds, she'd bitten the bullet and bought them. They'd been sitting at the bottom of her wardrobe ever since.

"I don't even know what I could wear them with."

"I don't think it would even matter," Caroline replied. "What about that little black dress you have? The one with the pockets."

Dresses with pockets, Holly had discovered, were infinitely better than ones without.

"Okay, I guess that could work," she agreed.

"Trust me, wear that, and Ben will not be able to keep his eyes off you."

Holly lifted her glass and polished off the rest of the lemonade. As much as she didn't want to admit she wanted Ben's attention, making him regret what he'd lost out on might make her feel a fraction better.

"I guess that's what I'm wearing then," she said, and raised her empty glass to clink with Caroline's.

"And don't worry, Michael and I will look after you. You have my word."

CHAPTER TWENTY-FOUR

It was going to be bad. Holly knew it from the moment she'd woken up. She'd had this feeling deep in her bones that maybe it would be better if she didn't get up at all and just slept all the way through until Wednesday. Unfortunately, she didn't have that option. With Caroline's in-laws doing the full night shift for Jamie's party, she'd asked to change her normal full day—which was Holly's regular day off—from the Tuesday to the Thursday, meaning she had to get up for work.

Listening to Jamie and Fin giggling first thing in the morning was not the way she wanted to start her day. It was innocent sounding enough, just two people enjoying each other's company, but it reminded her too much of how she and Ben had been just a week earlier. It seemed impossible that life could change so drastically in such a short period. Of course, it wasn't the first time it had done a full one-eighty, and splitting up with a new boyfriend was nowhere near as dramatic as it had been the year before, with Dan. But it still felt dreadful.

Wanting to drown out the noise, she treated herself to an

extra-long shower, during which she pressed her hands against her stomach and thought about the test she'd bought. Surely she would know if she was pregnant. She was nearly thirty. It was just the upset of the breakup that was messing with her. That was all.

When she stepped out of the shower, she retrieved the test from her room and slipped it into one of the bathroom drawers.

Tonight, she said to herself. There was no point dragging it out, particularly when it was going to be negative, anyway.

At work, rest was the last thing on offer. Before she'd even opened the shop, a large bag of mint imperials burst and spilt all over the floor. Of all the sweets for this to happen to, mint imperials had to be the worst. They simultaneously bounced and rolled away in every direction, and even after she'd spent ten minutes with a dustpan and brush and then reaching under the bottom shelves with a broom to hoick out more strays, she was certain that someone was going to slip on one, go flying and sue her for every penny she had. Every now and then, she'd catch a glimmer of white and find another one that had managed to lose itself between the bags of toffee pennies or the sticks of rock.

By midday, the roll of paper in the card machine had jammed not once, not twice, but four times. A child had dropped her sherbet pips only seconds after the parent had paid for them and she felt obliged to give her a replacement and then had to clear up all those, too. And as the *pièce de résistance* that the fates had in store for her, the traffic warden had been on the prowl and ticketed the cars of three of her customers who had parked outside.

Being on her own meant there was no chance of a lunch break and when she rang up the bakery to ask if they would do a delivery, it turned out they were short staffed too and couldn't send anyone over.

By the time she got home, she needed a large sandwich and a long a soak in the tub. Unfortunately, they were not only out of bread, but her bathroom was already occupied.

"You know that your room has an en suite, don't you?" Holly yelled at the door, hands on hips, waiting for him to appear.

When Fin finally came out and jumped in surprise at her standing right there in front of him, it at least gave her a modicum of satisfaction.

"Holly?"

"I said, you have your own shower, remember?"

For a moment, he just blinked as if he couldn't understand what she'd said. Then he cleared his throat and spoke.

"I realise that, but I can't get to grips with all the buttons. You know, the rain or pressure setting. I used to just have simple, outdoor showers and I just find the bath easier. It's all wiped down. I've even left some of my cucumber-and-apple body wash in there. It's made with essential oils. Organic ones, obviously."

She pressed her lips together, trying to work out what was so peculiar about this situation, other than Fin preferring to use her bathroom, that was. But he hadn't finished.

"I'm going to drive down to the restaurant in a bit. I've already put up all the decorations, but there are a few other bits and pieces I want to do. I've got to fetch Jamie, too, of course, the whole surprise thing, but I don't mind doing an extra run … If you don't want to walk, I can take you."

"No, I'm good. Provided I can get into the bath, that is."

With a nod, Fin quickly stepped to the side and let her past. She scratched her head wondering about the conversation they'd just had. He'd been babbling, just the way she did when she was nervous. But at least this time he'd actually been wearing a towel, which was definitely a step up from their previous bathroom encounter. Maybe it was Jamie's party that had got him all worked up. That would make sense.

With her bath filling, she flicked off the cap of his apple and cucumber body wash. He wasn't joking. It smelt really good. She poured an ample helping in the running hot water and stripped off, ready to get in. That was when she saw the drawer. It was only slightly ajar, barely more than a couple of centimetres, but she had definitely closed it properly that morning. Her heart hammered in her chest as she stepped forwards. There on top, her pregnancy test was on full display.

Fin had seen it.

A hundred possibilities ran through her head. What was she supposed to do now? she wondered as the foam mounted up. He'd seen it. So what? It was her bathroom. She could keep whatever she wanted in it. It could have been an old one or one she'd bought for a friend, for all he knew. Yet no matter how much she tried to talk herself out of it, a feeling of dread swirled within her. Was he going to tell Jamie what he'd seen? Did it even matter?

Either way, there was one thing she knew for certain. She had to do the test. Now.

It was only when the water started to gurgle in the overflow that Holly came back to reality. Standing up, she switched off the tap, pulled out the plug and then sat back down on the toilet.

She, Holly Berry, was pregnant.

Pregnant and single.

She'd read and reread the instructions on the back on the box, checking if there was some way she could have misinterpreted what the little cross in the window meant, but she knew deep down there wasn't. She was pregnant with Ben's child. But Ben was still in love with Ella, and she didn't even have anywhere to live. Not really. Not somewhere she could raise a child. The last thing that Fin and Jamie would want in their love nest was to be woken up six times a night by a wailing baby. How would they manage to go to work after that? Come to think of it, how was she going to? Maybe she could strap the baby to her chest in one of those carrier things during the day, although that would only work until it was mobile. Then she'd have to think of something else. But what? She could barely afford to give herself a decent living wage. How could she possibly raise a baby on that? Maybe she couldn't. Maybe the best thing would be if she didn't have it at all.

She quashed that thought before it even had time to form properly. If this last year had taught her anything, it was that you had to make the most of what life threw at you. Never would she have dreamed that Dan cheating on her would be the best possible thing to happen to her, yet it had been. Maybe it would be the same with this baby. Yes. It would be. She would make it work. She just didn't know how yet.

The front of the test box claimed it to be 99.9% accurate. That meant there was still a one-in-a-thousand chance that she wasn't pregnant, then. They didn't feel like great odds. Maybe she would buy another one tomorrow, just to check.

With her mind whirring, she still hadn't left the bathroom, when her phone rang.

"Where are you?" Caroline hissed down the line. "Fin wants to get Jamie and everyone's here except you."

"Oh, crap."

Holly picked up her watch and checked the time. Somehow she'd lost forty-five minutes. It would take her at least another twenty to get dressed, made up and down to the restaurant, assuming she walked. Maybe it would be better now if she just missed the meal altogether. She certainly had a perfectly valid reason.

"Don't you dare," Caroline said, reading her silence perfectly. "There is no way you're skipping out on tonight. I can come and pick you up, if you need me to.

A standard refusal started to form on Holly's lips. After all, if she ran, she could probably get there a couple of minutes quicker. But should she do that, given her condition? It wasn't like her body was used to that kind of exertion at the best of times.

"That would be great if you could. I'll be outside in ten minutes."

"Make it five. I'm coming now."

Never could she remember getting dressed so quickly. Ignoring the fact that she hadn't even had her bath, she dashed into her bedroom, pulled her dress off the hanger and slipped on her boots. She'd been hoping to have time to do a bit of makeup. At least attempt to appear she hadn't been falling apart since Ben had dumped her, but as it was, smudged, end-of-work-day mascara was the look she was going with as she raced down the stairs and jumped into Caroline's car. She had at least brushed her hair, though apparently that wasn't enough of a repair job for her friend not to notice the state she was in.

"What happened?" she said. "Are you okay?"

"I'll talk to you about it later."

"No problem. We can catch up over the meal. We've already got a bottle of wine on the go."

Holly buckled her seat belt.

"Trust me, this is not a conversation for company."

"Now you've really got me interested," Caroline said, with a smirk.

When Holly didn't reply, she reached across and squeezed her hand.

"Look, it's just one night. You can manage that. We have wine, remember?"

"Wine I can't drink," Holly muttered.

This time, Caroline didn't reply. Holly could feel her friend looking at her, but she couldn't face her. Instead, tears welled up in her eyes.

"Oh Holly."

Cutting the engine, Caroline wiped away a tear from Holly's cheek.

"Is it what I think it is?"

Holly snorted an ugly gulping breath.

"Can you think of any other reason I wouldn't drink right now?"

Another pause followed. Holly wished she could stop crying, but the floodgates had been opened. There would be no stopping it now.

"Does Ben know?" Caroline asked. "Have you told him yet?"

Holly sniffed.

"I just did the test. It might not even be accurate."

"I hate to tell you, but those things are pretty well spot on nowadays. Trust me."

She paused, the silence heavy in the air.

"What are you going to do?" she asked. "Have you thought about it yet?"

The truth was, she didn't need to think about it. She knew

without a shadow of a doubt, but that wasn't something that she wanted to discuss right now. Not even with Caroline.

"I have. And I'll have all that to deal with soon. But right now, what I'm going to do is go to Jamie's party, enjoy myself and try not to think about it for the rest of the night."

A worried expression lingered on Caroline's face, but she smiled all the same.

"That sounds good to me."

CHAPTER TWENTY-FIVE

Holly pushed the restaurant door open. It was one of the swankiest in the village, on a back road that ran parallel to the river. It had gone through several renovations and reinvented itself over the years since her departure, changing from a greasy spoon to a high-end sushi restaurant and plenty of other incarnations between. But it had spent the last two years as an Asian-American fusion restaurant, which as far as she could tell meant it could serve whatever it wanted on the menu—from battered fish and chips to a chow mein—and no one was allowed to call it out. Still, it had stood the test of time and got consistently excellent reviews.

She had been here twice before. Once for Caroline's birthday and for dinner with Ben on New Year's Day. They'd only been together a couple of weeks at the time and were still in the honeymoon stage. Unfortunately, with both herself and Ben being rather well-known figures in the community, they couldn't get longer than five minutes without one person or another coming up to speak to them. In the end, they'd got their food to-go and left it on the kitchen table to get cold and disappeared upstairs in a fit of giggles.

Holly tried not to think of this as she stepped inside, taking care not to trip on the threshold. While the boots may have looked pretty stunning, they were a darn sight higher than she was used to wearing, and she'd felt herself tottering from the moment she'd put them on.

Back in London, she'd usually worn heels to work. Nothing massive, just an inch or two to give herself a bit more height. But she'd been sitting at a desk all day there, only needing to walk to the small kitchenette to make a cup of tea or fetch a sandwich from the fridge.

Now, she spent all day on her feet, racing around the shop floor, sprinting up and down the stairs and climbing their mini ladder to reach the bottles on the very top shelves. As such, she only ever wore flat shoes, trainers mostly. So the three-inch heels on the boots felt utterly alien to her. There would be no running away tonight, however much she might want to.

With that thought in mind, she slipped through the main part of the restaurant and into the back room to a small, private area that they'd booked for the night's event. To her surprise, origami birds hung everywhere.

"Wow," she said, looking up and turning slowly around to take it all in. "It's like an aviary. A paper one."

There must have been a hundred of the brightly coloured birds hanging at different heights on near-invisible threads and stirring in the current of air created when anyone moved. They looked for all the world like they were flying. They came in every size, from long, crane-like creations to ones that appeared to be swallows and others that looked more like sparrows. It felt more like she'd stepped into an exhibition at the Tate Modern than a restaurant in Bourton-on-the-Water.

"This is incredible. I didn't know they had this here," she said.

"Oh, they didn't. Fin created it. He's been here all afternoon, apparently," Caroline said.

"Fin? Really?"

Holly dodged one of the lower hanging birds. Most of them were well and truly above her head height, but there were more than a couple that might cause a problem for someone taller than her.

He must have paid someone to make them, she thought to herself as she weaved her way through them. Bought a load off the internet. All he'd had to do was hang them up, although he obviously had a good eye for decorating. Perhaps tonight she'd find out what he actually did for a job. Assuming he had one, of course. Maybe she could employ him as a babysitter if he was desperate. Then again, she wouldn't be able to afford to pay him.

Pushing thoughts of Fin and her pregnancy to the back of her mind, Holly turned her attention to the long table that was buzzing with chatter and laughter. She recognised most of the guests. There were people Jamie worked with and some she volunteered with, too. Although, it was as if there was a magnet drawing her eyes to one particular spot. The seat, three places from the far end, where Ben was sitting, looking directly at her.

A flush of heat rose through her entire body and a throbbing started in her abdomen that must have been entirely imaginary. She grabbed Caroline's hand and squeezed it tightly.

"I'm just going to the ladies. I won't be a second. Make sure that you save me a seat between you and Michael."

Caroline nodded.

"It's already sorted, but be quick. Jamie's going to arrive any minute. Fin's already gone to get her."

In the toilets, Holly doused her face with cold water. This was ridiculous. What on earth was she doing? Why was she here, at a party, pretending everything was normal? Everything wasn't normal. It wasn't even close. With water still trickling down her face, she studied her reflection in the mirror. Would Ben be able to tell? she wondered, before dismissing the thought as ridiculous. Of course he wouldn't. She hadn't even known herself. Had it not been for her dad's comment about the chocolate limes, goodness knows how long she could have gone without putting two and two together. She stayed there a minute longer, before drawing in a deep breath and pulling her shoulders back.

"Here goes," she said to herself.

As promised, Caroline had saved a seat between herself and her husband, which Holly slipped into, avoiding anyone's eyes. The boots were now pinching her toes, and she wondered if there might be a way of subtly slipping them off under the table. Then again, she reasoned, maybe they'd be more comfortable when she was sitting down.

"Michael," she said, turning to him. "How are you?"

While Holly had gone to school with Michael, he was barely recognisable as the geeky, awkward boy who used to sit at the back of the class and listen to emo music on his Walkman. He now sported a fairly robust beard and thick-rimmed glasses, which together gave the impression of him being a cool science teacher, or perhaps someone who worked in tech. The fact was, he was neither, although Holly was never completely sure what his job did entail. They got on well, although at that precise moment he was looking at her as if she'd grown an extra head. His lips twitched.

"Holly, let me get you a drink," he said, jumping up from his seat. "Wine? Sorry. No. What was I thinking? Um. Water? Lemonade? Coke?"

He was stuttering like he was fifteen again and trying to chat someone up. And it didn't take a genius to work out why he was so flustered. Holly turned to her other side, where Caroline was staring intently down the stem of her wine glass as she held it to her lips.

"You told him!" Holly hissed. "I was only gone one minute! Why on earth did you do that?"

"I'm sorry," Caroline whispered, her face crumpled in remorse. "I just didn't know what else to do. He knew I was hiding something. He read it in my face the moment I stepped in."

"Then you should have told him you'd crashed the car, or I had a drinking problem, or something."

Heat surged through her again. She covered her face with her hands and let out a deep sigh.

"It's okay. It's fine. Just keep quiet, the pair of you, will you?"

"Of course," Michael said immediately.

"I won't tell a soul. Or another soul, I mean," Caroline stammered. "I won't talk to anyone all evening. Other than you two. Okay?"

Not knowing whether to laugh or cry, Holly was about to speak again when a large whoop went up from the table. The birthday girl had arrived.

CHAPTER TWENTY-SIX

Cheers erupted from around the room as Jamie stepped inside and lifted her hand to her mouth in mock shock. She could look just as at home in a pair of dungarees splattered with paint as she did in a ball gown. Her outfit that night fell somewhere in between. She was wearing a long, silvery skirt and a short black top, which she'd combined with a pair of killer heels that made Holly's boots look like she was in ballet pumps. Hopefully Fin was as strong as he looked because he was likely going to be carrying her home, Holly thought.

"Oh my goodness," Jamie said, stretching out her arms. "All my favourite people here in one place, I don't think that I could have planned this any better myself."

Like everyone else who'd stepped into the room, her eyes went quickly to the magnificent display of birds. One dangled just in front of her, at shoulder height. She reached out and brushed it with her hand, setting it spinning on its thread.

"These look spectacular. Is this you?" she said to Fin, looking up at him, with stars in her eyes.

"I thought it might remind you of something."

"It does. It definitely does."

A meaningful look passed between the two of them, before they locked lips. It was an extremely passionate kiss, considering they were in company, and to make matters worse, it lasted an uncomfortably long time. Even Caroline shot Holly a look, to which she mouthed *I told you so,* before Fin and Jamie finally remembered there were other people present and released one another.

"Isn't he talented?" Jamie said.

"Honestly, it wasn't that much," he smiled.

"You're just being modest. Fin took me to an aviary on our second date," she explained.

"I told Jamie that I was into aviation, and she asked if it was something to do with birds."

The pair of them burst out laughing in that annoying way that couples do that leaves everyone else feeling they've missed the gag somehow.

"Obviously, I was only joking," Jamie said. "But smart aleck here thought he'd take me to an aviary."

"Before we went up in a plane."

"That's right. You should have put up little paper aeroplanes, too."

"Maybe I'll do that for your next birthday."

They locked eyes once again, as if they weren't aware that there was anyone else in the room. Was this what she and Ben had been like when they'd been together as part of the group? She really hoped that wasn't the case, but she had a horrible feeling it might have been. Well, that had all gone up in flames quicker than anyone could have predicted. With a bit of luck, Fin wouldn't still be in the picture on Jamie's next birthday.

After greeting everyone with smiles and kisses, they took their seats, Jamie directly opposite Holly, and Fin opposite

Caroline. It could have been worse. She could have been looking straight at Ben. Tonight, she was going to count her blessings.

"So you made all these yourself?" Caroline asked Fin as a waiter brought the drink menus. "That must have taken forever,"

"Actually, I found once I was in the rhythm, it became almost meditative. I was listening to an immersive sound bath. It really helped me connect with the purpose of what I was doing."

"Folding paper?" Holly asked, unable to hide the sarcasm in her voice.

"They're actually made from seed paper. It's harder to get the sharp lines, but I think it was worth the effort. It gives the birds a really great texture. And after this, I thought we could go for a walk and throw them in some nearby fields."

"Are you allowed to do that?" Holly asked, genuinely curious. "Just dump seeds anywhere you want?"

"They're all indigenous, wild-flower varieties," he told her. "I chose them especially to ensure they wouldn't cause any disruption to the natural ecosystem."

"Of course you did," she muttered under her breath.

"I love seed paper," Caroline said, ignoring Holly. "I was at a wedding once where someone had all the favours made out of it. I can't remember whose it was though, can you Mike?"

"I have no recollection of that at all," her husband replied, helpfully.

Caroline smacked her lips together.

"Are you sure? Oh, that's going to drive me mad," she said, scratching her head. "Don't you remember, we helped with them? Stamped little messages on the back. I can see it in my head. I hate it when I forget things like that. Jamie, can you remember where it was?"

Whilst it could have been Holly's imagination, she would have sworn Jamie squirmed a little at this question.

"No, I can't," she said, offering Caroline a look that was bordering on a glare.

"Are you sure? We stamped initials on the front, too. What were they? M and E …? S and B …?"

"E and B," Ben answered from down the table.

"Yes! That was it!"

Caroline looked visibly relieved, as if it had been causing her actual trauma not knowing.

"You remember it, too? Who's wedding was it?"

Even before he spoke, Holly knew exactly what he was going to say, and her whole body tightened in anticipation.

"It was mine," he said. "We ended up with a whole stack of favours we couldn't even give away because we'd stamped our initials on them. We ended up throwing them away."

If ever someone had wanted the floor to open up and swallow them, it was Caroline at that moment. Her cheeks shone fluorescent red.

"Oh Ben … I'm so sorry. I didn't think."

"It's fine."

It was only when Ben locked eyes with her that Holly realised she'd been looking directly at him, and then she couldn't look away.

"It's fine," he repeated. "Honestly. I'm over it."

A lump came to her throat. She swallowed hard, trying to clear it, although she could do nothing about the sweat beading on her forehead.

"Is someone going to bring us the food menus?" she asked,

looking towards the door and ignoring the various eyes on her. "I think it's time we ordered, don't you?"

"I'm so sorry," Caroline whispered to her. "I really didn't think."

"Don't worry. I just have no idea how I'm going to get through this without a drink."

Whether Jamie had heard this comment or not, Holly wasn't sure, but she immediately noticed her abstinence.

"Why don't you have some wine?" she asked. "We've ordered some bottles for the table. You don't need to worry about the expense."

"Oh, well ..." Holly could feel a babble about to begin.

"She's doing dry January," Caroline blurted out. "Only she started it late. We both did. We're doing dry January. In March."

Jamie's eyes narrowed before they lowered to Caroline's wine glass.

"But you're drinking?"

Gritting her teeth, Caroline glared past Holly, straight at her husband.

"Michael. This is your fault. What did I say about dry March? You were meant to remind me. Well, I've ruined it now. I might as well keep drinking."

Michael looked up, wide-eyed at his wife's sudden outburst.

"Sorry?" he said.

Caroline tutted, before taking another sip of her drink, then touched Holly's knee gently under the table and offered her a brief smile.

The crisis had been averted, but they hadn't even ordered their food yet. It was going to be a very long evening.

CHAPTER TWENTY-SEVEN

While Holly had never been pregnant before, she knew only too well from friends that there was a standard list of things that were definitely a no-go when it came to food. Items that every doctor, nurse and health-care worker would warn you against. The only problem was, she had no idea what they were.

"Spicy Tom Yum soup?" she whispered to Caroline, who abruptly shook her head.

"It's got prawns in it," she whispered back. You need to stay off seafood."

"Pineapple fried rice?"

"Nope, not pineapples."

"Seriously?"

"Just get a chicken curry, but make it a mild one, though. You don't want too much spice. Do you know how far along you are yet?"

"You two are being very secretive over there. What's all that whispering about?"

Jamie had picked the most inopportune moment to stop

ogling Fin and turn her attention to them, although her line of sight was somewhat impeded by a rather large, orange crane that was drifting in the air between them. Holly had already caught her wrist on it when the waiter had passed her a drink from the other side of the table. Thankfully, she hadn't brought the whole thing crashing down. A wave of nausea swept over her.

"Oh, nothing. I was just asking what was good, that was all. Caroline's been here a couple of times."

"Oh, right," Jamie said, but her eyes lingered on Holly, almost as intently as she'd been looking at Fin.

Holly shrank back in her seat. Had he told her about finding the test? she suddenly wondered. And, combined with her not drinking, had drawn the obvious conclusion? No. No, she couldn't have. Could she? At this rate, everyone around the table was going to know before Ben did.

"You should speak to him, you know," Jamie said.

Holly felt the blood rushing from her head.

"What? Why?"

"What do you mean, why? Because you two were friends. And you're my friends, and it upsets me to see you like this. Maybe later tonight, you could just check in on one another. I think it would do you both good."

Holly wasn't sure how she was managing not to pass out and was somehow still sitting upright.

"Well, anyway, I'm glad you're both here."

When the food had been ordered, the table resumed chatting. Jamie was busy talking to the person to the left of her, who Holly vaguely remembered was someone she worked with, while Caroline and Fin were engaged in a conversation about wildflowers and meadows and the best place to see bluebells locally. Next to Holly, Michael seemed to have decided he should be her guardian and was taking his new role very seriously.

"I can ask them if they've got another cushion for your back. You want to make sure you support your adnominal muscles from early on. It can save a lot of pain later. We learned that with our second."

"I'm fine, Michael," she said, sotto voce, hoping he would get the hint to tone it down or, better still, stop talking altogether.

Unfortunately, that wasn't the way his mind worked, and every few minutes, he suggested something else, from sleeping positions to orthopaedic shoes. His loquaciousness was being fuelled by all the wine he was putting away. He obviously felt the weight of his new responsibility would be eased with several drinks.

"Do you want me to get you some ice? It helped Caroline a lot with the sickness."

"I'll be fine," Holly said. "If you can please, you know … just stop mentioning it."

"I know, I know. I'm sorry. But it's exciting, isn't it? Well, I'm excited. I guess it's different for you with Ben and everything."

Taking as many deep breaths as she could without hyperventilating, she looked around the table. As much as she wished they wouldn't, her eyes repeatedly fell on Ben, who was sitting next to a woman who volunteered at the Willows Care Home with them. She watched as she repeatedly threw back her head in laughter. No doubt they were talking about the residents and their recent antics. Yet each time it happened a smile flashed on his face, and a pang of jealously went through her. It was strange, having him sitting down there. He would normally be right next to her or across the table, at most only one seat away. The jealously morphed into bitterness.

"So, Holly, I was hoping to come down to the sweet shop tomorrow, if that's all right with you? Jamie's told me so much about it and I'd like to see the place for myself."

It took her a moment to realise that someone was talking to her, and another to realise that person was Fin.

"Sorry, I missed that. What did you say?"

"I said I was going to come and visit the shop tomorrow. Maybe buy a few things."

"I'm not sure many of the things I sell will match up to your organic, toxin-free standards," she replied, somewhat harshly although he just smiled.

"Oh, I allow myself the odd cola bottle, now and then," he said. "Besides, my nephews and nieces in the States love all the old sweets you've got going on over here. I think it's time I put a parcel together for them. It's going to be a while before we see them in person."

"Fin, what is it exactly that you do?" Caroline said, thankfully joining the conversation so that Holly didn't have to come up with any more vacuous small talk of her own.

But before he could answer, the waiters appeared with the starters. Jamie leapt to her feet, tapping the side of her wineglass with her knife.

"If I could just have your attention for a moment, please, everyone."

One by one, the voices around the table fell silent, all eyes turning to her.

"Don't worry, I'm not about to make a speech although, let's be honest, it would be amazing if I did that."

Laughter rippled around the group. When it had died down, she continued.

"I don't want to get all sentimental on everyone, because I'm far too tough and cool for that, but having you lot here today, all the people closest to me, sharing my birthday, is really special, and I feel really grateful. Thank you."

This was met with a cheer, which Jamie quietened with her hands.

"I want to say a special thank you to my amazing Fin. As I'm sure you'd all agree, he's done an incredible job on this room. So amazing, in fact, that the owners have asked him if it could stay up when we go."

"Wow."

Caroline's voice echoed Holly's own grudging approbation. She might have shown more enthusiasm herself, had her outlook not been tainted by the snake who'd created the display, she thought. She hoped that Jamie was done now, given that everyone had a starter sitting in front of them going cold.

"Don't worry, I'm nearly done," she promised, obviously reading the looks around her. "I would just like to propose a toast. So, if you can all grab your drinks, alcoholic or not ..." she said, looking directly at Holly, who picked up her glass only feeling slightly judged by her friend.

"To good times and great friends," Jamie said.

"Good times and great friends," the rest of the table followed, turning to clink glasses with those around them.

Holly gulped back a large mouthful of lemonade while, next to her, Michael polished off the rest of his glass of wine and then reached for a bottle to top it up again. With the smell of spring rolls causing her stomach to growl, she was just reaching for her knife and fork, when Jamie spoke again.

"Just one last thing," she said. "Don't get too comfortable. You're going to be moving when you've finished your starter."

"What do you mean?" Michael asked, in a somewhat slurred voice.

"It's something I saw on the internet, and I thought we'd

give it a go. You change your seats between every course. That way, you get to talk to different people throughout the evening. Great idea, right?"

Holly's eyes immediately whipped along the table to Ben, just at the very same moment that he looked up at her. And she knew he was thinking the exact same thing as she was.

Crap.

CHAPTER TWENTY-EIGHT

As could have been predicted, when everyone had finished their starter and Jamie's plan was set in motion, chaos broke out. Everyone ended up stumbling around each another, laughing as they tried to grab a new chair at the same time as someone else. It was like musical chairs, without the music.

"Don't forget, you're not allowed to sit next to anyone that you've sat next to before," Jamie shouted across the mayhem, already in a new seat near the far end of the table.

"But I want to sit next to Holly," Michael complained at a volume that proved Caroline had definitely been right about him not being able to handle his drink. "I'm looking after her."

"Michael," Caroline hissed, as if she were dealing with a recalcitrant child. "Find another seat, and stop being ridiculous."

"But Holly needs me. Don't you, Holly?"

"I'll be okay," she replied, grimacing.

In any other situation, she would have found Michael's drunken behaviour amusing, but in this instance, it was drawing far more attention to her than she wanted. She could almost feel Ben's eyes burning into her and could guess what he'd be thinking: that she'd asked Michael and Caroline to see to it that she didn't have to sit with him. And even though this was true, it didn't stop her from feeling bad about it.

Avoiding his gaze and keeping her head down, she took a seat at the very end of the table, thinking that at least that way she'd only have someone to her right, which might pose less of a risk, especially if the person opposite was engaged in conversation with the one next to them.

A middle-aged man, called Vic, plonked himself down beside her. He worked with Jamie and was obsessed with German Shepherds. After a brief introductory chat about the state of the weather and what they thought of the plan to put more houses up on the Rissington Road, he quickly steered the conversation onto his favourite topic.

"Did you know, it was a German shepherd that was chosen as the first guide dog?" he said, as their mains arrived.

"No. I didn't," she replied.

"No, most people don't. They assume it was a Labrador because that's what they usually see, nowadays. But it wasn't always like that. They're the third most intelligent breed, too, you know. Shepherds that is. Smarter than Labs. And people don't realise that either or that they aren't just brown. They come in a whole range of colours: sable, liver, blue …"

Having quickly realised that Vic could keep this up for hours, Holly just let him ramble on, adding the occasional, *really? I didn't know that,* just so he'd think she was paying attention.

At the other end of the table, Jamie and Ben had found themselves next to each other and, by the looks of things, she was chewing his ear off. Holly's stomach churned nervously. No doubt she was giving him the same talk about speaking to each other and staying friends. She was distracted from this train of thought by Michael, who was currently trying to get help remembering the name of a song by inflicting a tuneless rendition of it on those around him.

With another seat change planned before the dessert course, sitting next to Ben was no longer Holly's only concern. She also had to ensure that Michael wasn't anywhere near him, either. A flash of anger sparked within her. How on earth could Caroline have thought it was a good idea telling her husband about the pregnancy? She knew what he got like when he'd had one too many. Although, to give Caroline her due, she seemed to be trying to make amends for her faux pas by showing solidarity with Holly and was also now drinking lemonade, while glowering at Michael, ready to shut him down, if necessary. So now she felt guilty for ruining another person's evening, too.

"Can you believe that?"

Vic's question drew her back to the conversation that she'd drifted away from so easily.

"Sorry?"

"Poodles. I don't believe it, if I'm honest. I know they're smart, but never as intelligent as shepherds, don't you agree?"

"Poodles? No, I mean yes," she replied, still not sure what he was saying but feeling it was the answer he was looking for, which was confirmed by the grin that spread across his face.

"Exactly," he said, sitting back in his chair and putting his cutlery down on his plate.

He wasn't the only one, she noticed. More and more people were finishing their main course. She needed a plan to make sure she could get through the last one, away from Ben. This was the final leg.

The most obvious choice would be to move to the seat

directly opposite her. That way, she would only be next to one other person again and she wouldn't have to navigate far between all the dangling birds, particularly handy as her toes were starting to cramp in her high-heeled boots, even sitting down. Perhaps if she was planning on wearing heels out again, she'd practise for a bit beforehand. Not that this would be happening in the immediate future.

She thought about the changes her body would be going through. She was bound to get hideously swollen ankles. And she would have to get those jeans where they cut out the stomach area and replaced it with elastic, although to be fair, they did look rather comfortable.

She suddenly felt in need of some fresh air.

"Will you excuse me?" she said, standing and picking up her handbag. She ducked under a low-hanging bird and started to make her way out to the ladies. She had only just reached the door when Jamie's voice called out again.

"Okay people, for the last time, find a new seat, and make sure you're not beside anyone you've already sat next to this evening."

"Crap!"

Everyone immediately stood up, laughing once again as they bustled around. From the way the volume and the amount of jostling had increased, the alcohol had definitely taken hold, but Holly didn't have time to think about that. She needed to claim her new seat, away from Ben, away from Fin and away from anyone who might ask her anything remotely personal. Forgetting about both her current state and the fact that she was struggling to walk, she raced back.

For a second, it was all going so well. There was a clear path to the empty seat she was aiming for. Yet, in a heartbeat, everything changed.

Later on, she couldn't recall the exact order in which the events had happened, whether her hair caught on the bird first or was it the chair being pushed out in front of her. In fact, it was the boots that were the catalyst for the complete disaster. But it didn't matter. The outcome would have been the same.

Everything seemed to go into slow motion. She reached up her hand, trying to untangle her hair, while simultaneously losing her balance. Her body lurched, the momentum of her initial sprint keeping her moving forwards. But with a chair now standing in her way, there was nowhere for her to go. Her elbow hit the table first, then her shoulder, sending her body twisting and then bouncing to the ground. Pain seared through her arms, legs and side, as tears of both distress and humiliation came to her eyes. Hands rushed to help her, and someone was feeling her arms and legs, checking nothing was broken.

But there was one voice that cut through all the rest.

"We have to get her to the hospital! We need to think about the baby!"

CHAPTER TWENTY-NINE

A stunned silence filled the room, and for a second, nobody moved. Holly was still on the floor, the throbbing in her knees now replaced with an intense fear that gripped her insides. She was trembling all over.

"We need to get her up and to the hospital," Michael said again, at which point Jamie erupted into laugher.

"Yeah right. Great one!" she said. "Brilliant. Come on, get up. Way to make a scene."

Michael was tugging at Caroline's sleeve, trying to get her to corroborate his story, while she shushed him and told him he'd had too much to drink.

Meanwhile, Jamie was still waiting with her hand out. But Holly couldn't move. And it wasn't just because of the burning in her kneecaps. Her eyes were locked on Ben, his look was asking the question Jamie hadn't even bothered to consider. She couldn't look away from him, even when tears filled her eyes and trickled down her cheeks. He was searching for a trace of humour in her face. A smile or a shake of the head that would tell him it was just a silly, drunken remark from Michael, but she couldn't offer him that. She couldn't offer anything other than more tears, which she saw reflected in his own eyes. The pain in her chest moved lower and a sudden cramp spasmed in her abdomen. Wincing, she clutched her belly and gasped.

"We need to get her to the hospital," Ben said, sweeping past everyone, hooking his arms underneath her and lifting her off the ground.

"What!"

Jamie's draw dropped.

"Thank you!" Michael said, lifting his arms into the air and dropping them again, relieved that someone was listening to him.

Holly couldn't hear anything other than the pounding of her heart and the blood rushing in her ears. She was struggling to make sense of anything now, other than all the different sensations of pain that were flooding her body. Was it possible that the fall could have hurt the baby? No, she didn't hit her stomach at all, just her arms and knees. So why was it suddenly so painful?

"Crap," Ben said. "I can't drive. I've had too much to drink."

"I can drive," Caroline jumped in. "I only had one."

Michael had gone from shouting with joy to sobbing while resting his head on Vic's shoulder.

"You need to get Michael home," Ben said. "Is there anyone else who hasn't been drinking? Anyone else who can drive us there?"

And Holly knew, before he had even opened his mouth, exactly who was going to reply.

It was fair to say that she'd had far more enjoyable journeys in her life, and the main discomfort didn't come from any of her throbbing limbs. Maybe it would have been more bearable if they'd been in a car and she could have sat in the back, less aware of the unspoken judgements flying around. But they were in Jamie's van, and she was squeezed between Fin and Ben on the front seat, all three of them staring at the road in silence. In such a confined space just breathing felt uncomfortably loud.

She couldn't even distract herself with the radio, singing along in her head, as Fin had decided that they should listen to whale song because of its calming properties. So, whale song it was, all the way there, plus a level of tension that she didn't think her muscles would ever recover from.

"Try to stay relaxed," Ben said to her at one point, no doubt noticing the rigidity of her body next to his. "I'm sure everything will be fine."

She didn't reply. Even if the baby was okay, everything was a long way from being fine.

When they reached the hospital, Fin drew the van up outside the entrance to A&E and cut the engine.

"I can stay if you guys want me to," he said. "I don't mind. Or I could go and get you dessert. Seems a shame you're going to miss that."

Holly smiled at that. She wasn't sure what kind of refined-sugar-and-fun-free dessert he would get them, if he was left to his own devices to choose, but the gesture was sweet.

"That's okay, thank you," she said. "I'll be fine from here."

"Yes, we'll be fine. Thank you, though," added Ben.

Something about his commanding tone irked her a little, though she didn't have the strength to comment.

"Please, just give me a ring if you need me to come back and pick you up," Fin said. "Jamie and I will be at home all day tomorrow. She assumed it was going to be a bit of a big night and didn't book any work in. Although I don't think any of us expected it to be this big."

"Thank you, Fin," Holly said, just a fraction firmer.

A moment later, he nodded, got back into the van and drove away, leaving her alone with Ben.

"I should go inside," she said, turning around towards the doorway, but before she could move any further, he grabbed her by the wrist.

"How long have you known?"

"About three hours," she replied, truthfully, not looking back at him.

"And you told Michael before you told me?"

"No, I told Caroline, because she'd figured it out. Caroline told Michael."

Ben nodded slowly.

"Makes sense. You shouldn't tell either of them anything that you want kept secret. One or other of them will always get drunk and end up blabbing."

She lifted her eyes and tried to smile a little, but she didn't have it in her.

"I know that now," she said.

They stood there in silence for a moment. Given that the longest walk she'd anticipated that night was from the centre of Bourton back to the house, she was only wearing a thin jacket over her dress. As a chill wind whipped the air, a shiver prickled across her skin, and she wished she had something warmer on. And something softer on her feet. And a way to travel back in time so that things hadn't turned out like this. All in all, there were a lot of things she wished.

"Let's get inside," Ben said. "You need to sit down."

For a Tuesday night, A&E was busier than Holly would have expected. A range of people were in need of help, from crying toddlers to weary-looking elderly people. There was a young boy clutching his leg in pain, while his left arm was already in a cast. Needless to say, his mother looked distraught and exhausted.

"I filled everything in for you," Ben said, coming to sit down beside her. "Everything I could, that is. They asked how far along you were and I said you didn't know. You don't, do you?"

She shook her head.

"I don't understand how this could have happened. I thought you were on the pill," he said next, in a tone that, to her mind, bordered on accusatory.

"I was on the pill," she defended herself. "I *am* on it. I don't know what went wrong. I truly don't."

Heat was building up behind her eyes and she could feel tears starting to form again.

"Whatever happens, we'll get through this together," he said. "You don't have to worry. I'm here with you, now."

And he reached out his hand and took hers.

Seated like this together, Holly thought about the last time they'd been here. She'd come in the back of an ambulance with Verity after she'd taken a fall in her own ridiculous heels. She and Ben hadn't been a couple back then, yet he had shown up, like a knight in shining armour, to rescue her just the same. But there was one big difference between that night and this one. That time, as he'd plugged in her phone to charge and fetched her decent-quality coffee to drink, she'd told him to go, that she didn't want him there, that she didn't need him at her side to guide her through every situation. But this time, she did.

More than that. She wanted him there.

CHAPTER THIRTY

After waiting two hours, she was finally seen.

"Holly Berry," a voice called.

She jumped to her feet, only to remember that it was a similar action that had landed her there in the first place and, taking Ben's arm, walked as swiftly as she safely could to the nurse, who directed them through a set of double doors and along a corridor to a small room where a hospital bed and ultrasound machine were waiting. Together with an exhausted-looking doctor.

"You must be Holly," she said, looking at the screen in front of her.

The woman had a decidedly motherly face, with rounded cheeks and greying hair.

"So, you're pregnant and you took a tumble. Is that right?"

She nodded. Her throat had gone dry, and she was having a hard time swallowing, let alone speaking. The doctor smiled, sympathetically.

"But you don't know how far along you are. Is that right, too?"

"Yes," Ben cut in at this point. "We thought she was on the pill. She *is* on the pill. We didn't think this could happen."

"And you're the father, are you?"

He nodded, rapidly.

"Yes, I'm … I'm the father," he replied in a strangled voice, as if the words wouldn't quite form properly in his mouth.

"Right, well, no contraception is one hundred percent perfect. We'll do a scan to see how things are, and from that I can probably give you an estimate of how many weeks pregnant you are, too. And you're happy for him to be here while we do this?" she asked.

"Yes, I'd like Ben to stay," she said, smiling at the woman, grateful for the consideration she was showing her.

"Okay then, hop up on the bed and I'll have a little look at you, shall I?"

Her love of trashy films and television meant that Holly had seen plenty of ultrasounds on a screen, but never had she been a party to one. She was surprised by the coolness of the jelly as it was squeezed onto her stomach.

"Don't worry, we'll wipe all this off when we're done here," the doctor said. "Now, let's see what we can find. Tell me, did you bang you stomach or back at all when you fell?"

She shook her head.

"No, I landed on my knees."

"Well, that's a good thing … as is this. Can you see?"

She pointed to the screen beside them. The image was a mass of grey and white, a swirl of pixels that swept up and down in entirely unrecognisable shapes. But there, in the middle, something was pulsing rapidly and when the doctor switched on the speaker, a loud, swooshing beat echoed around them.

"Is that ..." Holly tried to speak, but a lump was forming in her throat. "Is that the baby?"

"That's your baby's heart beating. And it sounds very strong. Spot on. And as for age, judging by the size, I'd say you're looking at about nine weeks. So, there you go. Now I can schedule you in for a check-up. Just let me know how you want to take it from here."

The little heartbeat would have been imperceptible, almost nothing, without the machine to magnify it. But at that moment, it was the entire world to Holly. This was real. Not just a thought in her head or a cross on a stick. In the end, it was Ben who said the words that she was thinking but couldn't give voice to for fear of what might happen if she let them leave her lips.

"We're going to have a baby," he said. "We're going to have a baby."

They decided to go from the hospital to a late-night pizza place just across the road. Whether it was down to the excitement of what she'd just seen or because the portions at dinner had been quite small, Holly was famished, and a slice or two of margherita was exactly what she needed.

They walked over to the restaurant almost in a trance. The doctor had given them each a print-off from the ultrasound, not that they could really interpret it. As they sat opposite one another, with their pizza cooling in front of them, they continued to stare at it, not quite believing it was real.

Holly knew they now had no choice. They needed to talk about things.

"So, this was unexpected," she said. "But I have to tell you that I want to keep it. I'm going to keep it."

If she hadn't been certain before, she was now. She'd been too unlucky in love to let it dictate whether being in a relationship would be the be-all and end-all of her having a family.

"I understand. I do," Ben replied. "Is it wrong that I'm really quite excited about this?"

"You are?" she said, clearly relieved.

While she knew he was a good guy deep down, that hadn't meant he would take this well. She'd wondered if he would even want anything to do with it. The fact that she wouldn't be raising the baby entirely without help was music to her ears.

"Of course I am. I mean, I won't deny it's not the way I imagined it would happen, and I think it would have been nice to find out under different circumstances, but I think this is great. This is really great. Terrifying, but great."

"Wow," Holly said.

She expected there'd be many boyfriends in the world who wouldn't respond anywhere near as positively as this, and yet here was Ben, her ex, with the breakup still very new and very raw, and he was truly embracing it.

"I think the best thing would be if we turn the back bedroom into the nursery," he continued. "It's quieter out the back, and I can take the front room as my study. That would work well. It's big enough to put a desk in there for you, too, for when you need to do work stuff at home."

"Sorry," she said, feeling as if she'd missed part of the conversation.

"I think it'll be big enough. But if we find we need more space then we can put the house on the market and look for somewhere else. We won't have any problem selling it."

She was frowning now, as she rubbed at her eyes and tried to make sense of what was going on.

"Ben, what are you saying? You want me and the baby to live with you?"

"Of course I do. We're a family."

"But we broke up."

She felt she was stating the obvious here, but one of them obviously had their wires crossed.

With a loud sigh, he reached across the table and placed his hands on top of hers. They were as warm as they always were, and yet at that moment, she found them too warm, clammy even, against her skin.

"I know I messed up last week, Holly. There were some issues. I can see that. But surely this is a sign that we should be together."

"Last week you couldn't face a weekend away with me, and now you're planning on us spending the next eighteen years with each other?"

"Our lives will be joined by this regardless. What I'm saying is that we want this child to have the best possible life and that would happen if we were both under the same roof."

"No," she said, firmly. "It would happen from having parents who love it and support it. Whether we live together or not doesn't matter."

"I disagree."

The feeling of joy and wellbeing that she'd experienced on seeing her baby's heartbeat was rapidly evaporating.

"You disagree?"

"I'm sure I can find articles on it for you," he said.

"And I'm sure I can find ones that prove that NASA faked the moon landing. It doesn't mean they're true."

Ben sat back in his seat. He wasn't usually a man who was

easily riled, but that didn't mean it never happened. Holly recalled all too clearly the way he'd spoken to her when she'd run out into the road in front of his bike, the first time they'd met. Right now, he was wearing the exact same expression.

"I don't understand why you're being so awkward about this," he said.

"You think I'm being awkward for not wanting to play happy families with a man who can't even tell me he loves me?"

A hissing sound came from his lips.

"Look, you're obviously tired," he said. "It's been an incredibly long night. I'll call us a taxi. You can have a good night's sleep and we'll talk about this again tomorrow. Or later in the week, if you'd prefer. We've got plenty of time to work out all the finer details."

In Holly's mind, this was a long way off finer details. This would dictate not only the next months of her life but her entire future. And if this was the way he planned on speaking to her throughout it, it wasn't looking great.

"You call a taxi," she said. "I'm going to have some more pizza … and probably an all-you-can-eat ice-cream dessert."

The muscles along his jaw twitched.

"That's all right. I'll wait with you."

"I don't want you to wait with me."

"Holly, you're being ridiculous."

"For expressing how I feel? Honestly?"

He'd now given up trying to hide his feelings. He was scowling just like in that very first encounter.

"Please, be reasonable. It's gone ten o'clock. You can't—"

"Yes, I can, Ben. I don't even care what you were going to say, because the fact is, I can. I can do whatever I choose. You and I are not in a relationship anymore. And even if we were, then I would still be able to do whatever I damn well chose, because I am a grown woman. So, if you want even the slightest chance of me considering what you've suggested, if you want me to contemplate it for even a millisecond, then you should leave right now. Because the way you're speaking to me makes me wonder if I even want you in my baby's life at all."

This was probably a rather dramatic response, judging by the faces of the diners at neighbouring tables which were now turned their way, but she didn't care. If he wouldn't listen to her normal way of speaking, then this would have to do.

Across the table, Ben had gone decidedly quiet and pale. His expression was drawn, and he seemed to be having difficulty looking directly at her.

Finally, he spoke.

"Okay. I understand. I'll leave."

"Thank you."

He stood up, pocketing his ultrasound picture as he did so.

"Do you have money for a taxi?"

"Ben!"

"Sorry. I'm sorry. But I'll speak to you tomorrow. Or later tonight."

This time all it took was a glare from Holly, before he came round to her, kissed her on the top of the head and left.

CHAPTER THIRTY-ONE

Holly was used to overindulging on sweets. It was part and parcel of being a sweet-shop owner that you could take whatever you wanted whenever you wanted it. And some days she wanted lots. But until that moment, she'd never eaten quite so much pizza.

After a slice of margherita, she went for the pepperoni, then the veg deluxe. Despite what she'd said to Ben, she found she wasn't in the mood for ice cream and ordered a large portion of apple pie, instead.

She'd probably been a bit rash, she thought as she took the first bite of her pudding. He'd only been trying to help, but the way he'd *told* her what she should do with her baby, with her life! She'd never let anyone speak to her like that before, and she wasn't about to start now, when she needed to be stronger than ever. Still, that didn't change the fact that a taxi from Cheltenham back to Bourton wasn't going to be cheap and she was —once again—going to need to save every penny she could.

She took her phone out of her pocket, ready to check the times of the buses, just in case, by some miracle, there was a late-night one running on a Tuesday, when a voice stopped her dead in her tracks.

"Now I think you're definitely following me."

In a reflex action, she dropped her head into her hands and let out a deep groan. A short chuckle followed.

"I utterly deserve that," Giles said, coming to stand next to her. He was dressed far more casually than she'd ever seen him before, in a T-shirt and jeans and wearing a broad smile which quickly faded as he looked at her.

"Are you all right? You don't look great."

"Trust me, the last thing I need right now is your phoney concern," she replied, shaking her head.

She'd assumed that being so blunt would make him move on, but instead, he slipped into the seat opposite her, where Ben had been sitting only an hour previously. A deep frown creased his forehead.

"Look, I know things between us were … messy, and I admit I was a bit of a twonk, but if you need someone to talk to, you might remember that I'm quite a good listener."

She scoffed.

"You tried to ruin my business, and you were very nearly successful. And let's not forget you said some pretty awful things, you know, before I pushed you in the river."

He looked pensive for a moment.

"Okay, maybe twonk is a bit of an understatement for how I behaved. And I wish I had an excuse. I really do. All I can say is that I was in a really bad place back then, and I thought having the shop would put all that to rest. I'm sorry."

He looked genuinely remorseful, but she knew he was a master manipulator and had heard that spiel before. She wasn't going to fall for any of his smooth talking again, even something as seemingly straightforward as an apology. Silence followed, and she was happy for it to remain. However, Giles seemed intent on talking.

"What are you doing here?" he asked, looking her up and down. "You're all dressed up. You haven't been to the hospital, have you? Is everything okay?"

She skipped over his question and asked one of her own, instead.

"Why are you here? This place doesn't have any Michelin stars, you know."

He laughed.

"Does it not? Maybe it should. The meat feast is amazing."

His eyes glinted, but when she didn't respond, he carried on.

"I needed to pop into the hospital."

"To visit someone?" she asked, assuming from all his banter that he wasn't sick himself. At least not A&E sick.

"Yes and no," he replied.

"Great. Never a straight answer, as usual. I should have known better."

He ran his hands through his hair.

"Sorry, I wasn't trying to be evasive, honestly. I'm going to the hospital in a minute. And I suppose I'm visiting someone but not anyone sick. I'm about to grab some pizzas and drop them off to my sister. She works there."

Holly wasn't sure which part of this took her more by surprise, the fact that Giles had a sister, or that he would take her pizza. She started with the first fact.

"You have a sister?"

"A half-sister, yup. She's a midwife. She only started here recently. She's the baby of the family. Anyway, her mum mentioned that she'd been finding it hard to even get the time to eat, what with all the crazy shifts and everything, so I come down here once or twice a week and drop off pizza for her and her colleagues."

Try as she might, she was having a hard time believing that Giles Caverty—the same one who'd helped his uncle acquire an old people's home only to sell it for development and who'd then set about trying to steal her shop from right under her nose—could be the same person who'd deliver food at nearly midnight to a maternity ward. Judging by the way he was now laughing, she wasn't doing a great job of hiding her scepticism.

"I know. Who would've thought it?" he said with a shrug.

A waiter appeared at the table.

"They'll be ready in about five minutes," he said to Giles. "Can I get you a drink while you're waiting?"

"No, that's fine thanks, Kev, but could you do me a favour and add whatever she's had to my bill, too?"

Holly immediately felt her hackles rise.

"No, thank you. I don't want you to do that."

"It's no big deal," he replied.

What was it with men trying to take over and do things for you when you didn't want or need them to?

"I said I will pay," she said.

He shrugged, casually.

"In that case, do not add her bill to mine. The lady will pay for herself."

He threw her a quick grin, which she didn't want to return but somehow did anyway. At least he had listened.

"So, what are your plans now?" he asked. "Assuming this isn't your final destination."

"Oh no. I'm staying here all night. I reckon I can manage at least another two apple pies."

"Wow, are they really that good?"

"They really are."

Pursing his lips, he sat back in his chair and tilted his head to the side.

“Well, why don’t you come and meet my sister if you’ve got nothing else planned? Then I can give you a lift home, if you’ve had your fill of pizza by then, of course.”

It was Holly’s turn to tilt her head as she considered what he’d just said.

“You want to take me to meet your sister?”

“Sure. Why not?”

CHAPTER THIRTY-TWO

It was very clear from the moment they stepped into the hospital, Giles' arms laden with boxes, that he knew where he was going, and that his line about coming here once or twice a week was probably true.

"Evening, Guv," said one the security guards.

"Evening, Sam."

"That time of the week already?" someone else said in passing.

"Comes around fast, doesn't it?"

He'd bought a dozen pizzas and Holly had no idea how he would've carried them and negotiated all the doors, had she not agreed to come with him. Then again, maybe that was the purpose of his invitation.

By the time they reached the maternity ward, he must have spoken to at least a dozen different people, all of whom had smiled broadly as she tottered by his side, feeling exceptionally conspicuous in her ridiculous boots.

He pushed a buzzer outside the door with his elbow.

"I should probably wait here while you speak to your sister. You don't want me hanging around by your side."

"Of course I do. That's why I asked you to come, remember? Besides, we won't go into the ward. They're funny about that. She'll come and collect them from me here. Yup, there she is now, right on cue."

If she had been asked to look at a line-up and pick out which woman was related to Giles Caverty, there was no chance she would have chosen the one who appeared through the double doors. Her dyed-pink hair was pinned back in a bun, although a fair bit had already fallen out and stray hairs were hanging around her face. There was not a scrap of makeup to be seen and no designer watch on her wrist. It was only when she saw Giles, and her face lit up with a smile, that Holly saw a slight similarity in the eyes.

"You're a legend," she said, grabbing some of the boxes from his arms. "We're famished. What a crazy night."

She dropped the ones she'd taken onto a table just inside the door. As she came back for more, she noticed Holly standing there.

"Hello?" she said, her voice hitching with curiosity.

"Faye, this is Holly Berry. Holly Berry, this is Faye, my sister."

"*Half*-sister," Faye said, quickly.

Carrying all this pizza over had been quite an impressive biceps workout, and Holly hoped Faye was going to relieve her of her load, but instead, she cocked her head, looking even more curious.

"Holly Berry ..." she said. "Why's that name familiar?" she asked. "I don't know you, do I?"

For a sickening moment she thought that her visit to the hospital that evening might have resulted in her pinging up on some national pregnancy database that every midwife in the entire country had access to, but she quickly dismissed that idea as ridiculous.

"Um, I'm not sure. Maybe it's because your brother tried to ruin my business last year and have my sweet shop shut down."

Faye's eyes widened as her jaw dropped in an expression that was somewhere between shock and admiration.

"You're right. That is it. Wow, I wouldn't have expected to see you here."

"That would make two of us," she replied, feeling her cheeks getting warmer.

She was about to shove the pizzas directly into Faye's hands, when another woman stepped through the doors.

"Tell me you've got me a vegan deluxe," she said, looking at Giles.

"As if I could forget you, Nick," he said, passing over the rest to her.

Despite the appearance of her colleague, Faye's attention was still firmly on Holly.

"Well," she said, "he must really like you to have brought you to see me. I rarely get to meet any of his girls."

"Oh, I'm not a girl," she replied. "I mean, I am a girl. Obviously, I'm a girl, but I am not *his* girl. No, not a chance. Trust me. There's no way I would ever be going there. Ever."

"Hey!" Giles said, nudging her with his elbow. "I'm not that bad, am I really?"

"Yes," she replied, confused that this would need confirmation. "Yes, you are definitely bad. Or have you forgotten the time, or should I say *times*, you called the Health Inspector on me?"

He winced in mock horror.

"Well, so much for people deserving a second chance."

"I don't think that rule applies to someone like you," she said.

Faye chuckled at this banter as she finally took the boxes from Holly.

"I like this one, you should try to hold on to her," she laughed.

"Trust me, that is never going to happen," she said.

"That's a shame. I could do with someone normal to back me up at family dinners. Anyway, I should get going. I want to grab a slice of this before it all goes."

She punched Giles on the arm.

"Thanks for these, Bro. And Holly, I'll see you again, I hope."

"That's highly unlikely, I'm afraid," she replied, laughing.

With a quick wave, Faye disappeared back into the ward.

"Right," Giles said, "that's my good deed for the year officially done, but if you promise not to tell anyone, maybe I can squeeze in another and give you a lift home?"

Her immediate reaction was to decline the offer, but in the quiet of the hospital corridor, she became aware of just how tired she was feeling. Not only her arms from carrying all those boxes, or her legs from the heels, but her eyes and her shoulders. Even her head felt heavy.

"Thank you," she said, looking at him and genuinely meaning it. "That would be great. Although do you think you could drop me somewhere else?"

CHAPTER THIRTY-THREE

Holly followed Giles through the carpark, looking for the small, green, sports car he'd taken her out in on their first date, not that it actually had been a date, just a way for him to get information out of her. However, when he clicked his key fob, it was the lights of a large four-by-four that lit up.

"I only use the other one when I'm trying to impress people," he said, reading her expression. "It's all very well in summer, but trust me, the heated seats are what you need in winter. Mind your step up, it's quite high, particularly in ridiculous boots like those," he smirked.

She would have normally offered some quick and witty retort, but she was far too tired and by now had concluded that yes, he was entirely right. They were ridiculous boots and would probably be going back to the charity shop the next time she had a spare five minutes. When that was likely to be, she had no idea.

It was only as she considered how her limited amount of

time was about to be stretched beyond all imagination, that she remembered the reason she'd been in Cheltenham. She was pregnant. Somehow, Giles turning up and taking her to see his sister had distracted her, even though that was in maternity.

"I am sorry, you know," he said, bringing her attention back from these thoughts. She noticed that, despite the fact they'd got into the car several moments ago, he'd still not started the engine or even put on his seat belt.

"What" she said.

"I'm sorry about the shop … about everything."

"You mean you're sorry you got caught," she said, bitterly.

To her surprise, he shook his head.

"No, I'm glad you found out, if I'm honest. It's difficult to explain. Faye, she's not like the rest of my family. I guess being a half-sister saved her from the worst of it."

"Ah yes, the poor little rich boy, who's struggled through his private education with only a minimal trust fund. I can't imagine how difficult it must have been for you."

"No, you probably can't," he chuckled. "And I'm not going to pretend there aren't people who've got it a thousand times worse than me, because I know there are, but that doesn't mean it was easy. The expectations that I constantly failed to meet. The legacies I constantly failed to live up to."

She waited for the punchline. There always was one with him that showed he was not being serious and reminded her she couldn't trust him in the slightest. But none came, and he wasn't even looking at her, waiting to read her response. He was staring blankly at the steering wheel. A second later, he shook his head and straightened his back.

"Well, that was far more personal and emotional than I normally do, so ignore that entirely." Giles reasserted himself.

"You're a terrible businesswoman, Holly, and I was an idiot to be outwitted by you."

This was better, much more normal for him, but even as he met her eyes and smiled, she couldn't help but see a genuine sadness swirling there. Then, in a blink, it was gone.

"Right then. Northleach."

Without a doubt, Holly's parents were far too kind and trusting. They were the type of people who'd spend fifteen minutes on the phone with a cold caller because they felt bad about all the abuse those people received. They would always let people with baskets go in front of them in the queue at the supermarket, regardless of how full the basket was or how little they had in their trolley. And they would always, despite her insistence that it was a security risk, leave their spare key under the flowerpot next to the front door.

"You're inviting a robbery," she said to them, repeatedly. "Will you please stop doing this?"

But as was often the case, they ignored her entirely, and at midnight on a cold Tuesday in March, she was incredibly grateful for this.

"I'll wait here," Giles said. "Just to make sure you get in all right. I can give you a lift back to Bourton then if you need it."

"Honestly, it'll be fine."

"Please, just humour me. Give me a wave from the window once you're in. That'll do."

She nodded and turned to get out, but before she could tug on the handle, he spoke again.

"I'm well aware that I don't deserve your forgiveness, but I'm trying to do my best now, and that's what I want you to know. I'm trying."

This was just another of his ploys. Another charm offensive.

If she fell for it then, sooner or later, it was bound to come back and bite her. So, as she opened the door and got out, she said, "Thank you for the lift, Giles. Maybe I'll see you around."

And with that, she disappeared into her parents' house.

CHAPTER THIRTY-FOUR

Holly had gone to London by the time Arthur and Wendy moved to Northleach, so she didn't have a bedroom in their new house. On the rare occasions that she and Dan had come to stay, her parents pulled out the massive contraption that was the sofa bed in the living room, but she had never got the hang of it, and the way things were going that night, it would probably just snap closed with her inside.

So, after waving Giles off, she found one of her dad's clean T-shirts on top of the tumble drier then threw the back cushions off the regular sofa and took one of her mum's quilted throws to use as a blanket. As uncomfortable as it was, she was fast asleep within seconds of lying down.

"Holly Bear? What on earth are you doing here?"

Holly blinked, confused by the brightness of the room and the voice that was speaking to her.

"When did you come in? Why didn't you wake us up?"

It took another moment of blinking and scrunching up her eyes before she sat up, with an impressively long yawn. When she finally opened her eyes fully it was to see Wendy standing there in a pink dressing gown and matching fluffy slippers.

"Sorry, I didn't mean to scare you," she said, stretching.

"You didn't. Well, maybe just a little bit. Is everything okay? Shouldn't you be at the shop? It's already quarter to nine?"

The tiredness that she'd been feeling only a moment before, vanished in an instant. She jumped up.

"Yes, I should be," she said, but no sooner was she on her feet than all the blood rushed from her head.

Dizzy and suddenly unable to stand, she dropped back onto the sofa just in time for a wave of nausea to sweep though her. Pressing her hands against her head, she attempted to control the swirling.

"Holly, darling, are you okay?"

Wendy came and sat beside her.

"You don't look right at all? Are you sick? I can ring the surgery and get you an appointment."

Holly didn't mean to laugh. It wasn't funny really, and she certainly didn't want her mum to think she was ridiculing her, but once the laughter started, she could find no way of stopping it. Even when her stomach cramped and a big fat tear rolled down her cheek, it took her another moment.

"I'm not sick, Mum," she said. "I'm pregnant."

As could have been predicted in any type of emergency, Wendy's first action was to put the kettle on and make them both a cup of tea. Holly couldn't help but notice that she'd put an extra spoonful of sugar in her own mug as well as hers. Apparently, the standard one sugar wasn't enough to deal with such news.

"Where's Dad?" she asked, as she sipped the over-sweet tea at the kitchen table, still wearing his t-shirt and a pair of old slippers that her mum had found in the shoe box by the door. "Is he in?"

"He's still asleep, love. And you know what he's like. Dead to the world. I know he'd never admit it, but I think him stopping work and getting some proper rest has actually done him a power of good. But I can wake him," she added hurriedly. "If you want to speak to us both together. If that would be easier."

Easier than explaining the mess she was in twice, she thought. Well, she suspected she was going to have to get through it several times before this baby was born so, stealing herself with a deep breath and another sip of the tea, she told her mother all about the fiasco, from her dad mentioning the chocolate limes all the way through to Jamie's party, her fall, Michael's drunken faux pas and the hospital visit with Ben. She decided not to mention the late-night pizza with Giles, or that he'd dropped her off. It just didn't seem appropriate, although she wasn't entirely sure why.

"Well, that sounds like a bit of a pickle, but first things first. How are you feeling? I was fairly lucky with you and didn't get much sickness at all, but I know it can be terrible for some women. Ginger tea and ginger nuts. I'm sure that's what they used to say."

Holly smiled, "The sickness is okay. Well, bearable. To be honest, I just thought I'd drunk some wine that had gone off at first."

Wendy raised an eyebrow at this.

"What? Don't give me that look, I didn't know I was pregnant then."

"Well you do now, and you need to start looking after yourself properly. No sleeping on sofas, for starters. You should have woken us up. And have you thought about living arrangements? I know it's probably not what you'd prefer, but we can always convert the spare room. If you're sure you don't want to patch things up with Ben, that is?"

There was a definite question mark at the end of that sentence, despite the fact that Holly had told her exactly how annoyed she'd been that he'd tried to dictate to her that she should move in with him so they could be together as a family.

"Thank you," she said, smiling at her mum's offer of a place to stay. "I just don't know about Ben. He wants everything to be organised, as he always does, and this has definitely thrown him. But I'm not going to get back together with him just because of the baby. That's not the right reason to be with a person."

"I do get that," Wendy said, and Holly could already sense the *but* coming.

"But surely a father who comes across as too keen to look after his own child is substantially better than one who doesn't want to have anything to do with it."

"You're right," she agreed. "It is. I'm glad he wants to be involved, but I need time to work out how much I want him there. I'll be honest with you, Mum. I'm more worried about how I'm going to cope with the shop. I've worked so hard to get it to where it is. It breaks my heart to think I might have to sell it."

Wendy looked far more shocked at this than when Holly had told her she was pregnant.

"You wouldn't have to do that, would you? Why?"

"Because all my money is tied up in it, Mum. I can just about afford to pay myself enough to live on, plus Caroline and Drey's wages and the bills. If I can't work, then I'd have to be able to afford someone else to be there full time, and I just can't do that."

"What about your father? I'm sure he wouldn't mind working a few more hours and for free."

Holly scoffed at this. She hadn't meant it to sound harsh, but they were having an utterly truthful heart-to-heart.

"To be honest, Mum, Dad's been a bit of a liability in the shop. If it wasn't for the fact that you'd asked me to give him the job and he's my dad, I would probably have already sacked him."

Wendy pressed her lips together, and the rosiness in her cheeks drained away. Holly waited for her to say something. A *give him more time, he'll get better,* line. Or perhaps, *you know how grateful I am.* But she didn't say anything at all. That was when she noticed the change in atmosphere, and she knew, before she'd even moved her head, what she was going to see. Her stomach sank, and all the relief she felt from talking to her mum was replaced with stomach-churning guilt that was worse than any morning sickness she'd experienced so far.

She turned to the doorway, where Arthur Berry was standing, having heard every word that Holly had just said.

CHAPTER THIRTY-FIVE

For probably the first time in her life, Holly had no idea how her dad would react. He wouldn't shout, she knew that much about him. But would he turn around and storm off? Would he confront her and her mother? Would this result in an argument that would end their thirty-two-year marriage? Relationships finished over far less, of that she was certain. Her heart hammered so hard in her chest while she waited, she was certain she was going to end up with bruised ribs.

"Dad …" she started, even though she didn't know what she was going to say next. "Dad, I didn't—we didn't "

"Oh hush," he said, waving his hand in the air. "You think I didn't know your mother put you up to it? I realised that was her plan long before you offered me the job."

"You did?"

Holly was still struggling to breathe.

"I did. And if I hadn't then, I would have when you didn't sack me for leaving the shop unattended. I will admit, that was not one of my wisest moves."

Both Holly and Wendy's mouths were wide open, as they waited for him to say something more, but he strolled causally over to pick up the kettle and fill it at the sink.

"You knew?" Wendy said. "How did you know?"

"I know everything. That's what happens when you're married to someone for so long. I saw all those calls you'd made to Holly on your phone, didn't I? And then the next week she came here asking me if I wanted work. Doesn't take a Sherlock Holmes to put two and two together. Though you did a good job of selling it, honey. I really felt like I was needed. I'm sorry, I was more of a hindrance than a help."

For the first time, his head fell, and Holly's guilt intensified.

"No, I'm sorry, Dad. It wasn't all your fault. I never would have left anyone else in the shop on their own on their second day. I was just a bit preoccupied, that was all."

"Ah well, you live and learn, don't you? Have to say, I did like meeting all the customers. You've got some nice folk there."

His eyes drifted off wistfully for a moment before he snapped back to the present.

"Anyway, it was fun while it lasted. Now, talking of the shop. Why aren't you there now? Is Caroline working?"

"It's closed for the day," she replied.

It felt alien saying that out loud. The shop had been open the entire year other than Christmas Day. No, that wasn't true. She'd had to shut when the Health Inspector found the dead mouse among the sweets and couldn't reopen until she was able to prove that Giles had planted it there.

"Why? What's happened? Is something wrong? Is that why you're here, love?" her father asked.

Rather than explaining herself all over again, she opened her handbag, found the ultrasound picture and held it out to him.

"You're going to be a grandad," she said.

Arthur went straight for a cup of coffee, with two sugars. Unlike Wendy, who'd focused all her attention on Holly and her wellbeing, he was, like his daughter, concerned about her business.

"You can't give it up. It's too special. We can make it work, love. Don't you worry about it. Now, I know I didn't have quite the sterling first week that perhaps we'd hoped for, but I'll learn. And your mother can help, too. Maybe with cashing up in the afternoons if she's finished with her cleaning jobs."

He looked to Wendy for confirmation, and she nodded.

"I'm sure I can switch some of my shifts around, too. Finishing earlier so I can do that. And I'm always free at the weekends."

"It's a lot to ask," Holly said. "And like I said, I'm not even sure whether I'd be able to pay you."

"You can pay us in cuddles with our grandchild," she immediately answered. "I know there's lots we don't know yet, but you've got another seven months to get us up to speed. You don't have to worry. We'll make this work. I promise you."

Hot tears pricked at Holly's eyes, but they were good ones. With her parents on side like this, she somehow knew it was true. She could manage it.

"Thank you," she said. "You guys are amazing."

"Well, we're a team, aren't we?" her father said, planting a kiss on her head.

His eyes were shining with tears, too, and the deepest love Holly thought she'd ever felt. But then his expression changed and suddenly he was frowning at her. A nervous tingle went down her spine.

"Is that my favourite T-shirt you're wearing?"

Wendy drove Holly home. She remained dressed in her father's top and her mum's slippers, but also wore a pair of her elasticated-waist pyjama bottoms. Her parents had never been ones for luxury, and when they'd been earning good money, they remained frugal, keeping the purse strings tight for the rainy days that hit them regularly and far more often than was fair.

The car they were in was a good example of their economy. If she had to guess, Holly would say that they'd owned the dark-blue hatchback for at least ten years. It could easily have been fifteen or more, and that was from second hand. The paintwork was now peeling around the bumper and at various other spots, and there were countless small scratches and dinks. These days, it didn't need to take them far. Her mother used it to get to her various jobs and occasionally they would go to Cheltenham, but that was about it. Every time she got into it, Holly worried that something might give way and they'd end up rolling down a hill out of control. Still, it was that or the bus today, and given her current choice of attire, this was definitely the better option.

"Do you want me to drop you at the shop or at home?" Wendy asked, as they slipped onto the main road.

"I think I should probably go home first. You know, get changed."

"Of course, yes. And what about Ben? He'll be at work now too, won't he? Are you going to speak to him today?"

"I don't know. I need to work out exactly what I'm going to say first. Get my head straight."

Wendy hummed in agreement.

"You could always write him a letter. It's a good way to get your thoughts across. Your dad and I always used to do that when we had something difficult to say."

Holly couldn't remember a time when her parents hadn't spoken openly to each other, regardless of how difficult the situation had seemed, but maybe that meant the letter idea had worked. Even if she didn't send him what she wrote, at least she'd know exactly what she wanted to say when they did finally speak.

"Thanks, I might just do that."

The highway between Bourton-on-the-Water and Northleach was the Fosse Way, the long, Roman road famed for its straightness. It was the most direct route between the two villages but got unfeasibly busy. Locals, like Wendy, always preferred to take the back lanes, which wound around farms and over hills and were teeming with wildlife, like pheasants and rabbits that would jump out from the hedgerows and scare Holly half to death. Given that and the frequent potholes, she wasn't a fan of going that way. And it wasn't only the constant twists and turns and sudden appearance of animals that she didn't like, but the endless ups and downs. Holly's own car would sometimes struggle when it was stuck behind a tractor, laden with bales, grinding uphill at an impossibly slow speed. But the noise that her mother's car made when faced with a steep incline was something else altogether.

A mixture of graunching and clunking shook the vehicle as Wendy dropped into a low gear and pushed her foot flat down on the accelerator.

"Mum, that doesn't sound too great," she said, feeling decidedly apprehensive.

She glanced back, half expecting to see a cloud of black smoke billowing out behind them. Thankfully, there wasn't, but it didn't make her feel much more confident.

"No need to worry," Wendy replied. "It's been doing that for the past four years. It still passes its MOT with flying colours."

Holly failed to see how that could possibly be the case, but kept quiet and gripped the sides of her seat.

A sleek sports car overtook them at speed, followed by another large car. It was hard to tell whether these vehicles were going fast, or they were going particularly slowly.

"I tell you, they think they're on a bloody race track," her mother hissed irritably. "They think they're invincible in those big cars of theirs. Makes my blood boil."

Barely another two minutes passed before they were overtaken again. Their hatchback's engine growled as if echoing Wendy's anger. A high-pitched whistle was now coming from Holly's side of the car, too, which unnerved her even more. It didn't make her feel great that her parents were driving around in something this rickety. Maybe if she'd still been in London with a well-paid job and a chunk of savings, she could have helped them put down a deposit on something a bit sturdier, but there was no chance of that happening now.

Her mind was drifting off again. She was wondering how she was going to keep her finances straight, even with her parents helping at the shop regularly. Maybe moving in with them would be a good idea when the baby was born, at least for a short while, to save on rent.

As she was busy mulling all this over, she was oblivious to the three events that were about to occur simultaneously.

The first was the arrival of a massive four-wheel drive, this time a pickup truck, that came out of nowhere and swiftly bore down on them.

The second was the appearance of a large pheasant—notably male from its characteristically bright plumage—which darted out into the road at the exact moment the truck sped past them.

And the third was the materialisation of a giant pothole directly ahead of them.

Wendy started to swerve to the right, only having to veer straight back again, sending the car bouncing through the pothole with a shock that jolted them up and out of their seats, straining them against their belts, as they careered onto the verge and into the hedgerow.

CHAPTER THIRTY-SIX

While the pheasant flew away unscathed, and the other driver sped off without so much as a glance in his rear-view mirror, Holly and Wendy were left gasping for breath, hearts pounding.

"Mum, are you okay?" Holly asked.

Wendy was sitting there as white as a sheet, and her hands were gripping the steering wheel so tightly that her knuckles were shining through her translucent skin.

"Are you okay?" she repeated.

"Holly, my love, I'm so sorry. Are *you* okay? Is the baby?"

"I'm completely fine, Mum. Don't worry," she replied, pressing her hands against her stomach, trying to reassure herself. The doctor had said the night before that the heartbeat was incredibly strong even after the tumble she'd taken. This had certainly been no worse, although she'd rather it was where the drama ended.

"Those bloody drivers. They should put cameras on these roads. That's what they need to do. I'm going to be writing to the Council about this. I can tell you that much. The moment I get in, I'm going to be penning a letter. And an email. And a telephone call, for that matter. Could have killed us, this road and the drivers combined."

As she listened to her mother's ramblings, she saw just how white she'd gone. She took her hand and clasped it in her own. She was trembling like a leaf.

"Mum?"

"I'm all right, dear. I just need a minute, that's all."

Sitting there like that, with the bonnet lost in a hedge and the rest of the car sticking out into the road, was probably not the safest thing to be doing. Holly didn't want to rush her mother, but she knew they were at risk of a further accident if they stayed where they were.

"What do you think?" she asked. "Can you reverse it out? Do you want me to?"

"I'm all right, love," Wendy said again, shaking out her arms and shoulders like she was warming up for a sporting activity. "Don't worry."

Holly was half expecting the engine not to start, but on the second attempt, it coughed and spluttered into life. But her relief was short lived when the car refused to budge.

"Let me get out and have a look," she said, but Wendy shook her head.

"Just give it a second," she said.

Unfortunately, the second attempt was just as unsuccessful, and still dressed in her mother's slippers and nightwear, Holly was left with no choice but to step out onto the verge, amidst the brambles and nettles.

The good news was that she didn't need a certificate in vehicle maintenance to know what was wrong. The car was wedged in, and the height of the verge meant that the front wheels were an inch off the ground. The bad news was that they were going to need pulling out.

She glanced quickly around, searching blindly for some solution to strike her, but there was nothing where they were, other than trees and fields and a freezing wind. Of course, the way she was dressed, it would be the coldest day in weeks.

What did they say about bad luck coming in threes? Surely her break up with Ben, Fin's arrival and this, not to mention her massive faux pas with her dad and, of course, the pregnancy should have meant she was well in the clear by now.

She opened her door again and leant in.

"We'll have to ring someone, Mum. There's no way we're going to shift it on our own. You should probably get out of the car, too. It's not safe to wait inside like this."

If Holly hadn't felt bad enough about loading her parents with the burden of her disastrous life, this was now the cherry on the cake. Groaning, Wendy slowly manoeuvred herself out.

"I'll ring your dad," she said. "Gerald, next door, has got a pick-up. He rescued Iris at number fourteen just before Christmas when she ended up in a ditch by Cold Aston."

"Are you sure you don't just want to ring the roadside services? It might need towing home."

"Towing? This car? Don't be ridiculous. It's been in worse scrapes than this, believe me."

Holly wasn't aware of when this could have possibly been, but she didn't feel that then was the time to argue the point. Instead, she let her mother do what she thought was best and ring her father.

As she stepped away to allow her some privacy, a car came up the road towards them, a similar model to their own, small and rather old, and it slowed as it passed. She thought the elderly man was going to stop. But it picked up speed and carried on again. Perhaps he thought they were sorting things out for themselves.

But a bigger car was close behind it and caught her attention. Something about the four-by-four's boxiness was remarkably familiar. It wasn't until she saw the driver that she realised why.

The vehicle drew to a stop just behind them. Despite their situation, she was unable to stop a smile coming to her face, which had to be a sign she was cracking up under the pressure of everything that was going on, she thought to herself. The driver's door opened.

"Holly Berry. Causing a drama again?"

CHAPTER THIRTY-SEVEN

"Are you sure you don't want me to drive you both somewhere? I can haul this to the nearest garage later. It's not far away."

It wasn't the first time Giles had come to Holly's rescue, having helped her back to the sweetshop after her collision with Ben all those months ago. But he'd had an ulterior motive then: to get as much information about her purchase of *Just One More* as he could. But there was no chance now that he could get his hands on the shop.

After ushering them into his back seat and out of danger, he knelt down on the ground to attach a tow rope, muddying his previously pristine chinos. She wondered what he could possibly gain from this.

Thirty minutes later, and the little car was back on the lane with them inside it again and a very muddy Giles was leaning through the window.

"You really ought to get it checked out first. Make sure it hasn't done anything to the tracking or the suspension," he said.

"I think that's a good idea, Mum."

Agreeing with him was something she never thought she'd do again, but she could see the good sense in his advice.

"And have them charge me a hundred quid to look under the bonnet and find everything's just fine? No thank you."

"Well, I can see where Holly gets her stubbornness from," he said with a smile.

Given how much he'd just done for them, she found herself reciprocating.

"Where were you driving to?" he asked, as Wendy went to start the engine. "I could always tail you there, then you can stop if anything feels wrong."

"You don't want to do that," she said, but Giles ignored her and looked at Holly.

"Where were you going?" he asked again.

"Mum was dropping me home, and then she was going back to Northleach."

"Where I dropped you last night?"

Wendy raised her eyebrows at this comment, and Holly just nodded, keeping her gaze away from her.

"Well, that's far closer than Bourton," he continued. "Why don't I tail you back to Northleach, then I can drive Holly back home?"

"We've already used up so much of you time," Wendy tried to counter, but he was having none of it.

"Trust me, when it comes to the Berry family, I've got a lot of karma to sort out. It really is no problem."

As much as she wished otherwise, Holly had to agree that this was the most sensible idea. She really didn't want her mum driving a long distance on her own in case a problem did develop, and it wasn't as if she was going to open the shop up today, anyway. What was another half hour in the grand scheme of things?

"That actually sounds great," Holly replied, before her mum could object again. "That would be brilliant. Thank you. Come on, Mum."

"That's very kind of you, Giles," Wendy said, knowing that she was beaten and starting the engine.

After negotiating a five-point turn to head back home, with Giles holding up the traffic, they set off again.

Holly knew what would be coming next, but the silence lasted longer than she would have expected. Her mum was normally as bad with them as she was, but she remained with her eyes fixed on the road and a tight smile on her lips, obviously waiting for Holly to be the first to speak. And Holly really didn't want to be. She didn't want to discuss Giles at all.

"How does it feel?" she asked, suddenly realising that she could be the first one to blink without having to mention the enormous elephant in the room, or car. Unfortunately, Wendy was not easily put off.

"So, that's Giles Caverty," she said. "I have to say, he's not what I expected. I'm not surprised you fell for him. He's very charming, isn't he? And helpful."

"And he's also a liar and utterly untrustworthy."

"Well, you'd know that better than me," she replied. "He did seem very apologetic though, you know. And he didn't have to do all this, did he? He seems genuinely fond of you," she said, glancing in her rear-view mirror at his vehicle following them. From the way his mouth was moving, he seemed to be talking to someone on the phone.

"What are you trying to say, Mum? That the week I discover I'm pregnant, having broken up with my boyfriend and father of my child, I should get romantic with the guy who, less than a year ago, tried to ruin me."

"I didn't say that," she replied with a smirk. "You two just looked comfortable together, that was all."

Holly huffed. She didn't know why this annoyed her so much, apart from the fact that it was probably true. It had frustrated her the previous night, how relaxed and easy she felt in his presence, given that she should have wanted to hurl her pizza straight at him. And him coming to the rescue was exactly the thing she didn't want. So why did it make her smile so much when she saw his car approaching?

"Here we are," Wendy said, turning into their driveway. "You'll ring me when you get home, won't you? Just so I know you're okay. And remember, I'm here, any hour of the day, if you want to talk about Ben or the shop or …"—she threw a glance behind her—"anyone else."

"I know, Mum."

Holly wrapped her arms around her mother and squeezed her tightly.

"I love you."

"I love you too, Holly Bear, and whatever happens, this baby is going to be very lucky to have you as its mother."

They got out of the car. Giles was already standing on the pavement.

"Nice to have met you, Mrs Berry," he said. "And just so you know, I've rung a friend of mine who runs a garage in Compton Abdale and he's going to come over and give the car a quick check over for you. It won't cost you anything. He's doing it as a favour to me."

"You didn't have to do that," Wendy said, taking his hands and kissing him on the cheek. "You've already done enough."

"I know I didn't, but like I said, I've got a lot to make up for when it comes to this family."

He turned to look at Holly.

"Right, home? Or were you planning on going somewhere fancy, dressed like that?"

CHAPTER THIRTY-EIGHT

By the time they reached Bourton, Holly's stomach was cramping, although this wasn't giving her any cause for concern, for the baby at least. What was worrying was how much Giles was making her laugh.

"Honestly, the way you stood in that road, fluffy slippers and baggy trousers, I thought, that's a lady who's got her life together. A woman who knows what she's after and isn't afraid to go out and get it. Conventional fashion be damned."

"Oh, sod off," she laughed. "I'm sorry. We don't all have an endless selection of pink shirts and cream chinos to choose from."

"Pink!" he said with mock shock. "I'll have you know this shirt is not pink, it is salmon. Which is entirely different. Much more masculine, to start with."

"Is that right?"

"Absolutely."

She chuckled to herself. Considering the disastrous day, the state of her life in general and present company, it was surprising how good she felt. She'd been so busy laughing that it took her by surprise when he cut the engine and she looked up to find they were outside her house.

"I guess you're not going to invite me in for a coffee?" he said with a smirk.

Thankfully, Jamie's van wasn't there. Apart from Holly, there were few people who detested him more than she did, and she had no idea how she would explain this situation to her satisfaction. Still, the idea of having him in the house didn't sit quite right with her.

"Like you said, you've got a lot to make up for, yet."

He nodded and offered her a sad smile.

"You know," he said, "I get that you probably don't want to, and there's no way in hell that I deserve it, but I would like to try to make things up to you, even if we could never be anything more than just friends."

Holly felt her jaw drop, but he wasn't finished.

"I was in such a bad place last year. I know I've said it before and there's no excusing what I did. But the silly thing is, when it was all over, and you had the shop, I didn't actually care that I'd lost or that my uncle cut me out of his life and his inheritance. I was just sorry that I couldn't speak to you anymore. I missed you."

There was no response she could give to that. It would be a lie to say she'd missed him. She had been far too furious. She had despised him with every fibre of her being. Her silence said everything.

"Well, that's enough of me being vulnerable," he laughed. "Go on, get out of here. I've got some decidedly dastardly deals I need to secure, and if anyone sees you dressed like this in my car, it'll ruin my reputation entirely. I'm only meant to date hot girls, you know."

"Hey!" she said, flicking out her wrist and hitting him on the shoulder.

"I'm not saying you're not usually hot, you're just a little, you know, unkempt at the moment."

"Right, I'm going," she said, laughing again and turning to get out. But her door wasn't the only one that was on the move. At the exact same moment, Ben's front door flew wide open, and he stormed out onto the driveway.

"Holly, where the hell have you been?" he demanded, running towards her. "We've been worried sick. You didn't open the shop, and you didn't answer your phone, and none of us had any idea where you were."

Seeing Ben stressed wasn't a new experience—a tense board game could be enough to tip him over the edge—but this was entirely different. His hair was a mess, and he obviously hadn't shaved that day, not to mention the fact that he was wearing odd socks.

"Why aren't you at work?" she countered.

"Why aren't I at work? Did you not hear me? Why are *you* not at work? Caroline had to open up. What the hell were you thinking of, disappearing like that and not letting anyone know where you were? You do realise I went back to the hospital again and to the pizza place?"

Holly wasn't sure how to respond to this. She could tell by his appearance that he really must have been running around like crazy all morning looking for her, but maybe he should have just slowed down and used a little common sense.

"I went to my parents," she said. "Where else would I go?"

The logic of what she'd just said hit him, and he took a step back. Then his gaze turned from her to the other side of the car, as Giles stepped out.

"Is everything all right here?" he asked.

"You!"

Ben marched forwards, pointing his finger at Giles.

"What the hell are you doing here? You're not allowed anywhere near Holly. I'll call the police."

"Don't be a prat, Thornbury, I just gave her a lift, that's all."

Ben snapped his attention back to Holly.

"What are you doing talking to him? If you needed a lift, you should have called me."

In less than a minute, she had remembered exactly why she'd got so annoyed with Ben at the pizza place the night before.

"I did not *call* him. And Mum I would have been in an awful lot of trouble if he hadn't come along and helped us. As for who I *should* call, I think that's up to me. Or it was the last time I checked."

She could see that Ben was seething. His jaw was clicking as he ground his teeth from one side to the other.

"You should have at least let me know where you were. You should have realised I'd be worrying."

For all her annoyance, she couldn't help but feel a slight pang of guilt. He was right. She should have known this would have happened, particularly when she didn't open the shop. But that still didn't mean she had to answer to him for everything.

"Look, I'm exhausted. It was a very long night and not a very comfortable one at that, so if you don't mind, I'm going to get some sleep before I decide what the hell I'm going to do with my life."

She took a couple of steps towards her door, only to change her mind and head over to Giles.

"Thank you for helping Mum with the car. I appreciate it."

"No worries, maybe I can give you a lift the next time you're hanging around a late-night pizza joint on your own," he smiled.

And just like that, Ben snapped.

CHAPTER THIRTY-NINE

There was maybe a split second of silence when Holly thought everything was fine and she was about to turn around and head indoors to possibly sleep all the way through until the next morning. But then she glanced back at Ben and saw the magenta tone that had flooded his cheeks.

"You have to be joking. You called *him* last night? *Him?*"

"I didn't call anyone. Giles just happened to come along after you left."

"Oh yes, how convenient is that? And I bet you had a great laugh at my expense, didn't you?"

"What are you on about?" she said. "It might have escaped your notice, but last night wasn't particularly great for me."

"Oh no? Well, it wasn't a bag of laughs for me either, finding out you don't want me to have anything to do with my own baby."

"When did I say I didn't want you to have anything to do with it?"

Holly was shouting now. A couple walking past with their dog looked nervous and sped up a little.

"I didn't say I didn't want you to have anything to do with the baby. Of course I do, you're the father. What I said was that I didn't want to jump into living together and playing happy families when you didn't even know if you wanted us to be together, before."

"You two are together? And having a baby? Wow, that is one combination I would never have picked."

Giles let out a long sigh before stepping towards Ben.

"Look, it's clear you guys have loads to talk about, but I think it's fairly obvious that Holly here needs a bit of space, old chap. You're being a bit clingy."

"Don't you dare speak to me like that!"

Ben was spitting mad, his eyes wide in a way that Holly had never seen before. Giles backed up a step, raising his hand.

"Look, I'm not trying to cause trouble. I'm just dropping her home. And I'll go the minute I see she's safe inside."

"You need to leave now," Ben hissed.

Despite his aggressive behaviour, Giles remained calm. Holly suspected this wasn't the first time someone had threatened him.

"Like I said, I'll go as soon as she's in her house."

"You'll go now, *old chap*. Go on *piss* off."

As cool as a cucumber, Giles moved towards Holly, but locked his eyes on Ben before he spoke.

"You know what, Holly Berry, I think you should invite me in for that cup of tea after all. I don't feel comfortable leaving you alone right now."

If she had thought it was impossible for Ben to get any more enraged, she'd have been wrong. In that instant, he completely lost it and lunged at Giles.

"Ben, what the hell are you doing?"

She jumped clear just as he landed a punch square on Giles'

jaw. It was enough to knock him back but not down, and in less than a heartbeat he had steadied himself and, without a moment's hesitation, was charging at Ben. He rugby tackled him to the ground and held him there with a hand planted on his chest, raising the other above his head.

"Don't make me hit you," he said, his eyes flashing with the same heat that she'd seen in Ben's but looking far more menacing.

"No! Stop! Don't! Don't!" Holly yelled, grabbing his wrist.

"Just so we're on the same page here, Thornbury, I don't like you. I have never liked you—"

"Well, that makes us even then."

Most unexpectedly, for Holly at least, Ben jerked himself forwards and head-butted Giles in the chest. It had little effect, other than to annoy him even more.

"As I was saying. I do not like you, and the only reason that I haven't already hit you is because I know it would upset Holly, and as she is aware, I am trying to be a better person. But I swear, if you speak to her like that again, or me, then I won't hesitate to bop you right on that irritatingly straight nose of yours. You hear me?"

If Holly had been in Ben's position, she would have considered very carefully what Giles had just said, particularly considering he was pinned to the ground, and it looked like he had little option. And she would have gambled her entire sweet shop on the assumption that Ben was going to admit defeat and slink quietly back off into his house.

But that would have been a bet that she would have lost. The second Giles started to release him, Ben brought up his knee to connect with his groin, toppling him sideways with a deep groan.

From that point, the confrontation turned into a fight of

flailing limbs and shouted abuse as they continued to punch and kick at each other, somewhat ineffectually.

"Stop it, the pair of you! What do you think you are doing? Stop it!" Holly shouted, to no avail.

Ben then let out a high-pitched cry.

"Did you bloody pinch me?"

"There's plenty more where that came from, you stuck up twerp!"

She made a move to separate them.

"Stay out of the way, Holly," Ben hollered

"Finally, something we agree on," Giles said as he swung his leg in a poorly aimed kick.

"Please! Stop it now!" she cried again.

There was no way she was going to be able to restrain them on her own. How were you meant to separate people who were fighting like a couple of mad dogs without getting hurt yourself? Holly's mind raced before she realised she had already answered her own question.

It took her less than thirty seconds to get to the hosepipe at the side of the house. Turning the tap on full, she pulled it back around to the front where she twisted the nozzle and aimed the spray of water at the two so-called grown men rolling around on her driveway.

CHAPTER FORTY

They stood there, dripping wet and shivering in the cold March air. It would have been a comical scene, Holly thought, if it weren't for the bruises blooming on their faces.

"What the hell were you thinking?"

She aimed her words at Ben first, but offered a swift look to Giles, too, so he knew she was placing just as much blame for this on him.

"This is ridiculous."

She imagined that this was what it must be like being a schoolteacher, trying to deal with a playground fight, minus the water of course. They both looked down, suitably chastised.

"Ben, go inside and get yourself dressed. And while you're there, grab some clothes for Giles. He can't go home like this."

"You're not serious," he replied, remaining in naughty-schoolboy mode.

Holly's look said it all.

"I'll come over and collect them as soon as I've sorted Giles out with a towel."

"You really don't need to do that," he said, speaking for the first time since the drenching.

"Well, think of it as extra karma you owe me now. A lot of extra karma."

She grabbed her keys and opened the front door, holding it for him to step through. As he moved into the house, he cast his gaze back at Ben.

"What on earth got into you?" she asked, once they were in the hallway, where he was quickly producing a large puddle of water round his feet.

"You're sure Jamie's not due home soon, are you?" he asked, looking around with a distinct air of concern, as if she might suddenly appear despite her van not being outside. "I don't think I can handle any more violence today. Not that you can use that term for what Ben managed. I'm pretty sure my two-year-old nephew can hit harder than him. Jamie, on the other hand, would be a different matter."

Despite how mad she was, Holly found herself smiling at the comment. It was no secret that he and Jamie didn't get on, and given the sweet shop incident, he was probably right to be fearful of a left hook from her.

"She'll be at work," she said. "Her boyfriend, Fin, could be home any minute, though," she added with a smirk.

Giles' eyes bulged.

"Jamie has a man living here? Are we talking about the same person?"

"She does."

"Wow, things have moved on."

He paused, and she knew what was coming next.

"Pregnant?"

One word was all he needed to say.

"Are congratulations in order? I mean, I can't condone your

choice in sperm donor, but a baby's still exciting, isn't it? Or is it not? It might not be."

She smiled to herself. There was something very refreshing about not being told how she was feeling about the situation.

"It is exciting," she conceded. "Just a bit complicated, that's all."

"Because of the stuck-up bank manager next door?"

"Because of lots of things, none of which are any of your business. Now, stay there while I get you a towel. If you get water all over the house, Jamie will have your guts for garters and hate you even more."

"No, I don't think that's possible," he grinned.

After returning with the towel and directing him to the bathroom to dry himself off, she took a deep breath, headed outside and knocked on Ben's front door.

Only one week ago, they'd been coming home from work and watching films together. Eating meals with large glasses of wine, chatting and laughing as if they were going to stay that way for, well, ever. Last year she'd learnt that it was impossible to predict how quickly life could change. But now she knew the truth; it took less than a day.

Ben opened the door almost immediately. His hair was still dripping wet, but he had taken off his clothes and had a towel wrapped around his waist. He was holding a bundle of sports gear in his hand.

"I figured these would probably be the best fit," he said. "I take it he's still there?"

There was no edge to his voice, but she didn't answer his question. Given that Giles' car was still parked outside, the question seemed pretty redundant.

"Thank you for these," she said.

As she moved back towards her house, he called after her.

"Holly, can we talk?"

A heavy weight settled on her chest as she turned around to face him. At least, for the first time in a while, there weren't any tears. Perhaps she was all out of them.

"It doesn't seem to go too well when you and I talk, does it?"

She tried to smile, but the corners of her mouth fell almost immediately.

By contrast, Ben remained completely stony-faced.

"I've been wrong," he said. "I've been wrong in so many ways. I understand that. I would just like a chance to talk to you. To explain. Please. Whenever you're ready. No rush."

Holly nodded. The tears may have stayed at bay so far, but she had a feeling that might not be the case if she didn't get away from him soon. Swallowing hard, she turned back to her own front door.

"I'll message you," she said.

"Thank you," he replied, but she was already back in her house, closing the door and wiping her cheeks again.

"You know he picked the most shapeless, tasteless clothes for me, don't you?" Giles said as he stood in the hallway, dressed in Ben's offerings.

It was hard to disagree with this.

While she thought it had been sensible, offering sportswear, the faded football shirt with its peeling number and the ultra-brief running shorts that left nothing to the imagination, did make him look a sight. His long, white legs were on full display and, all round, he looked as if he were dressed for some charity event. Even she wasn't naïve enough to think Ben's choices had been accidental.

"Well, at least you can't comment on my clothes now," she said.

"You're enjoying this, aren't you?"

"I think I'm owed a laugh or two right now," she replied.

To her surprise, his face adopted an unusually serious expression.

"I know you've got good people around you, but I meant what I said about trying to make up for the past and doing better. And that doesn't just apply to you. It might surprise you to know, but I've upset quite a few people in my time."

"No, that doesn't surprise me."

"Well, if I can do anything. If you need anything, I'm here. Any time, day or night."

Then he turned and opened the door.

"See you around, Holly Berry," he said.

CHAPTER FORTY-ONE

It was only when Giles was gone and the quiet hit her that Holly suddenly thought about the shop.

Plugging her phone in to charge, she waited a minute for it to come back to life, before dialling. No one answered. Ben could have been wrong, she thought. Maybe Caroline hadn't opened up. After all, it wasn't her day to work. She tried the number again, and this time it was answered after the first ring.

"Thank God," Caroline sighed. "I'm so sorry about Michael. I shouldn't have said anything to him. But are you okay? Don't worry about the shop. Everything is fine here. God, I am so sorry."

Holly chuckled.

"It's not a problem, honestly. It would have come out at some point. I'll admit it was a little more dramatic than I'd expected, though. Thank you for covering at the shop."

"Don't be silly. After all the trouble I caused you last night, it was the least I could do. Holly, I really am so sorry."

"It's fine," fine said.

Caroline's guilt was rubbing off on her, now.

"How is Michael today?"

"Oh, he's in so much trouble, believe me. He called in sick to work. Obviously I made him do the kids' breakfasts and packed lunches and take them to school. And he's going to be doing bedtime and dinner for the next month, at least."

"Don't be too hard on him."

"Oh, I will be exactly as hard as he deserves," she replied. "I've got to go, Holly. There's a large group heading this way. But I'll ring you later, okay? Let me know if I can do anything else for you. And don't worry about coming in today at all. It's not that busy and I've got it. Besides, Michael will be picking up the kids, obviously."

"Thank you."

"And if you need another day, let me know. We can sort this out. We will sort this all out, you know."

"Thank you," she said again and hung up the phone.

Only when she'd taken a seat and closed her eyes in relief did she realise how exhausted she was. It wasn't surprising, given the lack of sleep she'd had.

She found her hands moving down. She was having a baby. And it still didn't feel real. Even when she'd been talking to her mum, she'd felt a certain detachment, like she was talking about some abstract concept. But the fact was that she was pregnant. She was going to have a baby. She was going to be a mum.

"Don't worry," she whispered, her hands still on her stomach. "I know it's all a bit crazy at the minute, but I'll sort it. I promise. You're going to grow up loved, little bear cub."

And then she did something that she'd been dying to do for several days.

She ran herself a nice, long bath.

She hadn't meant to go to sleep, and certainly not for so long, but when Holly opened her eyes, she realised that someone was sitting on her bed. She blinked a few times, waiting for them to adjust to the light, only to realise that there wasn't any.

"Hey sleepy head. Way to upstage my birthday party."

Stretching out, she rolled over and sat up.

"I'm so sorry about last night. Did I ruin everything completely?"

"No, of course not."

"Crap, I haven't even said thank you to Fin for driving me to the hospital. I should have done that by now."

"Don't worry about it. I think he was grateful to get away from all the drinkers. The pub scene isn't really his thing, as you probably guessed."

She nodded, grateful that Jamie wasn't making her feel bad about the situation or not deliberately, at least.

"So, I'm going to be an aunty then," Jamie said, grinning. "That's exciting."

"Yeah, I guess so."

"Well look, about living here, Fin and I think it would probably be best—"

Holly's stomach plummeted. Her parents and Ben had all been quick to offer her alternative choices of accommodation, most likely because they knew she couldn't stay where she was with Jamie.

"I understand. I do. There's no need to worry. I know I can't stay here."

"What? No!"

"Wasn't that what you were about to say? That it was probably best if I moved somewhere else."

Jamie's jaw dropped, as if she'd just been told that Holly had soaked Ben and Giles with a hose to stop them fighting, but that would have to come later.

"No, I was not going to say that. Of course, I wasn't. This is your home, for as long as you want it to be. I promised you that when you moved in, and nothing's changed because of your situation or because of Fin moving here. In fact, what I was going to say is that if you wanted to, we could swap rooms. You could take mine and Fin's and we'll use this one."

"Sorry?" Holly said, confused by the unexpected turn in the conversation.

"Well, to be honest, it was Fin's idea, so I can't really take any of the credit, but it does make sense. It's quite a lot bigger, which will give you room for the crib and the changing table and all the other millions of things babies need. It also means you'll have the en suite, though the baby will still have to use the bath, obviously."

Holly stared at her friend, wide-eyed and speechless. Of all the things that Jamie could have said to her, this wasn't anywhere on the list.

"This was Fin's idea?"

"He's a good guy. I know you two might not have got off to the best start, but he really is amazing. And think, you'll have a world-champion skateboarder on hand to teach the little one when they're old enough to start riding."

"What?"

Holly felt as though they'd skipped into a whole new conversation without her knowledge.

"What do you mean?"

"What do you mean, what do I mean? Fin, he's an ex-world-champion skateboarder. I thought you knew that. Obviously, it was quite a few years ago, so now he designs skateparks. Are you sure I didn't tell you that?"

"Positive," she said, struggling to cope with the fact that her new house mate was some semi-famous sports personality. "I think I would have remembered something like that."

She was about to ask for his surname, so she could look him up online and verify that this was true, when the doorbell went. Still smiling at Holly's shock, Jamie stood up.

"I'll get that, but let me know what you think about the change-of-room idea. There's no rush, obviously. And it's entirely up to you."

As Jamie's footsteps retreated downstairs, Holly remained seated on the bed, contemplating the outcome of her day. So far, Caroline had taken the helm at the shop without so much as a message from her. Her parents had offered to work there and make room in their house for her and the baby, and now Jamie was willing to reorganise her home for them. A deep warmth spread through her chest. Whatever the situation she was in, this was going to work out. She could feel it.

In the quiet of her room, she heard her stomach rumble but not the front door opening. Maybe she'd just missed it. A few seconds later, Jamie reappeared.

"This just came for you?" she said, holding up a small envelope.

There was no postage stamp in the corner, and no name and address, other than, *Holly* … in Ben's handwriting.

"I can leave it downstairs if you'd prefer?" Jamie said, keeping hold of it. "You can read it when you're ready. Or else I can take it back if that would be easier. Say you need more time. I know it doesn't feel like it right now, but you have got plenty of time to sort all this out, you know."

Holly nodded. She was right. She could easily go another month or two without making any decisions about where she was going to live or how running the shop was going to work, but what was the point of that? It would only delay the inevitable.

"It's fine," she said, reaching for the letter. "I'll read it."

With a worried smile, Jamie nodded and relinquished the envelope, though she remained hovering in the doorway.

"I'm just here, if you need me."

"I know. Thank you."

She waited until Jamie's footsteps were no longer audible before she ripped it open and started to read.

CHAPTER FORTY-TWO

My dearest Holly,

I think it's fair to say that I have messed up royally. I don't know if I can ever make amends for the way I have treated you this past week, and probably before that, too, but I want you to know part of the reason why I behaved the way I did, because the truth is that, even though I didn't say it, I love you Holly Berry. I love you and I will regret not telling you that before now, possibly for the rest of my life. But anyway, I wanted you to know.

As you might have noticed, I'm not that great at talking about my feelings. I've never been that good, but with you, as hard as it might be to believe, I really did feel like I was getting better. Even so, that doesn't explain my actions. Why I was so controlling when it came to the baby, to our baby, but hopefully this will.

As you know from our previous conversation, which again didn't go well, I proposed to Ella in Paris. I'd been planning it for several months and had the ring for the best part of a year, knowing that I would do it at some point. What I hadn't planned for was that, three weeks before we left for the trip, we would find out that she was pregnant.

It came as a surprise, but a great one, and made me even more positive that Paris was going to be the perfect place to propose. And it was. I won't go into details, but she said yes. That part you already know. She said yes, and all our family and friends, who'd been in on the secret, were overjoyed. But while they knew I was going to propose, they didn't know that Ella was pregnant. The only other person who did was Jess, and as such, you may have noticed that she's a little overprotective of me.

We were in Paris for six days, and I proposed on the second night. For the next two days, we did all the touristy things, visiting the Louvre and the Eiffel Tower, but on the fifth day, Ella was exhausted. We didn't think anything of it. She was pregnant. That was normal, we thought. So she decided to spend the day in bed reading, and I went off on my own. I had a wonderful time, hopping on and off the metro, walking along the Seine. I stopped at a patisserie for my lunch and picked up a lemon tart for Ella, just in case she hadn't eaten. By the time I got back to the hotel, I'd been gone for a little over six hours and I found her huddled in the bathroom. We'd lost the baby.

Like I said, we hadn't told anyone at home, so when we arrived back, everyone was full of congratulations about our engagement. Our parents had arranged a party and had already put together a list of wedding venues for us to look at. Ella didn't want the celebration. She just wanted to hide away and grieve. But I didn't give her the time. I took her around to all the places on the list and started organising caterers and flowers and she just went along with it all.

I thought it would be better if I acted like everything was normal, not dwelling on the baby, and we could go back to the way we were before. And if I could do that, then why couldn't she? It was only when she left me that I truly understood the emptiness she'd been feeling all those months and what it was like to lose a part of yourself. But I know my pain can't compare to what she'd gone through. I just didn't realise how deep it went. That's what cost me my relationship. Ella may have been the one who left me, but I was the one who'd deserted her long before that.

When Michael let slip the news last night, I knew that whatever happened, I couldn't let things go the way they went before. I couldn't ever let you feel you were on your own or that I wasn't there for you at every turn. And so I went too far. I know that, now. I just want you to understand why.

I love you Holly. And I might not be able to say it as easily as other people can, but I love you so much, and I know that whether we're together or not, we are going to give this baby the best life it could ever dream of.

I am here, waiting, whenever you are ready to talk.

All my love

Ben

CHAPTER FORTY-THREE

She read and re-read the letter until her eyes could barely focus on the words in front of her. It all made perfect sense now. It explained why he'd been so overbearing. And why he'd freaked out about Paris. He wasn't joking when he'd said the place had memories; she wasn't sure she'd ever be able to go back somewhere something so traumatic had happened. She now understood his actions and responses to so many things. But what she didn't know was how they were meant to go from here.

She knew that love didn't disappear in a week, but was that really what she and Ben had felt? He'd written down his feelings, but that was a darn sight easier than living them out. And even if she loved him, was she really in a position where she could raise a child with him? But then what was the other option? Raising it on her own, in her best friend's house?

A knock on the door brought her back from her thoughts.

"Come in," she called.

She'd expected it to be Jamie, checking whether she'd read the letter and if she needed some emotional support, but instead, it was Fin. His long hair was knotted into a bun, and he was holding a handful of the paper birds from the night before.

"Hey, I brought you a little gift," he said, coming into the room. "You know, in some countries these are called peace cranes. I thought you could do with some of them. After your fall, the restaurant owner decided they might be too much of a hazard to keep there permanently."

Holly chuckled as she took them from him.

"Thank you. They really are lovely."

"I can teach you to make them if you like? It's very meditative. If you're into that," he added hurriedly. "I really am sorry about the plants, and if I come across a bit too full-on, it's just part of who I've had to be, you know. When you work in a competitive industry like I do, you have to make yourself stand out. But I promise, I'm not that bad when you get to know me."

Holly reached out and clasped his hands in her own.

"Tell me then, what do my energy channels look like now?" she asked.

Taking a step back, he squinted at her.

"I'd say they're telling me that you're very determined. Like you know your own mind, and you will go out and get whatever it is you want."

"That sounds about right."

"And—" he stopped, cutting himself short.

"What is it?" she asked, her face falling.

By contrast, Fin's broke into a wide smile.

"It looks like a lot of those blocks have gone."

And because she honestly felt it was true, she smiled back at him.

Ben answered the door in less than a minute. He was dressed now but in slouchy tracksuit bottoms and a T-shirt, still a long way from his normal choice of attire.

"I wasn't expecting you to come tonight," he said. "I didn't mean to rush you."

She nodded.

"I know, but there's no point dragging things out, is there? We need to have this conversation."

He went pale and stepped back to let her in.

"Come in. Sit down. Would you like a drink? I don't have any juice or anything, but I can get some if you want. It won't take me long to run to the shop."

"Water will be fine," she said, as she slipped off her shoes and walked through into the kitchen.

She'd gone through the main points that she wanted to make at least a dozen times in her head before going round, but now she wished she'd written them down, as she was struggling to think straight. As Ben got her a glass of water, she tried to recall how she'd intended to begin.

"Do you want to sit in here or in the living room," he asked, handing her the glass.

"I think we should sit in the living room," she said, "if that's okay with you."

"Of course it is."

She let him lead the way although, of course, she knew it very well. When they reached the lounge, he waited for her to choose a seat, before he opted for a straight-backed armchair, where he sat looking rigid and uncomfortable.

"Thank you for the letter," she started. "It explained a lot."

Relief flooded his face. He drew in a deep breath, as if it had been the first proper one he'd taken all day.

"Everything that happened triggered a lot of bad memories, you understand. My reactions weren't about you. Not entirely."

"Yes, I do," she replied, slowly, "but I also know that if we're to have any chance of raising our child together, then how you behave needs to be centred around *this* baby, not panicking about what happened in the past and not comparing me to anyone else."

"I won't. I wouldn't. There *is* no comparison, Holly, I promise you. I meant everything I said in my letter. I love you, I really do, and I love the person you make me. The person I want to be."

She pressed her lips together, swallowing back the tears that she'd promised she wouldn't allow herself.

"And I love you, too," she whispered.

Within a second, he was on his knees in front of her.

"I promise you this will work. You won't regret anything," he said

But she didn't move. She still had things she needed to say. Things she thought he might not want to hear.

"I agree that, practically, me moving in here makes the most sense," she said. "But not just yet and not for certain. I would like us to see someone first."

"See someone?"

"A counsellor. A marriage counsellor. I know we're not married, but having a baby is the biggest commitment we can make, and I think we both have issues we need to resolve."

"I understand. I do."

"And when the baby arrives, I'm going to need you to go part time at the bank."

"What?"

He jerked backwards.

"It wouldn't be forever, but with the cost and problems of

childcare, we're both going to have to make sacrifices. I can't give myself maternity leave and pay, but the bank has probably got a good package. You're going to need to take whatever they have available."

This piece of news took a fair bit more swallowing than the suggestion of seeing a counsellor, though after a minute he nodded his head.

"Okay, I'll talk to HR tomorrow. I'll find out what the deal is."

"Slow down," she said, also getting to her feet. "We need to talk things through together first. Make plans."

He nodded, then got to his feet, took her by the hands to join him and then kissed her softly on the lips.

"I'm so sorry, Holly, I really am. And I promise I will never let you or this baby down."

Her smile was tentative, but it felt good and the next time he kissed her, she allowed herself to kiss him back.

"Will you stay here tonight?" he asked. "I've missed you so much. I just want to cuddle all night. Can we do that, please?"

"I might have missed you a bit, too," she said, "even if it means I don't get to stretch out as far as I want to anymore."

"You can stretch out," he said. "You can go full starfish. You can kick me out, and I'll sleep on the floor. I don't care. I just want you here with me."

Holly dropped her head against his chest.

"I love you, Holly Berry," he whispered in her ear.

"If I'm staying, I need to get a few things," she said.

"Get whatever you need. I can empty some of my drawers. Or not," he said, quickly catching himself. "If you want to take things slowly, that's fine. No drawers. No cupboards. No space at all."

She laughed.

"Perhaps one drawer would be good."

"Great, one drawer."

He pulled her against him and kissed her on the forehead before stepping back and freeing her from his grip.

"Right. Go. Because I want you back as soon as possible. And, as it's a special occasion, I'll even let you pick the film."

"Ah, did I not mention that complete control of the television remote was one of my terms for coming back?"

He frowned.

"This is one thing we might need to raise with our counsellor."

She laughed and walked to the hall, slipped on her shoes, and left.

Fin and Jamie were sitting in the living room, laughing too although it stopped the moment she shut the front door.

Before she could even take her shoes off, Jamie was standing in front of her.

"So, how did it go?" she asked. "Are you two okay?"

Holly nodded, slowly.

"We'll get there, I think."

"That's great news!" she yelled, jumping forwards and wrapped her arms around Holly so tightly she yelped.

"Careful. Baby in here, remember?"

"Sorry, I'm so excited that I get to be an aunty soon."

"It's still early. I've not even reached the twelve-week mark yet."

"So we need to make sure there's no stress, and lots of healthy eating," Fin called through to them.

The women caught each other's eyes with a smile.

"I've just come to collect some things," she said, moving to the staircase. "I'm going to stay at Ben's tonight."

"Cool. Oh, before I forget, there's a parcel for you on the

kitchen table. Not sure who it's from. There's no postmark or return address.

The intrigue of the mystery parcel outweighed Holly's desire to sort out her things for the night, and while Jamie went back to Fin, she ambled through to the kitchen, where a large, brown box sat on the island. Her first thought was that perhaps Ben had bought her some more flours, but she would have thought he'd have mentioned that, and anyway this box was a fair bit smaller. With her interest truly piqued, she took a pair of scissors and opened it up.

Four jars of prenatal, multivitamin tablets were on the top, while underneath the packing paper were four larger bottles. As she went to pull one out, she saw a note and took that instead.

Just trying to even out my karma. See you around, Holly Berry.

She chuckled as she removed one of the bottles and read the label: Non-Alcoholic Wine.

"Giles Caverty," she smiled to herself, then slipped it back into the box.

She was probably going to need a lot more than that to get through the next seven months. Then, moving from the island to one of the cupboards, she pulled out a large bag.

Chocolate limes.

Exactly what she needed.

ACKNOWLEDGMENTS

To Cherie, whose beautiful covers really help this series stand-out, thank you as always.

Thank you to Carol for her wonderful, and ever patient, editing.

Huge thanks to the amazing team of proofreaders who have done their utmost to track down those persistent typos that work so hard to sneak through every round of checking.

Lastly, thank you to all you readers who have taken Holly into your heart. I hope very much that her antics continue to bring you joy.

NEXT IN THIS SERIES

HIGH HOPES AT THE SWEET SHOP OF SECOND CHANCES

A successful summer has seen Holly Berry's sweet shop thriving, and she is high hopes about the future of *Just One More* for the first time since she bought it. However, it is not only her business prowess that has been growing. In a little over a month she will be trying to run the shop with a baby on her hip.

If only her love life was so easily managed. With things far from solid with Ben, and Giles back on the scene, Holly might find herself changing more than nappies.

Make sure you catch up with your favourite sweet shop owner and get your copy of ***High Hopes and the Sweet Shop of Second Chances*** today.

Available from Amazon

ABOUT THE AUTHOR

Hannah Lynn is an award-winning novelist. Publishing her first book, *Amendments* – a dark, dystopian speculative fiction novel, in 2015, she has since gone on to write *The Afterlife of Walter Augustus* – a contemporary fiction novel with a supernatural twist – which won the 2018 Kindle Storyteller Award and Gold Medal for Best Adult Fiction Ebook at the IPPY Awards, as well as the delightfully funny and poignant *Peas and Carrots series.*

Her latest works include retellings of classic Greek myths and saw her win her second IPPY Gold Medal for the first book in her *Grecian Women Series*, the heart-wrenching *Athena's Child.*

Born in 1984, Hannah grew up in the Cotswolds, UK. After graduating from university, she spent ten years as a teacher of physics, first in the UK, then in Thailand, Malaysia, Austria and Jordan. It was during this time, inspired by the imaginations of the young people she taught, she began writing short stories for children, before moving on to adult fiction.

Nowadays you will most likely find her busy writing at home with her husband and daughter, surrounded by a clowder of cats.

STAY IN TOUCH

To keep up-to-date with new publications, tours and promotions, or if you are interested in being a beta reader for future novels, or having the opportunity to enjoy pre-release copies please follow me:

Website: hannahlynnauthor.com

Alternatively sign up to my newsletter and receive a free book.

Sign-up to Newsletter

REVIEW

As an independent author, I do not have the mega resources of a big publishing house, but what I do have is something even more powerful – all of you readers. Your ability to offer social proof to my books through your reviews is invaluable to me and helps me to continue writing.

So if you enjoyed reading ***Turmoil at the Sweet Shop of Second Chances***, please take a few moments to leave a review or rating on Amazon or Goodreads. It need only be a sentence or two, but it means so much to me.

Thank you.

Printed in Great Britain
by Amazon

80176460R00161